Deck the Fire Halls

HARTBRIDGE CHRISTMAS SERIES
BOOK FIVE

N.R. WALKER

For Ruby

Blurb

Doctor Robinson O'Reilly is burned out. Exhausted, jaded, and disillusioned with the bureaucracy of his profession, he's ready to throw away his entire career. Convinced to take a part-time position in a small town instead, he packs his medical bag for Hartbridge, Montana.

Who knows, maybe the change of pace and mountain air will do him good.

Firefighter Captain Soren De Silva moved to Hartbridge two years ago. He loves the town, the people, his job. What he doesn't like is the lack of queer men. Well, the lack of available queer men. There are a few queer couples in town whom Soren can only look at with envy.

He wants what they have.

There's a new doctor in town; not Soren's usual type, but there's something about him that Soren can't ignore. A friendship sparks between them and Soren can't help but wonder if that Hartbridge Christmas magic the others joke about is real.

Because a spark leads to flames, and this is not a fire Soren wants to extinguish.

Copyright

Cover Artist: Hoja Designs
Editor: Boho Editing
Publisher: BlueHeart Press
Deck the Fire Halls © 2024 N.R. Walker
Hartbridge Series

ALL RIGHTS RESERVED:

TRADEMARKS

Deck the
FIRE HALLS

N.R. WALKER

Chapter One

ROBINSON O'REILLY

I WOKE with a start and stared at the strange ceiling, wondering what had woken me when I heard it again.

A motorcycle.

A big, loud motorcycle kickstarted to life right outside my bedroom wall, by the sounds of it.

New town, new house, new start.

Which also meant new sounds to get used to.

A Harley Davidson before seven on a Saturday morning was not a great way to start my day, nor was it something I wanted to get used to.

My real estate agent said the house was old but well-loved, that the street was quiet and the neighbors were great.

She was right about the house, but she never mentioned anything about said neighbor owning a Harley freaking Davidson.

I'd arrived in Hartbridge, Montana, late last night, grateful for central heating and that I didn't have to get a fire started, and also grateful that I'd had barely enough energy to make my bed before I fell onto it and was finally getting some decent sleep. My first decent sleep in far too long . . .

Until a thundering motorcycle almost rattled me out of my bed at far-too-early o'clock, before it roared off down the street.

Not a great start to my very first day in town.

I threw back the covers and grumbled as I got out of bed, sighing as I shuffled down the hall into my living room. I frowned at the boxes stacked around me, a reminder of the day ahead of me, and headed to the kitchen.

Where I immediately regretted not setting up my coffee machine last night.

After ripping into the boxes on the table marked *kitchen*, I found my machine and the coffee beans, and a short time later, was gratefully sipping on a double shot of espresso out of a drinking glass.

Once I'd had some caffeine, I could admit that the house was quaint. A two-bedroom, single story bungalow, a small porch at the front, and an enclosed porch at the back. The walls were a tad too yellow for me, and I entertained the idea of having the whole house given a fresh coat of paint. Maybe in the summer . . . maybe by then I'd know if I had any intention of staying.

I'd looked at renting, but with the holidays approaching, options were limited, so I asked to see homes for sale instead. I hadn't had any intention of buying again, not until I found the place which I wanted to make my permanent home. But given the price of real estate in Hartbridge, compared to Seattle where I'd just sold my very nice condo, it was just easier to freaking buy something instead of renting.

So maybe I'd have the walls painted, or maybe I wouldn't.

I wandered out into the living room with my coffee and almost caught myself smiling at the sunlight streaming in through the white lace curtains.

Almost.

I think I'd forgotten how to smile.

Not a fake smile for the sake of pleasantry. I mean an honest smile from happiness.

I think I'd forgotten what happiness was.

I felt beaten down by life, by my job, by the career I'd fought for my whole life. Like the people I'd called friends, my medical colleagues, were excelling and thriving, while I was going under.

I'd almost walked away.

I'd been so close to throwing everything away. Just getting in my car and driving to Canada or Alaska or flying anywhere—the next plane to literally anywhere—just for a chance to breathe, when Alaya Ross took one look at me and pulled me into her office because she was concerned for my well-being.

To cut a really long story short, I ended up taking on a general practice position three days a week at the Hartbridge Medical Center.

If I couldn't handle that?

Then I'd know I was well and truly done.

I was only thirty-six years old. I was young in this job.

Maybe I'd gone too hard too fast. I'd worked insanely long hours; double shifts were standard. I'd been promoted before my peers, my dedication was commendable, blah blah blah.

My dedication had almost killed me.

Which is why I found myself in a very small town in the middle of the mountains in a small but cute house surrounded by boxes that needed to be unpacked.

That was my weekend plans, anyway.

Before going to the clinic for my first shift on Monday morning. I was trying to be optimistic. Maybe this was the fresh start I needed. Maybe it was the change of pace my mental health deserved.

Maybe it would decide my fate once and for all.

I told myself to give it a year, even two. Give it a fair trial run. Even if I was half-convinced I was already leaving.

Doomed before I begin, I thought as I drained my coffee, then put myself to work.

By late afternoon, I was almost done. I had a pile of flattened boxes I had no clue what to do with, my kitchen and clothes were sorted and put away, books unpacked on the bookcases in the spare room, and I had the TV set up.

I tried not to let it bother me that my entire life took just a few hours to unpack.

There wasn't much of me. My entire life had been my job. I had a few photos of my parents and my sister. A candid photo of me at college, young and carefree, laughing with abandon, so oblivious to the path I was taking.

I wasn't sure why I kept it. It felt a little self-serving, vain perhaps. But it was a good photo. I didn't have many, and it was a good reminder to myself that I *did* use to smile.

God, that younger version of me had loved life. Full of adventure and a heart big and brave enough to take on the world.

Enough.

Stop it, Rob.

Get out and clear your mind.

Before I could let my thoughts spiral and have a full-blown what-have-I-done panic attack, I grabbed my coat and my keys, locked up my house, and walked outside.

Fresh air—albeit a little too fresh—warm sunshine, and a quick trip to the local store for some essentials was a great idea. The Home Mart itself was not much bigger than a 7-Eleven, but I managed to find some almond milk and some of that grain bread I hadn't had in years. There was a small but decent supply of locally grown fruit and vegetables, which I had to admit . . . if it was in my closest farmer's market back in Seattle, it'd have been five times the price.

The woman behind the counter gave me a bright smile. "Good afternoon," she declared. "Find everything you were after today?"

At first I thought she was a little too over the top, but the way she paused for my answer to greet an older lady as she walked in with—"Oh, Mabel, I was going to call you. We got the yarn in you were looking for. It's in aisle two, right alongside the others."—I quickly realized she was maybe just that cheerful.

She turned her smile back to me and I'd almost forgotten she'd asked me a question. "Oh, yes, I did, thank you."

"Just passing through?" she asked as she rang me up. "Or . . ."

"No, not passing through." I wasn't sure if anyone just passing through town would buy bread, milk, and a supply of fresh produce, but maybe I was out of practice with the art of small talk. "Just moved here, actually, from Seattle. Got a place on Elmwood Lane."

Her eyes lit up. "Oh, how wonderful! What's your name, love?"

Love?

I stopped short on the salutation of doctor. "Rob."

"Well, Rob, I'm Rosie. Nice to meet you. I hope you're happy here. It's a great little town. Carl's Diner on Main Street has some of the best coffee and cake you could ever want. And a whole range of meals, better than anything you could find in the city. Pizzeria, if you'd prefer. There's a menswear store, Tania at the hairdressers, oh, and a hardware store if you need anything at all for your house. Go in and see Ren, he'll fix you right up."

Carl, Tania, Ren.

Right, then.

"Excellent, thank you," I said, paying my bill. "I'll keep that in mind."

I thanked her and managed a smile as I left. It was only a short walk back to my house, but I spent every step wondering if I'd stepped into the Twilight Zone, or if small towns were really like this. Where everyone was on a first name basis.

I was going to have to get used to it.

As I walked up the two steps to my porch, I heard a rumble coming down the road, and by the time I juggled my groceries and got my key in the door, the very loud

Harley slowed right down and pulled in next door. Male rider from the size of him—huge bulging biceps, broad shoulders—though he wore a helmet, so I couldn't see his face. But my god, the sound was so damn loud.

I pushed inside and closed the door. The noise cut off a few moments later, the resulting silence overly loud in its absence.

Or maybe it just seemed so loud because the rest of the town was so quiet?

With an annoyed sigh, I put away my groceries and pretended I hadn't just bought a house right next door to a motorcycle gang member . . .

Which was probably a gross exaggeration and an awful stereotype, but as a doctor who'd spent way too many hours in the ER tending to riders of motorcycles and the occasional gang member, it was easy to presume such things.

I was disillusioned with the world. I was allowed to be mad about it.

I tried not to dwell on it though. Made myself my first home-cooked meal in far too long and put myself to bed with a book I'd been meaning to read for years.

I didn't give my Harley-riding neighbor another thought. He had been quiet all night, thankfully no loud music or parties for a Saturday night, and I'd managed another decent night's sleep . . .

To be woken again by the loudest, sleep-shattering rumble of that damn motorcycle.

I shoved my pillow over my head to drown out the noise, unsure if I wanted to weep in frustration or yell in anger. The rational part of my brain knew that going outside in my pajamas to yell at the guy probably wasn't the best way to establish new neighborly relations, especially if he was in some motorcycle club.

But then the ruckus faded as he drove off, leaving blissful silence in its wake. I sighed and tried to doze off again, wondering if the bone-deep exhaustion would ever leave me.

Maybe it was part of me now.

Along with the jaded pessimism and general crankiness at life.

I never used to be like this, and I needed to shake off the mood, the funk. I needed to start looking at the positives. This was a new start, a new life. I'd left the darkness behind me and needed to start appreciating the good things.

Like coffee and sunshine through my living room window.

So with that in mind, and considering I was now very much awake, I threw back the covers, put on my robe and slippers, and headed for the kitchen.

I switched on the coffee machine to warm up, taking a few moments to breathe in the peace and quiet and the first rays of sunlight coming in through the living room window, casting shards of white on the yellow walls and sending dust motes into a spin.

Peace and quiet.

I could get used to this.

I inhaled deeply and let it out slowly, trying to breathe in the serenity.

I made my coffee, almost smiling as I took my first sip . . .

Until an all too familiar sound came thundering down

the street, closer, slowing in front of my house before turning into his driveway.

My neighbor from hell.

Anger bubbled up inside me, irrational and stupid, and with my coffee in hand, I stomped out my front door, across the frosty front lawn, and met my inconsiderate motorcycle gang member neighbor in his driveway.

"Hey," I yelled. I couldn't even hear myself over the roar of his stupid motorcycle. "Hey!"

He cut the engine and my voice carried over the silence.

He sat on his huge motorcycle, wearing blue coveralls and a leather jacket. He lifted his hands and took off his helmet. I was expecting a hard face, scars, or neck or face tattoos.

But what I saw stopped me in my tracks.

Short brown hair, sun-kissed skin, smiling hazel eyes and a grin that stole my breath. "Morning," he said, voice like velvet. Then he looked me up and down, and I swear he chuckled. "Nice pajamas."

I looked down at myself, horrified to see my robe open and my navy pajamas with pink flamingos and rainbows on full display. They were old. I'd bought them for a Pride Pajama Party at med school, and everything else I own had been packed. I'd kept them out with the intent of throwing them out once I got settled in . . .

"You okay?" he asked, concerned now. "You just moved in, right? Need help with anything?"

His kindness threw me for a second, not to mention his ridiculous good looks. "I, uh, I'm, um . . ." I looked down at the cup I'd forgotten I was holding. "Coffee," I said.

Like an idiot.

Then I noticed the Hartbridge Fire Department logo on the breast of his coveralls, under his leather jacket.

Oh my.

Of course he was a firefighter.

"Hi, coffee," he said, smiling obscenely. "My name's Soren. It's nice to meet you."

Chapter Two

SOREN DE SILVA

"What the . . . ?"

I stood up from my desk and walked to the open doors of the fire hall.

"What is it?" Chucky said, coming to stand beside me.

Hartbridge Firehouse was on Main Street and traffic wasn't uncommon before eight o'clock as people went to work and school, but a now-familiar Audi SUV pulled up across the street at the medical clinic.

Nothing too unusual about that either. Except the clinic didn't open until nine and the fact *that* car had been parked next door to my house for the last two days.

"That's my new neighbor," I admitted quietly.

We watched as he got out of his car, dressed immaculately in tan trousers and a black coat. His short sandy-grayish hair was neatly brushed, and I couldn't help but smile. "Except he looks a bit more put together now than when I saw him yesterday," I added.

His hair in disarray, his navy robe falling open to reveal

his pajamas with flamingos and rainbows on them. Pride pajamas, if I ever saw any.

I'd asked him if he was okay, and he'd stammered that he was fine, and sorry, said it was nice to meet me and that he was busy, and ran back into his house.

It was all a bit odd, not gonna lie.

And I'd considered going over and introducing myself properly later on but figured I'd give him a few days to get moved in and settled. Moving was stressful, after all.

"Is he the new doctor?" Chucky asked.

He had a brown messenger bag over one shoulder and was carrying an archive box from his car. He tucked it under one arm so he could unlock the door, and disappeared inside. "He's got keys, so he must be?" I shrugged, still unable to get the flamingo pride pajamas out of my head.

"Imma be right back," I said, heading out, just as Doug came out of his office.

"Where are you going?" he yelled.

I half-turned and held up two fingers. "Two minutes."

I ducked across the street and up to the clinic door. It was open, and I popped my head in as he was sliding his box onto the reception desk.

"Uh, hey," I said.

He spun around, startled. "We're not open." He held his messenger bag defensively. "I should have locked the door, sorry. If you'd care to come back in an hour—"

Shit. He thought I was gonna jump him.

I stepped inside and smiled at him with my hands up, wanting him to see I was no threat, and a little disappointed he didn't recognize me. "My name's Soren," I said. "Your next-door neighbor at home and here, it seems." I gestured to the fire hall across the street. "Just over there. I saw you pull in. I recognized your car. You just moved here, right?"

He blinked and he flustered a little. "Right, yes. Ugh. I'm so sorry about yesterday. I don't even know what I was thinking."

"That those flamingo pajamas are a bold statement?" I was aiming for funny . . .

His whole face scrunched up in the cutest way before he buried it in his hands. "Oh my god, I'm so horrified."

"Don't be embarrassed. I liked them."

One cautious eye appeared from behind his fingers.

"I'm serious," I added, as nonchalantly as I could. "Anyway, I recognized your car and saw you come in and just wanted to say hi and welcome you to town. I didn't want you to think we got off on the wrong foot or anything." I took a step toward him and held my hand out. "Soren De Silva."

He stared at my hand, and for a long moment, I thought he wasn't going to take it. He seemed to shake off his embarrassment and took my hand. "Rob O'Reilly. Doctor."

It made me smile.

He was kinda cute, in a professional, clean-cut way. Not usually my type but there really was something about him that struck me. He was . . . god, there was something about him.

He was older than me by a few years, at a guess. He was pale, as if he hadn't seen the sun in years. And he had dark, tired circles under his eyes.

But under that . . .

His blue eyes hid a story I wanted to hear. His lips looked as if he worried them with his teeth too much.

Realizing I'd been staring a beat too long, I nodded to the box he'd carried in. "First day?"

"Uh, yeah," he said. He slid his messenger bag onto the counter and opened the archive box, revealing some stationary, a small medical skeleton thing, and a certificate frame. "Need to get acquainted, I guess."

Yeah, there was definitely a story in those eyes.

He carried the box into the second office, and given he hadn't told me *not* to follow, I assumed I was supposed to. He paused a moment to look around, then slid the box onto the desk and took the frame out first. He looked around at the walls. "Hm. I'll need a hook. I should have thought about that."

"I can put a hook up for you," I offered.

He looked over at me and blinked as if surprised to see me. "Oh. No, it's fine. I can . . . get one of those stick-on hooks or something."

I pointed my thumb to the door. "We have all kinds of stuff at the fire hall, it's no problem."

He hesitated so I took it as a green light.

"I'll be back in a minute and get it fixed up. You open at nine?"

He nodded.

I grinned at him. "Plenty of time."

I jogged back across the road, unable to stop smiling.

"Oh shit," Chuck said when he saw me. "Boss, he's got that look."

Doug came around from the side of the truck and looked me up and down. "Longest two minutes I ever saw."

I grinned at him as I opened the drawer, took out a one-inch nail, and lifted the hammer from the hook on the wall. "Gonna be another two."

"What the hell are you doing?" Doug asked.

He was my superior, but he loved me. He'd scowl at me, I'd grin at him, and he'd grumble but let me off. It was how we rolled.

"Just doing my civic duty and helping the good doctor."

Chuck looked at what I was holding. "By nailing him?"

Doug told him to shut it, and I snorted as I went back across the street to the clinic. "Hello," I called out as I opened the door. "It's just me."

He poked his head out of his office. "Oh, hey. You really . . . you really didn't have to come back."

"It's no problem," I said, grinning at him. "It's a small-town thing. Helping out, it's what we do."

He opened his mouth and closed it again, blinking a few times. He had a flicker of emotions steal across his face that I wasn't yet sure how to read. "Guess I need to get used to that."

"If you plan on sticking around, then yeah."

Was I fishing for information? Yep. Was I subtle? Absolutely not.

He nodded slowly. "I, uh . . . I'm not sure." He looked around the clinic. "A year, maybe. Possibly two. I'm not sure if this is . . ." he trailed off with a shrug.

Damn. He looked so well put together, like a doctor should, I assumed. But he was . . . I wasn't sure. Running from something?

"Not sure on Hartbridge?" I asked. "It's a great little

town if you give it a chance. People are real nice. It might take some getting used to if you've come from a big city and all."

"It's not the town," he said quietly. He frowned, and taking in a deep breath, he shook off whatever thoughts he'd had and tried to smile. It was half-hearted, but maybe it was all he could afford right then. "And I'm actually looking forward to the slower pace. And the peace and quiet—" He smirked at me. "Actually, the peace and quiet would be great, except I have this new neighbor who has a really big motorcycle that he likes to start right by my bedroom window . . ."

I barked out a laugh. "So that was the reason you came out in your pride pajamas." I grinned at him. "Were you gonna give me a piece of your mind?"

His cheeks went pink and he scoffed, his gaze looking anywhere but at me. "They're not . . . those pajamas were . . ."

I grinned at him, making full eye contact. "Those pajamas were awesome. I already told you I liked them."

Read into that what you will, doctor.

His eyes flashed with understanding, his cheeks flushing a darker pink.

Oh yeah. He read it right.

"So," I hedged. "Did you move here alone?"

He balked at my bluntness.

I chuckled. "Sorry if that's too straightforward. Well, too forward, I should say. Because straight isn't something I am. If you get what I mean."

He cleared his throat, that blush creeping down his neck. "I, uh . . . I understood the reference, thank you."

He said nothing more.

Damn, he really was hot. In an older, silver fox kind of way. Not that he was silver . . . well, maybe there were a few flecks at his temples. His sandy colored hair hid it well.

Before it could get awkward, I held up the hammer. "Anyway. Where would you like the frame put?"

He swallowed hard and turned back to his office. "Uh, here, if that's okay. You really don't have to do this . . . I do appreciate it though."

"It's no bother, but I better not keep you. You're about to have your first patients, and my boss is gonna be all out of the other kind if I'm not back soon."

He looked a little confused.

"Patience," I clarified. "He pretends to be grouchy but he's really a big softie."

He smiled and nodded slowly. "Right. Yes, patience."

I fixed the nail with two quick taps and stood back. "Okay, I'll let you do the honors of hanging your diploma."

He rolled his eyes, but with a deep breath, he hung the simple black frame and straightened it. "Done. Thank you."

Then I read it.

Robinson O'Reilly.

"Robinson," I murmured. "When you said your name was Rob, I just assumed your name was Robert."

"Everyone does."

"I like the name Robinson," I said, not sure why. I mean, not sure why I told him that.

His eyes met mine, those blue eyes a little less guarded.

"Hello?" A soft voice called out.

We both turned for the door and I knew who it was

before I saw her. Katie stood by the reception desk in her blue slacks and purple cardigan. She held her handbag nervously.

It was pretty clear that Rob hadn't met her yet. "Hello," he said gently. "Can I help you?"

"My name is Katie Hawkins. This is my workplace. I work here. Today is your first day and I was told to be early."

She was nervous, poor thing. So unlike her.

"Hey, Katie," I said warmly. "This is Doctor O'Reilly. I was just helping him hang up his frame in his office. Doctor, Katie has worked here for years and she keeps the whole place running. Dontcha, Katie?"

She gave a nod. "Hello, Soren."

"Well, Katie," Rob said with a smile. "It's nice to meet you. I'm glad you're here and if you know how everything works, then you're in charge, okay?"

She smiled at him. "I need to turn my computer on, then I'll go buy the milk. I get the milk on Mondays. You didn't turn the heat up. Doctor Humphries turns the heat up."

Rob smiled again, a more natural one. "Perhaps you can make me a list of all the things I'm supposed to do."

"After I buy the milk."

"Of course, yes."

Katie nodded and turned the computer on, then pressed a button on the thermostat so the screen came to life. "You just press Day, and don't touch it after that," she said.

"Understood," Rob said.

Then we watched as she put her coat back on and went out the door.

I don't know why it made me happy that his first interaction with Katie was so wholesome. He was a doctor, after all, and I should expect nothing less, but some people treated Katie's Down syndrome as a weakness.

"I better get back to work or Doug will come yelling," I said. I went to the door and pointed my hammer at the thermostat. "Don't change the temperature."

His eyes met mine, warm and filled with humor. "Wouldn't dream of it."

I went outside into the brisk air, smiling at the blue sky and the warm sunshine on my face.

I had a real good feeling about him. I dunno how or why, because he was certainly not my type, but there was something—*something*—about Robinson O'Reilly that made my heart take notice.

Doug met me in the doorway, standing with his arms crossed. "Is two minutes different in your world than it is in mine?"

I laughed, my good mood unshaken. "Just doing a good deed for the new doctor in town, sir."

"Hm-mm." He was doing his stoic, unimpressed-dad thing. "Your next good deed for the day is washing the truck. Get to it."

Yeah.

Not even that could ruin my mood.

In fact, pulling the fire engine out the front and spending a few hours in the sunshine sounded like a great idea.

"On it, boss."

He scowled at me. "Don't act like you like it. It's supposed to be a punishment."

Chucky laughed as I collected the keys, and then Doug turned to him. "And you can help him."

"What did I do?" Chuck protested. Then it was me who laughed, and Chuck gave me a shove. "Thanks a fucking lot, man."

We got busy with the truck, cleaning inside and out, working up a bit of a sweat. I had to undo my coveralls to my waist so it was just my T-shirt showing, and man, the sunlight felt good.

It was an unusually warm day for November, and we'd soon be under a few feet of snow and freezing winds, so I wasn't about to waste any chance I got to absorb some vitamin D.

I kept a random eye on the clinic across the street every now and then, noticing people going in and out as they usually were. But I must have gotten lost in my work until Chucky gave me a shove. "Eyes at nine o'clock."

I turned and saw Rob standing out in front of the clinic, staring, before he realized he got caught and hurried down the street.

Chuck laughed. "Good deed, huh?"

I was grinning, feeling a buzz I hadn't felt in far too long. "Good indeed."

Chapter Three

ROB

Of course he was washing the fire engine. Because of course he was.

Of course he was wearing his coveralls rolled down to his waist, and of course his gray T-shirt clung to his ripped body like a glove.

Of course it did.

I had a coat on with the collar up against the cold and my hands shoved into my pockets, and he was wearing a goddamn T-shirt while he washed the fire engine.

And he was gorgeous.

I don't mean a little bit gorgeous. I mean the whole way. Tanned, ripped, dark, glittering eyes, and that smile. And don't even get me started on the perfect bone structure of his face.

Or his lips.

Did I mention his lips?

And the way he always seemed to be smiling?

And the way he held my gaze and said he liked my pride pajamas. Pride. And that he wasn't straight.

He said these things to my face.

Admittedly, I'd been a hermit by Gay Seattle standards. I just hadn't had the time, the energy, or the inclination to bother.

I was also a sad and sorry mess.

Who the hell would want to deal with a guy who was one minor inconvenience away from getting into his car and driving away from his entire life?

I had issues. I had a problem with how the world worked, and I was cynical and angry at a system I couldn't change.

No prospective guy wanted to deal with that on top of me working ninety hours a week.

Hell, I didn't even want to deal with me.

I could have hooked up. I could have used a dozen apps to find a random one-nighter, but I didn't even have the energy for that.

Or the libido.

I had nothing left to give.

And the only reason I noticed Soren was because he was my neighbor. And because he woke me up with his stupidly loud motorcycle. And because he worked across the street from me, wearing that damn firefighter outfit, washing his sexy red fire engine.

He was a cliché and I was a mess.

That's all it was.

I shook my head at myself and walked to the diner. Katie told me it was the best place for lunch. She also told me my lunch was at 11:30 because the usual lunch hour was when people came for doctor appointments, and Doctor Humphries preferred to have an early lunch instead of a late one, so that was now my lunch time as well.

Hard to argue with that logic.

Kinda hard to argue with Katie at all. She was efficient in everything. When Soren had said she ran the clinic, he wasn't joking. She had lists for every single thing and ran the time schedule like a drill sergeant. She clearly liked routine and schedules, and honestly, so did I.

Patients greeted her warmly, and she treated every person the same. She was also the no-nonsense type and I appreciated that the most.

So, I took myself off to the diner. It was like something out of a movie from the 1960s, with a door that chimed overhead, and vinyl booths and retro tables and chairs. Only it wasn't *retro*, it was original in impeccable condition.

Places in big cities paid a fortune to replicate this, most not even coming close.

It was also warm and smelled amazing and the few customers looked happy. There was a guy behind the counter with brown floppy hair and a warm smile. "Good morning," he said with an accent.

English? South African?

"What can I get for ya today?"

Australian.

"Uh, hi," I said, trying to scan the chalkboard menu above the counter, not sure where to start. "Uh . . ."

"Just made a fresh batch of roasted tomato soup," he said. "Lunch special with grilled cheese."

Damn.

"Sounds perfect."

He grinned. "Take a seat, I'll bring it over."

I slid into the furthest booth, hiding away as I usually did, and a few minutes later, I had a huge bowl of the best-tasting tomato soup I'd ever had. The grilled cheese was the thick kind of bread with oozing cheese. It might have even been pan-fried in *real* butter.

Best lunch I think I'd ever had.

God, living in Seattle, my entire life had been green, clean, and lean. Jeez, some days I consumed enough calories to make myself function, and sometimes not very well.

"How was it?" the guy from behind the counter asked. Except now he was standing beside my booth with an anticipatory smile.

The fact I'd stopped short at licking the bowl clean told us both how much I'd enjoyed it.

"You know," I said, "I've always tried to keep my dietary habits secular."

He tilted his head, confused.

I nudged the empty soup bowl. "But this was very near a religious experience."

He threw his head back and laughed. "I wondered where you were going with that."

"It was delicious. I've been told I simply had to come to the diner, and now I can see why."

"Ah. I thought you were new to town."

"Oh?"

"Well, new face and all, but also no gloves." He smiled at the huge windows overlooking the street. "It's looking pretty cold out there."

"Ah, yes. I do have gloves, I just left them at home," I said. "I'll remember to bring them to work tomorrow."

"Work?"

"Oh." I let out a bit of a sigh. "Yes, I've just started at the health clinic in town."

Recognition flashed in his eyes. "Ah, right, yes. Old Doc Humphries said he was semi-retiring and a new guy was taking over. That's you?"

I gave a nod. "That's me. Rob O'Reilly."

His grin widened. "Jayden Turner."

"Nice to meet you, Jayden."

"Likewise. So, how are you finding Hartbridge?"

"Oh, it's fine . . . so far. I bought a house on Elmwood Lane."

"Perfect," he said. "It's a great little town. People here are the best you could meet. Where did you come from? If you don't mind me asking."

"I don't mind. I'm from Seattle."

He grinned again. "So, just a small change in pace, huh?"

"That's why I'm here," I said, without really meaning how it sounded. I mean, I meant it. I just didn't mean to say it to a random stranger. "Well, I better get back. Katie has me on a tight schedule."

Jayden laughed again. "I bet she does. Here, give her one of these," he said, ducking back behind the service counter and taking a chocolate walnut brownie out of the cabinet. "These are her favorite. She'll think you're the bee's knees."

Bee's knees. That made me smile.

"Then I should most definitely take her one."

The door chimed behind me and two guys came in, but not wanting to keep Jayden from his work, I paid quickly and took the white paper bag with Katie's afternoon snack in it. "Thank you so much."

"Doctor O'Reilly," one of the men behind me said.

I turned to find none other than Soren, with his breathtaking smile and those damn firefighter coveralls, which he had done up now. Sadly, no tight gray T-shirt on display.

"I'm beginning to think you're following me," I said.

His grin widened. "Oh, I absolutely am. Watched you walk in here and told the boss I was going to lunch."

My heart stuttered a little and I hated that he and his damned smile had this effect on me. I'd known him for all of two minutes. For some stupid reason, I couldn't seem to take my eyes from his.

"Your boss must be a very patient man."

Soren snorted. "He's the opposite of that. But I'll take him back some pie and he'll be fine. And Chucky."

"Chucky?"

"Yeah, Chuck. He's like my work partner. Well, his real name is Danny but his surname is Norris, so . . ."

Chuck Norris. I nodded. "Makes sense."

I had to make myself break eye contact. *What the hell is wrong with me?*

I looked back to Jayden and gave him a nod in thanks, to find him standing with the guy Soren had come in with. He had dark hair and a beard and was clutching Jayden's sleeve, staring at Soren and me as if we were the most wondrous thing he'd ever seen.

"It's happening again," he whispered, nudging Jayden.

"I know," Jayden replied. "This needs to be studied."

Um, what?

"What needs to be studied?" I asked.

Soren intercepted and ushered me to the door. "Nothing. Ignore the Australians. They get a little crazy this time of year." He opened the door, and all but shoved me out onto the sidewalk into the cold. "Say, how about I come over to your place. I'll bring dinner. Seven o'clock? Perfect. See you then."

The door shut in my face, and the man with the dark beard let out some kind of squeal and I heard Soren shush him.

That was weird.

And what was even weirder was that Soren had just invited himself to my place for dinner.

And I . . .

Well, I could go back into the diner and tell him no.

But I wasn't going to.

To be honest, mid-afternoon I was back at my desk and *still* thinking about the whole interaction—and whatever the weird thing was with the Australians, as Soren had called them—and I still wasn't even mad about Soren inviting himself over.

Was I looking forward to it?

Undecided.

Liar.

Pardon?

Liar, liar pants on fire.

I shook my head at my own subconscious.

Okay, so I was excited for conversation. Excited for a meal and having an actual conversation that didn't revolve around a medical case or insurance and copays and legalities.

I couldn't remember the last time I'd done that.

Med school, maybe?

Far too long.

And I was neither blind nor stupid; I could see Soren was interested. He wasn't shy about flirting. Hell, he'd admitted it to my face that he'd followed me to the diner.

I wasn't mad about that either.

Did I want something with him?

He was gorgeous and sexy and seemed to be interested in me. For what, I could only guess. Something casual and physical? A one-night stand?

Apart from getting way ahead of myself, I knew virtually zero about him. He was a firefighter, drove a motorcycle, and he'd dropped everything to help me hang my diploma in my office, which told me he was kind.

Did he have ulterior motives?

Nothing his wicked grin and sparkly eyes didn't already convey. He certainly didn't hide his interest.

Unless he was like that with everyone?

Unless he was the town flirt and man-whore? Or maybe it wasn't flirting at all. Maybe he was just a super nice guy.

Maybe he was incredibly unstable and one bad day away from being on *America's Most Wanted*.

No, that didn't seem likely.

Not that I knew him at all.

But if things didn't work out between us, if they progressed no further than friendly neighbor dinners, then I'd be very okay with that too.

Jeez, Robinson, listen to yourself.

Already talking about possible relationship scenarios with a guy you've just met.

I was so out of practice. Maybe a guy being no more than nice to me was sending me into a tailspin. Especially when that guy was younger and hotter than anyone I'd ever been with.

Why was he even interested in me?

Was he even interested in me?

Could I even act on it? If he was interested? I wasn't sure I *could* act on it, even if I wanted to. I was the local physician.

God, was he a patient at this clinic?

Stop it, Robinson.

I was letting my mind get away from me.

It'd been far too long for me, obviously.

One flirty smirk from a hot guy and my mind went to pieces. I'd been here for three days!

Maybe I was more stressed out and defeated than I'd realized.

I needed to focus.

"Doctor O'Reilly," Katie said from the door. "Mr. Thornton is here to see you."

Startled, I stood up. God, I really had lost my mind. "Yes, thank you, Katie. Send him through, please."

Mr. Thornton was an older gentleman in for a general check-up and a chinwag. I got the feeling he was also here to check on me, but he was a lovely man and I didn't mind the curiosity.

"Katie told me you brought her in her favorite sweet treat from the diner," he said with a bit of a smile. Then he nodded and winked. "You won her over already."

I chuckled. "Well, I had a bit of help from the man working at the diner. Was his name Jayden? He told me which was her favorite. I can't take all the credit."

"Ah, yes," he said, nodding slowly. "Jayden. He's getting married, you know. To another man."

Oh.

My defenses went up with my placating smile, because I knew how these conversations usually ended.

"The guy with the dark beard?" I asked. "He seemed nice."

"No, no," he said. "That's Hamish. The other Australian guy. He's married to Ren Brooks, at the hardware store. Jayden is getting married to Cass. He runs the bed and breakfast out on Ponderosa Road."

"Oh."

God, there were two gay couples in this small town?

"Well, that's exciting," I said, still trying to gauge his reaction and about to change subjects.

"And there's Clay Henderson. Lemme tell you, that was a surprise to the whole town. He's run the local sawmill his whole life with his dad, Cliff. As tall and broad as a door but met a newcomer to town. Smaller, quiet type. Gunther or Gunter, I can't remember. He's starting up the youth center. Nice fellow. And then last year another newcomer to town, a young Englishman he is, got pulled over by the deputy for speeding, and that was that." He pointed his gnarled finger at me. "You might want to watch yourself, being a newcomer to this town. Might find yourself in the sights of a man." He winked.

"Well, I . . ." Good freaking lord. What the hell?

"I dunno what's in the water in Hartbridge," he went on, "but it sure weren't in the water when I was a youngin. There's nothing wrong with that, mind you. My granddaughter told me it was accepted now, and people being in love is better than people being hateful, and I guess she's right."

I wasn't about to tell him that it sure was in the water back when he was a youngin, folks just had to live in hiding, but I didn't think it was appropriate. He certainly wasn't being disrespectful. In fact, he was very accepting. "Your granddaughter sounds very smart."

"Oh, she is," he said, his gray eyes lighting up. And then he gave me the rundown on her schooling and the clubs she's in and how she helps around the house. He clearly adored her, and he clearly adored chatting.

I kept thinking of the time, a stopwatch in the back of my mind counting the seconds, telling me I needed to wrap up this appointment, because time was money and there was a never-ending line of patients and insurance companies and hospital board quotas I had to meet . . .

But I didn't.

Not anymore.

So I took a few minutes to chat with Mr. Thornton, and when he left, he left with a clean bill of health and a smile. And for such a simple thing, a ten-minute chat with a kind old man, it made me smile too.

My next appointment didn't mind waiting a few minutes and came in with a smile of her own. Mrs. Shelly had to have her blood pressure checked and a new prescription, and it took all of five minutes, and then she and Katie talked about an up-and-coming sewing club meeting.

The following appointments were relaxed and easy. A sinus infection, a baby's six-month check-up, a toddler's ear infection, a cholesterol check, a strained back.

And maybe in a few months' time I'd be bored out of

my mind, but my god . . . the change of pace was like a breath of fresh air.

The simplicity, the quietness.

No hectic and stressful ER events. No accidents, no assaults, no shootings. I hadn't been sworn at, spat at, or threatened.

No directors yelling at us to treat people faster, cheaper. No boards to please, no quotas to meet.

Admittedly, I hadn't met Doctor Humphries yet. He was the doctor who had been Hartbridge's only doctor for forty years, and he was cutting his hours back getting ready for retirement.

Which was really him getting the townsfolk ready for his retirement.

All the patients I'd seen on my first day told me how much they liked Doctor Humphries, so I knew I had some pretty big shoes to fill. And as my first day wrapped up, I thought I'd done okay.

"People liked you," Katie said. "They said you were nice."

"Oh, thank you," I said, genuinely touched.

"They said they preferred Doctor Humphries, but that's not surprising."

I almost snorted. Her bluntness was part of her charm.

"Not surprising at all," I agreed. "Are you going home now?"

She was standing there with her bag, with everything turned off, so it was pretty obvious. But still . . . "Yes," she said with a nod. "I finish at five o'clock."

"Very good. Then I'll see you tomorrow."

"At eight fifty a.m.," she reminded me. "I get here at eight fifty a.m."

"Perfect."

"You have the list I made for you," she said.

I couldn't help but smile. "I do. And I'll make sure to adjust the heat."

"Thank you for the brownie. I kept some for tomorrow. It's in the fridge. Please don't eat it."

I had to purse my lips so I didn't smile. "I won't, I promise."

She clutched her bag and stepped closer to the door. "Bye, Doctor O'Reilly."

"Bye, Katie. Thank you for being so helpful today."

That earned me a smile before she ducked her head and disappeared out the door. I locked everything up and was home by 5:20 p.m.

I hadn't had an eight-hour workday, ever.

I wasn't quite sure what to do with myself. I couldn't even make my dinner because Soren said he was bringing it.

I had no clue what Soren expected. Was I supposed to have wine? Dessert? I had no clue and nothing to go on.

My house was clean and tidy, and I hadn't broken a sweat all day, so it wasn't as if I needed a shower. Normally after a double shift at my last hospital, I'd need a steaming hot shower to scrub away the day and decompress before crawling into bed.

Today I felt energized, almost.

It was weird.

I did a quick spray of deodorant and was going to brush my teeth but told myself not to be stupid—I was getting waaaaaay ahead of myself—so I opened a bottle of wine instead.

I'd barely had two sips before there was a knock at my front door.

It was far too early for Soren, so I had no idea who it could be. With equal amounts of curiosity and dread, I opened the door . . . to find Soren standing there holding a pot of something that smelled amazing, covered with tinfoil, and a loaf of some kind of bread on top. He was wearing a blue sweater and jeans and a smile that made my stomach swoop.

"You're early," I said, in a not-so-polite greeting.

"Saw your lights on, car in the driveway. And I was hungry, so I figured I'd come over. If that's not okay, I can come back," he said, looking back to his house.

"No, please. Forgive my rudeness. Come in," I said, holding the door open in invitation. "Whatever that is, it smells amazing."

He carefully handed it to me and began to take his shoes off. "It's my mom's famous casserole." He got one shoe off and placed it inside the door, then his other. "I'd like to take credit for the recipe, but I'd be lying if I said it was mine."

I walked through to the kitchen and sat it on the cook-top. "And the bread?"

"Ciabatta. Totally store bought," he said.

When I turned to face him, the front door was closed and he was following me into my kitchen. Closer than I'd anticipated, and we were very much alone.

I looked for the closest distraction. "Glass of wine?"

"I can have *one*," he said.

"Are you on-call?"

"Never not on-call," he said with a shrug.

My god, he was so incredibly good-looking. It was baffling to me that he was in my kitchen, looking at me with those smiling eyes.

I poured him a glass and he took it with a smile. I was disappointed when our fingers didn't brush . . .

Jeez. Get a grip, Rob.

You don't even know if he's interested, or inclined to be interested, or just being nice.

Though I was pretty sure I was reading this whole thing correctly.

"I didn't hear your motorbike come back," I admitted.

He grinned. "I didn't take it today. Pretty sure it wakes my new neighbor up and I don't want to get on his bad side."

I gave him a wry smile. "Sorry about that. I don't mind now that I know about it. And now that I've started work, I won't need to set an alarm, so it's fine."

He chuckled. "I don't take it every day anyway, so you might wanna keep setting that alarm. I'd hate to be the reason you're late." He grinned behind his wine glass. "And anyway, I got to see your flamingo pajamas, so it wasn't all bad."

My cheeks burned. "I'll never live that down."

His eyes met mine and held my gaze for a beat too long. "Nope."

A moment passed between us, not awkward—far from awkward—and a staticky thrill ran through me.

Wow.

What the hell is this?

"So," he said, taking a sip of his wine. "Robinson is an unusual first name."

"It was my great-grandfather's name," I admitted. "His first name. He was English. Came over here in his twenties. I don't know much about him, but my father has a cricket trophy with his name on it. That's how I know."

"Nice."

"And your name?"

"Soren De Silva," he said. "My grandparents moved from Argentina to Canada after the war."

"Canada?"

"Yep. I'm actually Canadian. Just across the border in Alberta though, so it's not even a two-hour drive from my house to my folks' place for a Sunday dinner." He nodded with a smile. "Been here in the States for six years now, Hartbridge for two."

"Hm," I said flatly. "So you're a Flames or Oilers fan?"

His grin was spectacular. "Flames to the bone. And you?"

"Canucks."

He groaned and let his head fall back. "Gah. I guess a gorgeous doctor from the West Coast had to have some flaw. Though they are Canadian, so you're forgiven."

Gorgeous?

I chuckled, ignoring the heat in my cheeks. "The Flames? And there I was thinking a Harley Davidson-riding firefighter who cooked me dinner didn't have any flaws."

His eyes were warm and shining. His tongue peaked

out at the corner of his smile. "I can take my casserole and go home if you'd prefer."

"No," I replied. Then I remembered him saying he was hungry. "Should we dish it up?"

He gave a nod. "We should."

My stomach felt all jittery, which was ridiculous. But damn, he was so freaking sexy and there was definite interest on his behalf.

The way his eyes caught mine, or the way his tongue would leave a wet stripe across his pink bottom lip.

He was flirting with me, and I liked it. It felt good.

It was the first time I'd felt anything in so long.

We took our plates and glasses of wine to the table and sat down. "You got yourself a nice place," he said, though I got the feeling he was just being polite.

I looked around my small living room, at the furniture from my expensive high-rise apartment that now looked out of place in a quaint small-town bungalow. "I, uh, I never spent much time at home, to be honest."

"Working?"

"All the time."

Soren took a mouthful of food and chewed thoughtfully. "Get the feeling there's a story there."

I laughed, though it wasn't really funny. "There is. Short version is that I burned myself out. Was about to quit medicine and a friend convinced me to come here instead. Take a step back and regroup, get back to basics with a general practice. Then if I still didn't love it, I'd have my answer."

Soren's eyes met mine and he gave a nod. "Sounds like a very smart friend."

"She is."

He nodded slowly and pushed a piece of beef on his plate around with his fork a bit, frowning at it. "So, is *she* a close friend?"

Jeez.

He was just asking outright.

"Kind of. A colleague first and foremost, but I'd consider her a friend."

Then his eyes met mine. "Oh, so not *that* kind of friend? Because I thought I was picking up on some single vibes, but if I was wrong—"

"You're not wrong," I replied a little too fast. "I mean, single yes. If you're asking me if I'm into men, then the answer is also yes. If those were the vibes you were picking up on." I couldn't help but smile.

"They were, yes." His eyes lit up and he fought a smirk. "Well, that and those flamingo pajamas were a bit of a hint."

"Oh my god, that's it. I'm putting them in the trash."

He laughed. "No, please don't. They're amazing."

I couldn't believe we were even having this conversation.

I stabbed some meat with my fork. "So what vibes exactly was I putting out there for you to think 'hmm, this guy's into men'?"

He laughed and sipped his wine. "Well, not counting the first day we met, when you came stomping over to give me a piece of your mind, wearing your cute little pride pajamas—"

Oh, dear god.

His grin widened. "When I took my helmet off and you almost swallowed your tongue."

"I absolutely did not," I replied, indignantly.

"Ah, yeah you did. And then when I was washing the fire engine, you were staring pretty hard."

"You were wearing a tight T-shirt, and you were wet, and I was pulling a coat on because it was cold. I had concerns for your health."

He laughed, such a pretty sound, and his eyes glittered with humor. "Hm-mm. Sure."

My face was on fire, and I didn't even care. "So, what about you? What vibes do you give off?"

"One hundred percent gay vibes." Then, as if he remembered something, he shifted in his seat and took another mouthful of stew, ripping apart some bread while he chewed. "And tragically single. And you said you were too . . . but is there not someone you left behind in Seattle? A handsome cardiothoracic surgeon who's going to turn up here to try to win you back, perhaps?"

I snorted. "I think you've watched one too many Hallmark movies."

He smiled, kind of. "That wasn't a no."

"There's no one. Cardiothoracic surgeon or otherwise. Hasn't been anyone in a long time." I sighed. "My entire life has been work. Hence the disillusioned, catastrophic burnout."

His hazel eyes met mine. "Disillusioned catastrophic burnout. Sounds bad."

"It was." I frowned, my appetite waning. "Sorry. Didn't mean to crash the mood."

"You didn't, so don't be sorry. You have nothing to apologize for."

"What about you? I can't imagine this little town of Hartbridge has a thriving queer dating scene."

He chuckled. "Dating, absolutely zero. As for queer guys, there's a few of us. All established couples, though. I've been the odd one out for a while." I knew about the couples but still mustn't have hidden my surprise too well because he laughed. "You seem shocked."

"Well, yeah. But not really about the fact there are gay couples here. More that you're single."

"Me?"

I gestured in his general direction, then up and down for good measure. "Harley Davidson-riding firefighter. I've seen you wearing a T-shirt washing the fire engine, remember?" I sipped my wine, wondering what I was missing about him. He was gorgeous, yes. But he was also funny and sweet and a good cook, and kind enough to offer to cook his new neighbor dinner.

He laughed as he swallowed his food. "Well, you see, there's this running joke in this town. Well, between us queer guys, that there's some crazy Christmas Cupid that sets his sights on queer men and makes them fall madly in love. I've been late to the party, apparently, because he missed me. Popped the other guys good and well, though."

I snorted out a laugh. "Cupid?"

He nodded. "Slings and arrows and all that."

Now I stared. "Did you . . . did you just quote Shakespeare?"

His eyes met mine. "I did, yes."

My heart thumped. "Okay, so a Harley Davidson-riding firefighter who quotes Shakespeare. I'm clearly missing something. What's the real reason you're single?"

He barked out a laugh. "Ouch. I don't know. I'm kinda new to town. Been here two years. Kept my head down for the first year, in respects to dating. I'd go back to Missoula to get any particular itch scratched, if you know what I mean."

"I believe I do know, yes."

"And I do shiftwork. We're only a small town, so we don't do twenty-four hour shifts like the bigger fire halls. One week, is seven a.m. till four p.m. Second week is three p.m. to midnight, and week three I do the solo graveyard, and I'm always on-call. Makes it kind of difficult to meet people and keep them when I don't keep normal hours."

"Oh, believe me, I know."

God, if anyone understood that it was me.

He smiled. "Last year, I thought for all of half a second I might've had a chance with the new schoolteacher who came to town, but he only had eyes for the deputy. The Christmas Cupid got them both."

"That's a shame."

"Not really. I mean, for me, maybe. But not for them. I've become pretty good friends with the deputy this last year, and they're so in love it could be akin to madness. I can see now that I was never in the running, because they're ridiculously perfect for each other."

I snorted. "Akin to madness."

Soren laughed and sipped his wine. "And the year before that it was another new guy in town and the guy from the lumberyard. And the year before that it was another newcomer and the owner at the B&B. Oh, that's the guy you met at the diner today. One of the Australians."

"Right."

"And the other Australian came to town and drove his car into a snowbank, met the owner of the hardware store, and bam! Total goner. Christmas Cupid got them too."

This was ridiculous. "And this happens every year?"

He nodded. "Apparently. I've only been here for two, but the guys swear it's a thing. Seems to me the only criteria is one of you's gotta be new to town before Christmas, and single." He made a face. "Hate to break it to ya, Doc, but looks like you're it this year."

I scoffed, because that was absurd.

"I'm not looking," I said. "I came here to . . ." To what? Find myself? Regroup? Learn how to live again? "It doesn't matter what I came here for. The fact is I'm a local doctor, and I can't be having any kind of relationship with a patient."

Soren's smirk was slow to spread, his eyes locked and loaded on mine. "Not everyone in town's a patient. For example, my doctor's in Missoula. I mean, just as an example. But I'm not on the books at your medical clinic at all." He held my gaze and I swore the temperature in the room went up. "You know, if you happen to find that information pertinent, for future reference. Or statistical curiosity."

Jeepers. He was just putting himself out there.

"Statistical curiosity, huh?"

He laughed. "Well, you're a doctor, I figured you'd appreciate data."

God, this was flirting. He was *actually flirting* with me. It had been so long since I'd flirted with anyone, and damn, it was invigorating. Consequences be damned, this was a rush.

I had to play too. "And what do firemen appreciate?"

His grin was wicked. "Heat."

Oh hell.

I laughed, but dear god, I was so out of my depth. So to break the spell between us, I pushed my plate away and shook my head. "I think you're playing a game I can't possibly win." I hated that I was such a downer, that I couldn't be fun and flirty and sexy as he was. "I'm . . . look, I'm flattered. It's been a long time since I've felt . . . well, since I've felt anything. But I came to Hartbridge to decompress and . . . I don't know. Find myself? Remember who I am and why I became a doctor. Find a sense of community. That probably sounds silly and wildly inappropriate. You were kind enough to bring me dinner and the flirting was fun, if that's what it was." I realized then, in a horrifying moment, that maybe I'd imagined it. "Oh god, was it flirting? See? I don't even know. That's how out of practice I am. I'm so sorry—"

Soren reached over and squeezed my hand. "It's fine. And yes, it was flirting. Though maybe I'm not as good at it as I thought if you weren't entirely certain . . ."

Now I was just embarrassed. "No, believe me, you were great at it. Too good, even. I'm just . . . I . . ."

He sat back in his seat, still smiling, but he seemed to understand something that I wasn't even sure I did. "You know what? Tomorrow is the first of December, right?"

I wasn't sure I followed. "Ah, yes."

"Perfect. Tomorrow night is the annual Christmas tree lighting ceremony in the park, and you're coming with me. The whole town will be there, and I'm going to introduce you to all the guys. You want a sense of community, then that's what I'm gonna give you."

"Oh."

His smile was bright and perfect. "Just you wait till you see Main Street tomorrow. First of December this whole town becomes something out of a Christmas movie. Believe me, you're gonna love it."

Chapter Four

SOREN

TAKING the bike to work was a great idea.

Well actually, I thought starting my bike before seven in the morning outside Rob's bedroom wall was a great idea. I hoped it woke him up, and I hoped it made him mad or smile . . . or just think of me in general.

He could pretend it annoyed him but the fact was, he'd mentioned me being a Harley Davidson rider several times as if it were a very good thing.

A Harley Davidson-riding firefighter.

As if it was some qualifier on the sexy scale.

So yeah, kicking my bike over before seven and giving the throttle an extra turn while smiling at his bedroom wall was a great way to start my day.

Like having dinner with him the night before was a great way to spend my evening.

I'd spent only a handful of hours with him in total, and I couldn't say I really knew him at all, but I liked him.

As in *liked* him.

There was something about him that drew me in.

Something I couldn't get out of my head.

"Hey," Chuck greeted me with a grin. "So? How'd it go?"

Of course he knew I was having dinner with Rob last night.

I couldn't help the grin. I squared my helmet, wallet, and keys away in my locker and turned to him, not even caring what my face gave away. "It went well."

His eyebrows almost met his hairline. "You banged already?"

I scoffed out a laugh. "No, dude. No. It's not like that. It's . . . I dunno. It's . . ."

"It's what?"

"I don't wanna say nice, because that sounds lame. But it's just . . . nice, man. I like him. And he's different."

"Different how? Like weird different?"

"No. Different from the others."

He stared and his mouth did some weird O thing. "I see."

"You see what?"

"You're down bad already after one date."

I laughed. "It wasn't really a date." Though it kinda was. "It was just dinner. We talked, ate some food, talked some more, and I went back to my place."

"No banging?"

"No."

"Did you make out?"

"No."

He squinted at me. "Did you kiss at all?"

"Nope."

He seemed confused by this. "But your entire game play

is the nail and bail while you wait for Mr. Perfect to fall in your lap."

I stopped and stared at him, my shoulders falling. "It is not."

Chuck raised one eyebrow. "Dude."

"Look, my previous casual approach was only because there were no dating prospects. Those guys had specific needs that I helped fulfill. They were bar hookups in a different town, nothing more." I shrugged. "If I still lived in Missoula and not just visited on random weekends, then maybe I'd have got to know them better."

"Like learn their first names?"

I snorted. "I learned their first names . . . of some of them."

He laughed. "But this new guy, you learned his name."

"I did."

He studied me for a second. "Holy shit, you really do like him."

I tried to play it cool. "I could like him. If it progressed any further, I could find myself liking him a lot. I dunno what it is about him. He's certainly not my usual type."

"Is he married?"

"What? No."

"And he likes guys?"

"Yes."

"Then that's all the type you need."

"What's that supposed to mean?"

Chuck shoved me toward the kitchen. "Just have some fun. It doesn't need to be wedding bells and forever. What are the odds that another gay man comes to town? Even if it's just casual fun, it could still be a good thing, right?"

"Well . . . I guess."

He sighed as he handed me my empty coffee mug. "I know you want all the bells and whistles, dude. And there's nothing wrong with that. So he might not be Mr. Right, but Mr. Right Now is still a win, yeah?"

I frowned at him. "Okay, first of all, I'm not that desperate for love that I'd settle for just anyone. And secondly, that's Doctor Right Now, thank you very much."

Doug chose that exact moment to walk in, carrying a huge cardboard box. He dumped it on the table. "Speaking of right now. We're out this afternoon and evening, remember, so I want it done this morning."

Then he turned the box around to show us the words *Xmas decorations* scrawled across it. He grinned. "Happy December first."

I LOVED WINTER. I loved snow and the holidays, the warm fires, and the idea of having someone to cozy up with in front of them.

Which got me thinking about what Chuck said. Now, I loved Chuck like a brother. And I knew he never meant any harm by what he'd said.

It had stung because it was the truth.

I *did* want to fall in love. I wanted a partner, a lover, someone to share my life with. I wanted what the other queer couples in town had—that perfect relationship with someone who accepted them exactly as they were.

Okay, so I was sure they weren't all perfect.

But I'd come to know Colson Price pretty well this last

year. After he'd met Braithe and come out of the closet, figuring we could both use a friend, I'd suggested we hang out and watch some game on TV. We'd become buddies and caught up often.

We actually had a lot in common.

He was a deputy; I was a firefighter. Both gay, both had been alone for a long while. We both loved hockey, and we had the same taste in men.

His partner Braithe was absolutely perfect for him, and I'd been a fool to think I even stood a chance with him. I'd just seen a cute little British twink and thought it was my chance at finally meeting someone in my town . . .

And Chuck's words hit a little closer to home.

Because yeah, I was kinda lonely. And desperate for love.

So maybe I needed to hold back the reins a bit with my new neighbor. If I came on too strong, he'd probably run a mile anyway. The thing was, I *had* gone to Rob's place last night with hopes of something physical eventuating. I mean, if he wanted to get off, I wasn't going to say no.

But I realized pretty quickly that he was guarded, and whatever had happened back in Seattle had left him in a bad place.

What had he called it?

Disillusioned catastrophic burnout.

So yeah, he was left reeling and had come to Hartbridge to find some peace. To see if he still wanted to be a doctor. To find himself, and a sense of community.

So instead of offering him a mind-blowing orgasm, I offered to take him to the annual tree lighting night.

Because if he wanted to find a community, he'd definitely find that here in Hartbridge.

"That's not even," Chuck said from the bottom of the ladder I was currently standing on.

I looked at the string of tinsel I was hanging. "Yeah, it is."

"I'm telling ya, it's not even close. It needs to be up another two inches."

"Is that what your girl says?"

He grumbled and shook the ladder and I laughed as I stuck the stupid tinsel up another few inches. Why we decorated the fire hall was beyond me, but Doug insisted we get into the holiday spirit with the rest of the town.

Clay Henderson's red truck pulled up out front and I climbed down the ladder to go greet him and Rusty.

"Morning," I said.

They got out of his truck and Clay gave me a nod. "Morning."

I'd met him more times cleaning up fallen tree debris off roadways than I had in any get-togethers with the queer group. He was a big burly bear of a guy, wore plaid and coveralls, and swung an ax like a machine. But he was soft as a kitten for his boyfriend, Gunter.

"Christmas tree time," I said, nodding to the back of Clay's truck where there must have been a hundred small, netted trees. They decorated Main Street every year, and damn, if they didn't look amazing.

"Sure is," Clay said, dragging a tree down.

"Hey, Rusty," Chuck said, giving Rusty a familiar bro handshake.

"Chucky," he replied.

"Perfect timing," Chucky said. "We were just getting some decorating done. We'll add some baubles and tinsel to the tree."

"I was getting the decorating done," I said. "You were holding the ladder."

They looked up at the front of the fire hall, to the sign that read Hartbridge Fire Department 1910 and to the tinsel that now underlined it.

"The tinsel's crooked," Rusty said.

"It is not!" I said, looking at my handiwork. Okay, so maybe it wasn't perfectly straight. I tilted my head to the side. "You need to look at it like this."

Chuck gave me a shove. "Dipshit."

Clay laughed as he cut the netting, and the little tree shaped out nicely.

Chuck, with his arms crossed, nodded to the new tree. "So if this little guy goes missing and accidently ends up in my living room, no one will be suspicious, right?"

Now it was my turn to shove him. "Dipshit."

Rusty laughed at us. "Well, we better keep going. Only got another hundred to do. Town has to look like a Christmas movie before the tree lighting tonight."

"Oh, Clay," I said. "That reminds me. Will you and Gunter be there tonight?"

He gave me an odd look before schooling it away. "I believe so, yeah. Why?"

"Oh, it's just . . ." I don't know why I felt so nervous for asking. "I was talking to the new doctor in town and thought maybe he'd like to hear about Gunter's start-up. Could be something he might be interested in helping out with, and if you'll both be there tonight, I could introduce you, that's all."

Clay seemed pleasantly surprised by this. "Sounds good."

"Oh look," Chuck said. "Speak of the devil."

And sure enough, Robinson's car came down the street and pulled up in the medical center parking lot. It was directly across from us, so the fact the four of us were standing there watching wasn't weird at all.

Much.

"He and Soren are dating," Chuck whispered.

Clay and Rusty both spun to stare at me. "We are not," I hissed at Chuck, giving him a much harder shove. "We aren't," I explained more civilly to Clay and Rusty. "He's my next-door neighbor, that's all."

"That is *not* all," Chuck added with a laugh, and I tried to kick him in the pants just as Rob got out of his car.

Of course he saw.

"Go and say good morning," Chuck said, and this time I did manage to connect my boot with his ass.

Of course, Rob saw that too. I just hoped he didn't hear.

But then Rob raised one hand, kinda awkwardly. "Morning."

Yep. He'd heard.

Clay and Rusty both laughed as they went on their way, but I raised my hand in a wave back at Rob. "Morning."

Rob ducked his head and went into his clinic and Chuck stood behind me waiting for me to turn around. He raised his hand and spoke in a baby voice. "Morning."

I was about to tackle him but Doug came out with a clipboard and an out-of-patience sigh. He handed the clipboard to me. "Hydrant report. Both of you. Now."

"Hey," I said when Rob opened his door. He was wearing dark jeans and a black sweater, which made his hair seem more salt than pepper.

God, he was handsome.

It was not lost on me that he was the first older guy I'd ever been attracted to. And when I say older, he had to be no more than thirty-five. I just meant older than me.

"Come in," he said, opening the door for me. "I'm almost done. Just finishing the dishes." He looked at my feet. "Leave your boots on. I won't be long."

I noticed he had shoes on so I didn't feel too bad, but I still wiped them on the doormat before stepping inside. I followed him into the kitchen. "So how was day number two?"

He pulled his sweater sleeves up to his elbows and dipped his hands into the soapy sink water. "It was good. I met Doctor Humphries today."

"And?"

"Nice guy. The townsfolk clearly love him."

"They do."

Doctor Humphries was a great man, and everybody did love him. He'd been the town doctor for forty years or something. But he had to be almost seventy. It was no surprise he was cutting his hours back.

"I have big shoes to fill," Rob said.

Which of course made me look down at his shoes. Then up his legs, the backs of his thighs, his ass. His narrow waist and shoulders, and how his hands washed the dishes. Jesus, that shouldn't be so sexy . . .

How was that sexy?

"He had an appointment in Mossley yesterday," Rob went on to say.

Right. Yes. Doctor Humphries.

"He was sorry he hadn't caught me on my first day, but Katie told him, in no uncertain terms, that my standard was, and I quote, 'Fine.'"

That made me chuckle. "Sounds like Katie."

He smiled as he pulled the plug and wiped his hands on a dishtowel, and holy hell, that was sexy too.

How was this man so damned sexy when all he was doing was drying his hands?

I wanted to step over to him, take his face in my hands, and kiss him. Feel his tongue against mine, feel his body beneath me, his hands on me . . .

"Soren?"

"Huh?"

He laughed. "I asked how your day was."

Oh. I was sure my face flamed as if he could somehow tell where my mind had gone.

"Oh, it was fine."

"No terrible fires to battle?"

"No, thankfully. There were fire hydrants to maintain and reports to fill out."

His eyes shone as he smiled. "Sounds fun."

"Not really."

"So what do firemen do when they're not fighting fires? When everything's covered in snow."

"Maintenance, fire prevention, education. Winter means more house fires, unfortunately. Wood fires, electric heaters, clothes drying in front of heaters, overloaded electric panels, circuits."

"Oh, of course."

"And we help clean up accidents and fallen trees, that kind of thing."

His eyes met mine and there was a kindness there that made my heart thump. "I guess I've never thought about what firemen do. Apart from putting out fires."

I chuckled. "And what do doctors do in quiet towns like Hartbridge?"

"Colds, immunizations, prenatal care, the cutest baby check-ups, and a sprained wrist from a horse-riding incident."

"Ouch."

"It's a nice change of pace for me."

"Don't find it . . . boring?"

He shook his head. "Heavens, no. I mean, it's only day two, but so far, I'm enjoying it."

"I'm glad."

Rob smiled and hung the dishtowel over the oven door handle. "So, are we heading out to the tree lighting thing everyone in town was talking about today?"

I clapped my hands together. "Yes." Then I checked my watch. "We have time, and it'll be a nice walk."

"Walk? It's dark and there's snow . . ."

I laughed. "Doesn't it snow in Seattle?"

"Well, it does . . . sometimes. But can we drive?"

"Nope. It's a few blocks, and honestly, it'll be quicker than if you tried to find a parking space." I chuckled at his expression. "Come on, city boy. You'll be fine. You gotta get used to it. May as well start now."

"City boy?" He raised an eyebrow. "I'm older than you." Then he made a face. "Well, I don't know how old you are, exactly, but I already know I'm older than you."

"I'm twenty-eight," I admitted, quickly jumping on this perfect opportunity to ask his age. "How old are you?"

"Thirty-six."

"You make it sound like you're fifty-six. You're still young." I put my hands on his shoulders and turned him toward his front door. "Grab your coat or we'll miss it."

Thirty-six.

Eight years older than me. Now, that wasn't a huge difference, and it certainly wasn't a deal breaker. It was just different from what I was used to.

He slid his coat on and pulled his gloves from his coat pocket, so I did the same, pulling them on as we walked down his front steps to the sidewalk.

"It's not even that cold yet," I noted. "And there's not too much snow." I toed the small mound of build-up on the edge of the sidewalk. "It's got a few feet to go yet."

He made a face, which was adorably cute. "Remind me why I moved here? In winter?"

"Just you wait till you see how pretty it is." I nodded to the direction of Main Street. "This way."

He wasn't too surefooted as we walked. "I never cared

too much for walking in snow," he said. "Seen far too many broken wrists and coccyx injuries for my liking."

"What injuries?"

He rolled his eyes. "Coccyx. Tailbones."

I laughed. "I just wanted to hear you say it again."

"Are you twelve?"

"No. Twenty-eight. We just had this conversation. Is your memory going already, old man?"

He stopped walking to stare at me, but his foot slid. I grabbed him—one hand on his arm, the other on his waist, and pulled him against me. His face was closer than I anticipated, his eyes bluer under the streetlight.

"I'm not an old man," he whispered.

"Oh, I know," I replied. My gaze went to his lips, and so help me, I wanted to kiss him. He was close enough that I could have. I had him in my arms and could feel his body warmth.

And I could so easily lean in that final inch and press my lips to his . . .

But then he pulled away, clearing his throat and brushing himself down. "I, uh, I, um . . . thank you. For not letting me fall over."

My heart was still hammering and my breath left me in a plume of steam. "I just didn't want you to hurt your coccyx."

His cheeks went red and he mumbled something under his breath before he began walking again. "So what is this tree lighting ceremony exactly?"

I fell into step beside him. "There's a huge fir tree by the river, and every year they cover it in lights and the mayor wishes everyone happy holidays."

Rob made a face. "Sounds . . . fun."

I laughed. "It's a community thing. It's not the big winter wonderland thing when they close the street off. That's on Christmas Eve this year. That's the fun one. People come from all over. There are food and craft stalls, a kiddie train, photos with Santa, and we bring the fire engine down by the tree so the kids can climb up."

That made him smile at least. "So why are we going tonight?"

"Because there's some people I want you to meet," I admitted.

He shot me a look. "People? I meet people all day."

"No, these are our kind of people," I said. "You said before you wanted a sense of community, so that's what I'm doing."

He stopped at the end of the block. "I didn't mean for you to . . . introduce me . . . God, is this going to be weird?"

He made me laugh. "It's not going to be weird." Then I reconsidered. "Okay, well, look. Hamish is a bit weird. He's one of the Australians. But he's lovely and funny; he just has no filter. I've only met him a handful of times. Since Colson and I became buddies, really. Braithe is good friends with Hamish, so I know him by proxy. But they're all great, I promise."

"And the two Australians are together?"

"No. Hamish is with Ren from the hardware store. And the other Australian is Jayden. He works at the diner sometimes, but he's with Cas from the bed and breakfast."

"Right. Sorry. I think I knew that."

"The guy I'm hoping to introduce you to is Gunter. He's with Clay Henderson. The big guy in the old sawmill truck who was dropping off all the Christmas trees up Main Street."

Rob looked concerned. "I'm going to need you to draw me a chart."

I laughed as I took his elbow and we crossed the street. "It'll be fine."

"Why am I meeting Gunter?"

"Because I think you guys could hit it off," I explained. "And he's started up a community youth group that I think you could really enjoy."

"Why would I enjoy that?" he asked as we walked down to where the crowd was gathering by the river.

"Because you wanted to find a sense of community," I explained. "And what's a better way to do that than helping out at a center for teenagers."

He looked about to object but Mr. Wilford spotted me as we edged into the crowd. "Soren," he said with a tip of his hat.

"Mr. Wilford," I replied. "Need someone to look at your heater again, drop by the station and give me a holler."

"Will do," he said.

Then Mrs. James from Cypress Street said hello. Then Rosie from the store, then Richard from the mechanics, and that was only the last thirty yards.

"Oh my god, do you know everyone?" Rob whispered.

"Mostly. It's a small town, and I do community-based work, which helps." I spotted the guys and gestured toward them. "This way."

Clay saw me first and greeted me with a smile and firm handshake. "Ah, good to see you again."

"Likewise," I replied. We kind of had the attention of

the group so I made a quick round of introductions. "Guys, this is Doctor Rob O'Reilly. He's new to town and was lucky enough to move next door to me."

"Uh, hi." Rob nodded and everyone said hello back.

I didn't miss the way Hamish and Jayden were grinning at me, but I didn't want to embarrass Rob, so I focused on Gunter. "Gunter, I was telling Rob about your teen support group. I thought he might be interested in helping out." I winced at Rob's clear surprise. "Well, I mean, once he gets settled in. He's only been here for a few days."

I hadn't really meant to throw Rob under the bus, but I really did think he would be a great fit for Gunter's organization. And it could be really good for Rob too.

Maybe I shouldn't have been so pushy . . .

Colson arrived with a clap on my shoulder, Braithe beside him. Colson was on duty, given his uniform, and Braithe was quickly absorbed by Hamish and Jayden, and Rob was soon talking with Gunter and Clay.

"Is this the new guy Braithe told me about?" Colson asked quietly.

"Yep."

Colson nodded slowly, smiling as Rob listened intently to whatever Gunter was saying.

"Hamish's dead certain that it's gonna be another one of those Christmas Cupid things. Hope you're ready."

I snorted. "He's been here for a matter of days. We should probably give him some time."

"That wasn't a no," Colson said. "Are you interested?"

Jesus.

"I don't know what I am. Intrigued, maybe," I allowed,

because that was a safer bet than just admitting I was interested. "He's a nice guy."

Colson glanced over at him again, then met my eyes. "Sexy older nice guy," he whispered.

I nudged him with my elbow. "You're not supposed to notice these things."

"I'm a deputy. It's my job to notice physical attributes about people."

I snorted, shaking my head at the ridiculousness. "There's something about him," I murmured. "But I don't want to read too much into it."

"Why not?" Colson shrugged. "Read away, my friend. Take whatever you can get. You never know how long it will last, and sometimes you gotta jump in with both feet and see what comes of it."

"Is that the best advice you got?"

"Look where it got me," he replied. "Braithe and I were just supposed to be a casual fling for a few weeks, and look at us now. Same with the others. None of us were supposed to be here, or stay here. Certainly weren't supposed to find the love of our lives." He shrugged. "But sometimes we have no say in it at all. This town has other ideas."

I scoffed. "You don't believe in that Cupid shit too, do you?"

"I didn't." But then he looked around the group of us, at the couples. "Kinda hard to ignore it, dontcha think?"

I ran my hand through my hair. "I dunno. He's . . . he's been through something," I murmured. "And he's here to regroup. Pretty sure he's not looking for anything."

Colson shrugged with a sigh. "And I'm pretty sure that

old Hartbridge Christmas magic doesn't care. And it *is* the first of December."

I rolled my eyes but couldn't help but smile. "You've been hanging around with Hamish too much."

Colson laughed, but he was called away by the sheriff, who I realized was talking to the mayor, and to Doug, my boss. Seeing Rob was deep in conversation with Gunter and Clay, I made my way over for a quick hello.

And then Chuck found us and I got busy talking shit with him and his girlfriend, Delaney, and it wasn't until the mayor called for everyone's attention, so they could flip the switch on the lights, that I headed back to Rob and the others.

I saw him looking around, looking for someone, and he smiled when he saw me. "Sorry," I whispered. "Had to say hello to my boss and the sheriff."

"Thought you'd bailed on me," Rob said quietly.

"I'm not the bailing type," I replied. Not meaning it how it sounded, but not taking it back once it was out.

I was trying really hard to put what Colson had said out of my mind. I didn't want to pressure Rob into anything he wasn't ready for, and the man had only been in town for a few days. I needed to chill the hell out.

This was absurd.

One gorgeous, smart single gay man turns up in town and I'm all over him like a dog in heat.

But then they flipped the switch on the lights and the huge fir tree came to life in gorgeous pastel colors against the dark night, and Rob gasped beside me.

His face lit up too, smiling and bright, the Christmas

lights reflecting in his eyes, and I swear the world stopped turning. I'd never seen anything so beautiful.

It took a few seconds for me to snap out of whatever spell *that* was, and I ignored the way Hamish and Jayden were smiling at me. Ren from the hardware store clapped my shoulder with a laugh.

"Merry Christmas, Soren."

Hmm, yeah. Right. Sure.

"Yeah. Merry Christmas."

Chapter Five

ROB

"You were right about everything," I said.

Soren and I were walking home. It really wasn't far and the snow wasn't too icy—I only almost slipped a few times —and despite the cold, it was a beautiful night.

"About everything?" he asked. "That the Flames are better than the Canucks? Because yes, that's correct."

I snorted. "Okay, so not everything."

He shoved his hands into his coat pockets. "About what then?"

"Tonight," I replied. "That it'd be fun. That the whole town would be as pretty as a Christmas picture. That the group of guys you were introducing me to were great. That Gunter's organization is something I could be interested in." Then I shrugged. "And that Hamish is a little weird." I waited for his eyes to meet mine before I laughed. "Just kidding. He seems totally nice."

He grinned at me. "He is. His husband is too. Ren."

"From the hardware store," I added. "See? I'm learning."

Soren grinned. "You'll be a local before you know it."

"I highly doubt that."

"I'm glad you and Gunter hit it off. I thought you might, and he's been working hard at getting his little center up and running."

"I'm going to stop in on my day off," I admitted. "Well, one of my days off. I have four days off a week, which is more than I've had in the entirety of the last decade, so . . ."

"Four days off in ten years?" He made a face. "No wonder you said you were burned out."

I gave him a sad smile. I was about to say it wasn't the hours that got me in the end but didn't want to ruin the mood. "Yep. Actual days off. I won't know what to do with myself, so helping out seems like a good place to start. Gunter said it was rewarding. He retired early and wanted to give something back. That's kinda remarkable."

"Some people'll surprise ya," he said as he stopped walking. "There are some truly decent people in this town."

I looked up and down the street. Houses with warm Christmas lights in their windows, looking cozy against the dark and cold, and utter silence. It was so peaceful and serene. Hell, even this street looked like a scene from a Christmas movie.

Then I realized we'd stopped in front of his house. "Oh." Then I noticed he also had Christmas lights in his window. "You have lights up." Then I realized something else kind of horrifying. "Am I the only one who doesn't?"

Soren chuckled. "Maybe. But you just moved in, so they'll keep the pitchforks at bay for a few days."

I made a face. "I better get busy on my days off. Tell me, where does one buy Christmas lights in Hartbridge? Is the

Home Mart my only option? Should I notify the pitchfork hoards that I may have to order them online and to expect a short delay? And a tree. I guess I'll need one of those too, lest they forgo in-house inspections, and I won't be burned at the stake in the town square." I faked a gasp, my hand to my chest. "Oh my god. Is that Hartbridge's deep dark secret? Little town appears perfect on the outside but harbors an insidious underbelly of Christmas rituals, and anyone who doesn't conform to supply the most perfect Christmas decorations will be sacrificed to the Christmas elves."

Soren snorted. "Yep. That's it. Christmas elves come kidnap you, and while there's not burning at the stake, they will torture you with Mariah Carey's Christmas hits album, non-stop until you beg for mercy."

I clutched at my chest. "Oh, the horror."

He smiled, his breath leaving him in a plume of steam. The tip of his nose and ears were pink. His eyes met mine and for a heart-stopping moment, neither of us spoke. I almost asked him if he wanted to come in for a drink, or a kiss, or an entire night of wild sex . . . It shocked me that I'd think that. That I would even want that.

And yeah, I think I wanted that.

Hell yes you do, Robinson. That thump-thump of your heart right now is anticipation and desire. I know it's been a while, but you remember how those things feel, right?

"I better go," Soren said quietly. He looked a little torn and I regretted my indecision. He took a step back. "Before, um . . . before . . ."

"Before?"

He took another step back. "Before it gets late. Or

something." He almost tripped on a clump of snow by his driveway.

"Oh, be careful," I said, kinda reaching for him but not close enough.

He laughed and looked at where he was putting his feet when he stepped back again. "Good night, Rob."

"Night." When he got to his porch, I remembered my manners. "Thank you, for tonight. I had a great time."

His grin lit up his entire face. "I'm glad. I'll see you . . . tomorrow or something."

I nodded, looking forward to it already. "Or something."

I took myself home, smiling as I unlocked my front door and kicked off my boots. I smiled at my cute house, welcoming and warm, and I was still smiling as I climbed into bed.

I hadn't been expecting to enjoy myself tonight. To be honest, when Soren had told me he was introducing me to a bunch of guys at a town Christmas tree lighting night, I'd very wrongly assumed it was going to be awkward and lame.

Oh, how wrong I'd been.

The guys were great. Well, what I knew of them so far. I was shocked that this little town had its own circle of queer couples, and I was shocked to find how much I liked them already.

Most circles of rich doctor friends I'd had back in Seattle consisted of pretentious social climbers and superficial snobs. Fine for a dinner party and a few glasses of wine, then after I'd leave early, I'd need a week to take the knives out of my back.

These Hartbridge guys didn't seem like that at all.

I really liked Gunter and Clay. I could see why Soren might think Gunter and I would get along. We were closer in age, probably. Closer in mental age, anyway. Definitely both quieter, introverted serious types, while Hamish and Braithe were the extroverts for sure.

Soren was definitely more at ease talking to the deputy, Colson, and Ren the hardware guy. And he'd been laughing with Clay when I'd seen him outside the fire station in the morning.

He seemed to fall into stride with the tops of the group, that was for sure. Not that I was presuming . . .

Yes you are. You're presuming and stereotyping.

No I'm not.

Yes, you—

No, it's called wishful thinking.

Wishful what?

Wishful thinking. You want him to be a top so he can take you to bed and rail you so thoroughly.

Oh my god. That's not—

You can't lie to me. I'm literally your brain.

I pulled my pillow over my face. *Shut up. It's just . . . he's sexy and flirty and it feels good to . . .*

To what?

To feel something.

I bet you want to feel his something.

"Oh, shut up," I said, rolling onto my side. "You're having conversations with your subconscious. Never a good sign." I sighed, realizing I was now talking out loud to myself.

This was ridiculous and absurd.

And yet, I was still smiling.

That wasn't good.

DOCTOR HUMPHRIES WAS in his office when I arrived. He was an absolute gentleman. From that generation of understated men who dressed well, tipped their hats to women, and spoke well-chosen words.

Except now he was muttering to himself.

I cleared my throat, not wanting to startle him. "Everything okay?"

He laughed as he hung his hat and scarf. "Just talking to myself," he said.

I almost laughed. I hadn't really intended to bring it up, but now that he'd mentioned it . . ." "Oh. Uh. Funny you should mention talking to yourself."

He paused as he hung his coat. "And why would that be funny?"

"Well, I, uh . . ." Jeez. There was no other way to say this. "I have found myself having conversations with myself a lot in the last few days."

His faded blue eyes sparkled as he hung his coat. "Don't suppose you've been answering yourself too?"

"Well, actually, yes."

He stopped then, when he realized I was being serious. "Listen, Doctor O'Reilly. I'm gonna tell you a little secret." He slowly put on his white doctor coat. "I talk to myself all the time. And I answer myself too, and I haven't found any reason for concern yet. Some days it's the most intelligent conversation we can have." He winked.

"Oh." I hadn't been expecting his sense of humor.

He smiled as he shook his head. "You're a good doctor and you've just left a high-stress, fast-paced career and moved to a new town with a population smaller than the number of people who probably lived in your old apartment building. You're allowed to be questioning things in your head, sorting out your thoughts, and putting them in order."

"I guess . . ."

"Do the conversations with yourself invoke thoughts of concern? For your well-being or safety of others?"

"What? Oh no. No, nothing like that. It's just me, and the voice in my head telling me I might actually be happy here, if I give it a chance."

He smiled then and nodded sagely. "Sounds like good advice."

I tried to smile in return. "Well, maybe . . . I just . . . I'm not really in the habit of having full conversations with myself in bed at night." I regretted saying that second part the moment it was out of my mouth. "Sorry. That was too much information."

Doctor Humphries studied me for a long while. "I can see you're worried, so I tell you what," he said. "If you think there's any reason for concern, and if it escalates, or if the conversations in your head start to involve voices other than your own, then come let me know. But for now, just give yourself a few more days to settle in. You're probably out of routine, in a new place, meeting new people. New job." He gestured at his office, to the clinic. "I think you'll be fine."

It was hard not to be reassured by him. He was so good at this. Because I did feel better. Kind of. "Okay, thanks."

"And for what it's worth," he said gently, "I think your subconscious is right."

"My what?"

"The voice in your head with which you've been having conversations."

"Of course." Right. Yes. "Uh, which part, exactly?"

"Where you were telling yourself to give Hartbridge a chance."

Now my smile was more genuine. "Gonna give it my best."

"Good," he replied, just as Katie arrived and our day began. It was a relaxed day with a steady stream of patients, and Katie kept everything running like a well-oiled machine. Me included.

And I liked it. The way she structured my day really suited me. I liked the no-nonsense professional but still polite way Katie did everything. I liked her. Everyone did.

My day was a breeze.

I got home with enough time and energy to make myself a delicious dinner of chicken, pasta, and salad. Even poured a glass of wine and watched some ridiculous show on Netflix.

It was glorious.

In my old life, I'd be home by maybe midnight if I was lucky, eat something out of a can or a frozen dinner, and collapse into bed.

Now I had my feet up on the coffee table, glass of wine in my hand, laughing at a TV comedy show that everyone'd raved about a decade ago that I was only now getting to watch.

And, and this was the crazy part, I had tomorrow off work.

In fact, I had the next four days off work.

I still couldn't get my head around it.

I had plans. Well, plans that consisted of a trip to Home Mart for groceries and Christmas decorations. I could even go for a drive through the surrounding towns, see some sights, and get my bearings.

Four whole days. And not just once, but every week.

I was just about giddy with the realization.

It wasn't until I was in bed that it occurred to me that I hadn't heard Soren's bike. Surely I'd have heard him . . . Was his bike parked at his house when I'd come home? I couldn't remember seeing it. Was he out somewhere? Was he out fighting a fire? Was he okay?

That was a stupid line of thought, because why wouldn't he be okay? Why was I concerned about his safety?

He could be out on a date for all I knew . . .

On a date . . .

With someone else. Someone who was not me. Was he . . . was he smiling at them the way he smiled at me? Looking at them with those intense eyes?

Was he . . . ?

Why was I thinking about that?

Soren was free to do whatever he wanted, free to see whomever he wanted. He was free to look at anyone the way he looked at me. Hell, maybe he was . . .

Maybe I was overreacting.

There's no maybe about it, Robinson. You are overreact-

ing. You're thinking about him in ways you're not entitled to be—

"Oh, shut up," I said out loud. "You were on my side last night."

The voice in my head shut up, as asked. And I made the mental note to maybe tell Doctor Humphries that my late-night conversations with my subconscious had taken a snarky turn.

THE PROBLEM with being efficient and an over achiever, and used to having zero time to spare and running on fumes, meant that I'd had breakfast and been to the Home Mart and was home again all before 8:00 a.m.

I put my few groceries away, made myself another coffee, and stared at the few boxes of new Christmas decorations, which sat on the dining table.

I could begin putting up lights out front but then I'd have everything on my to-do list done by midday, and then what would I do with the other three and a half days off?

Plus, I reasoned, maybe I could ask my neighbor for some help. A certain neighbor who was handy with ladders and whatnot. Like a firefighter, perhaps.

Oh, and I'd need a Christmas tree.

I figured I could stop by Gunter's center to see it in action, and asking about finding a tree would be a good ice breaker. His boyfriend Clay was the one to ask, apparently, but Gunter would be a good place to start.

The center was just off Main Street. Unsurprisingly, most things in Hartbridge were. But this was a short-paved alley on the river side that could be a short mall if it tried harder. It was past the menswear store and the hairdresser, at the end of the dead end. The store directly next to it was empty, same as the one across from it. It was a quiet, tucked-away spot, and the trees and river on the other side made for privacy and it was perfect for a youth center.

The store front was glass, and maybe it had once been an office at some point. I opened the door and stuck my head in. Gunter was sliding a box onto one of the tables and he grinned when he saw me.

"Hey," he said.

"You open?" I asked. It was only nine o'clock in the morning after all.

"Sure, sure," he said, gesturing for me to come in. "Please, come in."

The space itself was maybe fifteen feet across and twice that long. There were bookshelves and beanbags, a small kitchenette, and what looked like an office at the back. There were posters on the walls, some pride flags, and some brochure racks with mental health cards and some sexual health ones too.

"Great place," I said.

He sighed as he looked around, smiling, proud. "Thanks. It's early days and I'm still getting it set up. There's a lot to do, but I'm happy with how it's going so far."

"Anything I can help with?" I didn't know why I felt so nervous. Almost as if I was asking if we could hang out, which was weird. We were both adults. I was a doctor, for Pete's sake. "I uh . . . I have actual days off for the first time ever and I'm not entirely sure what to do with myself. I had a to-do list for my first day off and was kinda done by eight, so . . ."

Gunter laughed. "So you're like me. You can't sit still, need to be productive."

"I guess, yeah. I rarely had any time off before, and if I did have a day, I slept."

"Sounds brutal."

"It was." I made a face. "Hence why I'm here."

His smile was warm and knowing. "I totally get it. I moved here, bought a fixer-upper, and buried myself in renovation work, and when the house was done, I started on the gardens, and when that was done, I tried to relax. I retired early, right? To spend my days leisurely doing whatever I felt like, but I was stir crazy after six months. Clay suggested I look into doing something community-based, and so I jumped right into this." He gestured around at the room. "Took a bit of red tape and background work, but here I am."

I found myself smiling. "I love that. I get the whole doing-something-community-based thing. I mentioned something similar to Soren and he thought helping out here would be good for me." I shoved my hands into my back pockets, nervous again. Or still. "That's why he introduced us the other night."

His eyes sparkled as he gave me a nod. "Ah, Soren. You're neighbors, right?"

My cheeks burned with . . . something akin to embarrassment. "Yes. He's, uh . . . he seems nice."

Gunter found that funny. "Nice, yes." Then he whispered, "Also a hot-as-hell firefighter. And he's single."

My face burned brighter. "So I heard."

He chuckled, but maybe for the sake of my embarrassment, he dropped the suggestiveness. "But seriously, he's a nice guy. I don't know him that well. Clay does. He works with him from time to time, you know, with forestry and fires, etcetera. He's become pretty good friends with Colson too, which is nice. He actually hasn't been in town too long. About the same as me, and I'm glad his circle now includes ours. Kinda need that, right?"

He meant his queer group of friends, his own little queer community.

"Never really had that," I admitted. "I mean, I did, but not really. My circle of friends was mostly doctors and there was no social life to speak of. No dating, even. Just casual . . . acquaintances."

His smirk told me he knew what I meant. "Ah, yes. Acquaintances of the Grindr community."

"They would be the ones." I snorted. "The Venn diagram of my community of friends and Grindr dates is pretty much one circle."

Gunter laughed. "Well, there's a community of friends here if you want. Though I should probably warn you about Hamish."

I snorted at that. "Soren said something similar."

"Nah, I'm just joking. He's great. He's one of my dearest friends now. We're actually meeting for dinner tonight at the diner. You're more than welcome to join us. There'll be a few of us. We try to catch up once a week or so, and with Christmas coming, Jayden and Cass get super busy so we need to get in early."

Oh.

"Oh, uh . . ." Could I join them? Did I want to? Hell yes, I really did. "That'd be nice, actually. I'd like that."

Gunter grinned. "Great."

He opened the box on the table, pulled out a roll of green and red tinsel, and handed it to me. "What are your Christmas decorating skills like?"

"I'm going to be very honest with you when I say below average."

"Perfect," he said with a chuckle. "Oh, and Soren's already invited to dinner tonight so you don't have to ask him."

Chapter Six

SOREN

I was already running late. I'd finished work later than expected and needed to shower to get rid of the smoke and sap, and I was just getting out of the shower when I heard a knock at my front door.

I wasn't expecting anyone and was in a hurry, so I just wrapped the towel around my waist. "Ah, coming!" I yelled out as I rushed to the door. "One sec, I'm not really decent." I peeked through the peephole to see Rob at my front door.

"Oh. Sorry," he said, a startled expression on his face. "I can . . . wait. Or come back. I shouldn't have just—"

I pulled the door open and grinned when he saw me, his gaze taking in my chest, the towel—lingering at the towel—before he even looked at my face.

He closed his eyes. "I'm so sorry."

I laughed, pleased at his reaction, and grabbed his arm and pulled him inside. "You're letting all the warm air out."

"My boots—"

"Your boots are fine." I shut the door behind him,

liking how we were standing a little closer than was probably necessary.

"I should have called first," he whispered. Then he cleared his throat. "Or texted."

"It's fine," I said, not moving back an inch. "I just finished work and I stank of burned pine and had sap stuck all over me."

He had great self-control to not avert his gaze from my eyes. Not even when I ran a hand over my chest, wiping away some beads of water. "You should probably get dressed," he murmured.

It was an effort not to grin at his reaction. "Probably."

He let out a slow breath and his eyes went to the wall behind me, to the ceiling. His self-control really was good, but now I was being cruel. I took a few steps backward, making sure to clutch my towel, right below my navel. Not to ensure it didn't fall, but to draw his eye downward.

It worked.

"I'll just be a second," I said, disappearing into my room. "So, to what do I owe the pleasure of this visit?" I called out while I pulled on some underwear and jeans.

"Oh. Uh, dinner," he replied. "At the diner. Gunter asked me to join them and he said you were invited. I was going to walk down and saw your light on. I thought I'd see if you'd left already. Your motorcycle wasn't at the side of your house, but I hadn't heard it the last day or so and I wondered—"

He stopped talking when I walked back into the living room wearing my jeans and pulling a T-shirt on, giving him another chance to see my torso before the fabric stole his view.

"She's in the shed," I replied.

He was still standing at the door. "She?"

"My bike."

"It's female?"

"She is."

"Does she have a name?"

"Harley."

"Imaginative."

"I thought so." I went to the sofa and began pulling on my socks. "And anyway, I haven't ridden her to work these last few days because she wakes up my neighbor. And although the prospect of him coming back out to yell at me in his flamingo pajamas is enticing—"

"Oh god."

"I don't want to get on his bad side."

"You're not on my bad side, though those flamingo pajamas are going in the trash. I'll have you know. If I had an open fire, I'd burn them, ceremonially."

I put my hand to my heart, wounded. "No, no burning. As a firefighter, that's a smoke hazard. And as a gay man, it's a crying shame should you bring harm to my most favorite pride pajamas in the world."

He looked a mix of embarrassed, amused, and a little mad. It was cute. He ignored all mention of the pride pajamas. "And I don't want you to walk to work on my behalf. That's unfair to you and inconsiderate of me. Plus, I'm awake at that time, so it's not a bother."

I finished pulling my socks on, then plucked my sweater off the back of the couch. "I don't walk to work."

"Oh."

"I jog."

He rolled his eyes. "Is that somehow better? Because I think it's actually worse."

I pulled the sweater on, giving my abs a pat before the sweater covered them too. "I need to keep fit. You're doing me a favor."

He blinked at my now sweater-covered midsection, then as if he'd lost his train of thought, his eyes met mine and he sighed. "I'm so sorry. Please feel free to ride to work. I don't want Harley to blame me . . ." He winced, presumably at himself. "You know what? I totally should have called instead of coming over. Your body is lovel—house. Your *house* is lovely. Oh my god." He put his hand on the door handle. "You know, on second thought, I don't think dinner is a good idea—"

I stalked over, pressing my hand on the door, caging him against it. He spun around and we were so, so close. "I think dinner's a great idea," I murmured. "And thank you for the compliment. On my house and my body. I like to take care of both. I feel a burning need to take care of everything I consider mine."

Was that ridiculously cheesy and laden with sexual innuendo? Hell yes. Did I care? No. Because it totally worked.

He sucked back a breath, his cheeks a wonderful pink. "Soren, I . . ."

That was beginning to sound a lot like a knock-back, so I smiled at him and gave him some space. "Hold on one sec," I said as I pulled my boots on, then took my coat off the hook by the door. I met his gaze, still smiling brightly, and acted as if he weren't just about to tell me this was a bad idea. "Are you ready? I'm starving and we're already a bit late."

He blinked a few times and swallowed hard. "Uh, sure." This time when he opened the door, I held it for him and pulled it closed behind us.

Now, if he genuinely didn't want to start anything with me, then I'd take his no for what it was. But I got the feeling that was just a knee-jerk reaction, a measure to guard his heart. From the way he looked at me, from how he blushed and kept looking at my lips, I was more than certain he did want something with me.

He just needed some time. Time to get settled, time to see that I was genuine. So I could give him that.

We fell into step beside each other down the sidewalk toward Main Street. The night was dark, cold, and crisp. Our breaths were steam, our boots crunching in the snow.

"You're already used to walking in the snow," I said, remembering how he'd slipped and slid a little the other night.

Then, right on cue, he slid a little and I was quick to grab his arm.

"Whoa," he said. "You jinxed me."

I laughed, reluctantly letting him go. "Sorry." I was really only sorry he hadn't fallen closer into me, brushed up against me, perhaps. "You okay?"

He nodded and we began walking again. "So you were out at a job today?" he asked. "You mentioned sap."

"Yeah. A barn fire out on Cottonwood Road."

His eyes met mine, alarmed. "Oh goodness."

"Nothing too serious, thankfully. Welding sparks and dust and hay are never a good combination. He wasn't hurt, didn't lose any animals or equipment. Gonna need some new walls though."

"Is that the kind of thing you have to deal with a lot?"

I nodded. "Yeah."

"Was it like that at your last job?"

"In Missoula? Not really. More house fires, warehouses, cars, abandoned houses, that kind of thing."

He made a face. "More of a human element."

"Yep. Not all bad though. Got to save a few people. Made it all worth it."

He smiled at me then and went for another slide on the sidewalk. He slid back, away from me this time, and I had to grab him with both hands. I pulled him close, purely so he didn't hit the ground, of course.

"You're okay," I murmured, still holding onto him. It wasn't a question, more of a reassurance.

He nodded anyway, our faces kinda close. He tried to straighten up, his hands were on my arms, and I moved one hand to his waist and lower back to make sure he was stable. "Thanks," he said. "I promise my motor skills are fine. I can actually walk."

I chuckled. "But we're gonna need to get you some proper footwear."

He looked down at his super trendy, expensive shoes. "I like these."

"Well fine, but I can't go everywhere you go to catch you. And then you're either going to break a wrist," I said, "or your cock-ix."

He rolled his eyes. "Coccyx. It's pronounced cossicks, not cock-icks."

I grinned at him. "I know. I just wanted to hear you say it."

He sighed and looked up the street. "I should have driven."

I laughed and took his arm, crossing the street. "Then we wouldn't get to talk, and I wouldn't get to stop you from falling, and I wouldn't be able to link arms like this, and where's the fun in that?"

He grumbled under his breath, but he was smiling, so it was hard to take his sulking seriously.

As we got to Main Street, it was also hard not to appreciate just how scenic it was. All the Christmas trees, the decorations on the lampposts and awnings, the way the snow on the ground illuminated in the moonlight.

"You were right about that," Rob said. "About how pretty this town could be."

"It's something, isn't it?"

"I thought you were joking when you said the whole town goes into holiday-mode with the decorations."

"We take it very seriously."

"Oh yes, the threat of Mariah Carey on endless loop. I remember." He chuckled. "I actually like Mariah Carey, so . . ."

That made me laugh. "We'd need to find your weakness. Something torturous."

"Elvis's Christmas album."

I gasped. "Nooo. Not the king."

"There is only one Christmas king, and that's Bing Crosby."

I snorted. "Fair call. But I'll make a note about Elvis

being your preferred method of torture. You know, should you not be forthcoming with the Christmas decorations."

"I bought some today," he said. "And I spoke to Gunter about ordering a Christmas tree from Clay."

That made me stupidly happy to hear. "Good. But you've made no effort to put any of them up yet."

"Well, no. I was hoping I could find someone with a ladder to perhaps help me." He gave me a side-eye. "If you . . . by chance know of anyone."

I couldn't stop my grin, even if I'd wanted to. "I do, by chance, know of someone."

"Is he free anytime soon?" he asked, trying not to smile. "You know, before the pitchfork-wielding townsfolk come for me."

"This weekend." Then, because I couldn't help myself, I added, "I'll check with Chuck. Pretty sure he's free this weekend."

Rob's eyes went wide with surprise and confusion. "Oh. Uh, sure . . ."

I laughed. "Just kidding. I'm free. And I have a ladder."

He gave me a playful nudge with his elbow but he didn't move his hand from my arm. And as we were getting closer to the diner, I didn't want to let him go, even though I didn't really have an excuse any longer to touch him. I held the door open for him instead. "After you."

He nodded, and if his cheeks were pink from the cold or if it was from blushing, I wasn't sure. I was indebted to the lights of the diner for showing me, nonetheless. "Thank you."

"Oh, here they are," Braithe said. The whole group was

there, evidently. They had three tables pulled together and everyone sat around them.

"We thought you two might have decided to stay in," Hamish said, wiggling his eyebrows with zero shame.

Ren gave him a nudge, and Jayden stood up, pulling out the two empty chairs. "Take a seat, guys." He then locked the door, turned the sign to *closed*, and pulled the blinds.

"We walked," Rob said as he sat down, pulling his toque off. I still wasn't sure if the pinks of his ears and cheeks was from the cold, but it didn't matter. It was cute as hell.

"And I was a bit late," I admitted.

"I told them you might be," Colson said. Yeah, of course the sheriff's office knew about the fire. "Everything okay out there?"

"Yeah. He'll have a bit of a clean-up job tomorrow, but he was grateful."

When I'd been invited for a get-together Christmas dinner at the diner, I hadn't exactly been aware that Jayden was closing the diner an hour early. He said it was a quiet night and Carl said it was fine.

It was an awesome way to spend the night though. We each threw in twenty bucks and demolished all the leftovers between us while we sank a few brews and sodas. I got chatting with Clay and Colson mostly, talking shit and nonsense, every so often looking over at Rob who was laughing with Ren, Cass, and Gunter. Jayden, Hamish and Braith were arguing and laughing about something, and this, this right here, was what I wanted for Rob.

This group of people. A great bunch of guys, living

decidedly normal lives with their partners in this little town tucked away in the mountains.

Away from the rat race he struggled with. Away from the soul sucking job that almost broke him. I wanted him to see that he could be happy here.

"So," Colson said quietly. "I dunno if you're trying to keep things on the downlow but you keep looking at him, and if it's supposed to be a secret, then I have to tell ya . . . You're really bad at secrets."

I chuckled. "It's not on the downlow. Well, not really. I haven't told him yet. In so many words."

"That you have it bad for him?"

"I don't have it bad," I lied. Apparently I was bad at lying too because Colson's eyebrow shot up. "It's just that I don't think he's ready or up for anything like that." I took a swig of my beer. "And you know what? Even if he's not, which is fine by the way, he still needs this." I gestured to the group. "This right here. So that's okay with me too."

Colson nodded slowly. "You looked kinda cozy when you walked in. I thought maybe something mighta happened."

"Something mighta almost happened," I mumbled behind my beer bottle.

His gaze shot to mine. "Details."

"I mighta accidentally on purpose kinda got real close up against my front door."

"Accidentally on purpose."

I nodded. "Well, I opened the door wearing just a towel."

Clay choked on his beer, earning us a few looks from the others. He wiped his beard and his shirt. "Sorry."

I avoided all eye contact and took another pull of my beer, but Colson just laughed. "And? He liked what he saw?"

"Pretty sure, yeah. But he also freaked out a little bit, so I backed off. Well, until he tried to leave and then I might have cornered him at the door, but I was dressed by then."

"And desperate for him not to leave," Colson added.

I gave a nod. "Something like that, yeah."

"Well," Colson murmured, "for what it's worth, when you haven't been lookin' at him, he's been looking at you."

It took everything in my power not to look at Rob right then. "Really?"

Colson's grin widened. "You can say what you like, Soren, but you got it bad. And maybe, just maybe—" He pointed with his eyes. "—you're not the only one."

Before I could turn or sneak a peek, Clay cleared his throat. "Oh, Rob," he said loud enough to make everyone stop. "Sorry to interrupt. I got that Christmas tree for you. Can drop it around tomorrow afternoon if that suits you?"

Rob's gaze went from Clay's to mine, back to Clay's. "Uh, sure. That'd be great, thanks."

Gunter patted Rob's arm. "Though he should probably have some help decorating it, because he helped me decorate the center today, which I am most grateful for, but . . ."

Rob put his hand to his chest. "I told you I was terrible at it."

Gunter laughed and gave him a playful nudge. "I'm just kidding. It was fine."

"It was terrible," Rob said with a laugh. "No need to call it anything other than what it was."

"No, it was fine," Gunter said again, but he leaned back

in his chair and shook his head. Then he looked directly at me. "But someone could help."

Then every pair of eyes turned to me, each and every one of them throwing me under the bus. Rob's cheeks went red, and before he could say no, I said, "Sure. Only too happy to help. Actually, I already said I would."

"Oh, you already asked?" Hamish asked Rob. "And here I was thinking we'd need to work a covert operation like *Avengers Assemble* or something."

Rob's cheeks were a darker shade of red. "Uh, I, uh . . ."

"Thanks, guys," I said flatly. "Thanks for not making it awkward or anything."

Clay laughed and clinked his beer bottle to mine. "No worries."

I dared to look over at Rob then, and when his eyes met mine, he shook his head and laughed.

It was hard to be mad at them when they all looked at me with such kindness. It was a fond humor, and maybe they knew I was interested in Rob and were trying to give us a gentle nudge in the right direction.

Or maybe they knew I was desperate to not be alone anymore and wanted nothing more in the whole world than someone to share my life with.

I wanted someone to hang out with, to cook with, to cuddle on the couch with. Sure, intimacy and sex would be awesome, but honestly, the intimacy of doing everyday things together, of sharing my life with someone, that was what I wanted.

Could I have that with Rob? Could I see myself laughing in his kitchen or snuggled up on his couch watching something funny on TV?

I was thinking I'd like to find out.

Considering I'd known him a matter of days, and the fact he'd moved here after burning himself out, it really wasn't my decision to make.

I'd have to leave it up to him.

"You okay?" Colson murmured, knocking his knee to mine. "Zoned out there."

I blinked myself back to the present. The conversation at the table had moved on, and thankfully no one was paying any attention to me.

"Uh, yeah, sure. Just thinking about some . . . thing."

He nodded slowly. "Mm-hm."

"I should, ah . . . I should get going," I said, grabbing my coat from the back of my chair.

"Are you good?" he pressed.

"Yeah, of course," I said. I clearly wasn't good, and although tonight had been great, I needed some fresh air.

"I'll come by the station this week sometime," Colson added.

I stood up and clapped his shoulder. "Sounds good."

Rob saw me stand. "Oh," he said, getting to his feet too. "Are we . . . ? I mean, are you . . . ?" He checked his watch. "Oh wow, yeah, it got late. I should go. You're going home? I'll walk with you, if that's okay?"

Everyone at the table was watching us, smiling.

"Yeah, of course," I replied.

Rob held his coat to his chest like a shield and winced. "It's just that . . . I don't own appropriate footwear and I slip a lot and he catches me . . ." He winced harder, and it was so freaking adorable.

How was a guy older than me adorable?

"Appropriate footwear is very important," Hamish said, grinning, his huge eyes like a cartoon character.

"Thanks for tonight, guys, it's been great," I said, trying to save Rob. "Jayden, you in particular, the food was amazing, as always. Let me know if I owe you anything extra."

He waved me off. "No problem. Anytime."

"We should all do this more often. Not just at Christmastime," Ren said.

I gave a nod as I pulled my coat on. "We should."

"I've had a great evening," Rob said, meeting me at the door. He put his coat on but his collar was tucked in, so without thinking, I reached up and straightened it for him.

Someone made a high-pitched *eeeeeep* sound. Hamish or Braithe, I wasn't sure, but they were *all* watching us, and Rob's face flushed red. He pulled his toque on his head as I opened the door and I gave a wave as I followed him out.

Jayden closed the door behind us, just in time to see Rob's foot slide out from under him. I grabbed him and pulled him against me, his face an inch from mine. "Jeez, you okay?" I asked.

Rob nodded, his eyes locked on mine, and he made no attempt to free himself from my arms. Until we heard Jayden laugh. We both turned to see him grinning at us from the glass door.

Of course he saw.

Then Hamish appeared beside him, and I linked my arm with Rob's and crossed the road.

"I, uh, I really need to get better shoes," Rob said.

"Well, probably," I agreed. "Not that I mind and all, but just in case I'm not close enough to catch you."

"Well, yes." He kept his arm linked with mine as we

began walking down Main Street, and damn, it felt nice. "I can't expect you to save me all the time."

"Maybe I can speak to Doug about the salt maintenance. He's buddies with the mayor, and it's a city ordinance issue. We usually get stuck with proper clean-up disposal of incorrect salting. People mean well but it's really bad for the river and the soil, especially with all the national parks around here."

"It's fine," he said. "I don't mean to be a bother. I'll just get some proper footwear and adapt to the conditions. And learn to walk like a functioning adult."

I snorted. "Didn't you spend your childhood winters skating or skiing?"

"You mean venturing outside? When there were perfectly good books to be read inside by the fire?"

That made me laugh. "Okay. I guess being a doctor and all, you were more the studious type than me."

"You grew up in Canada. I grew up in Seattle where it snows much less frequently and with considerably less severity. And," he said with emphasis, "it snows *outside* the house, where I tended to avoid being because of the aforementioned books by the fire."

I laughed again, and as we made it to our street, I relished walking in comfortable silence with him, his arm linked with mine.

The street was lit by soft streetlights and colorful Christmas lights on houses and fences, and I swear I wasn't going crazy, but Rob was definitely leaning into me a little.

"I can't believe this is my life now," he said. "Look at this place."

I chuckled. "It's pretty, huh."

"And tonight? I think I can say tonight was the best night I've had in a long time. I can't even remember . . . years. And I hate to sound like I hated my old life, because I didn't. It was everything I'd worked so hard for, but it simply became my entire life. I slept at the hospital more than I slept at home, and it was fine because that's what it took to be the best in my field, and in the beginning, I loved it." He sighed. "Until I didn't love it anymore."

"Until it wore you down."

"Oh yeah," he said with a nod. "But here, I get to be a doctor. A back-to-basics doctor. A general practitioner three days a week. I get days off. Like actual days off. I helped out at the youth center today. And by help out I mean put up decorations that I'm pretty sure Gunter fixed after I left." He let out a laugh. "Then dinner tonight with a great group of guys. I can't believe this is my actual life."

"Do you . . . do you think you might get bored with it?"

"With this?" He gestured at the picturesque street before us. "Are you kidding? Did you miss the part where I said I now work three days per week and had the best night I can remember having?"

"Well, I'm glad. Just remember, if you get bored and start missing your life back in Seattle, I can give you a list of things to do to keep you busy."

"Things to do? Such as?"

Uh, me.

"I don't know," I replied instead. "What hobbies do you have?"

"None. Work. Specializing in emergency medicine for ninety hours a week doesn't leave much time for hobbies."

Jeez.

"Well, we can find you a hobby."

"Oh god, like what? Please don't say fishing."

I laughed and slowed our walking to a stop. "Wouldn't dream of it."

He noticed where we were. "Ah. My house. The void of darkness amidst a sea of blinking Christmas lights."

"I can help you tomorrow afternoon, if you'd like."

Please say yes. Please say yes. Please say yes.

"I would like that, thank you." He smiled at me, then at his feet, before his eyes met mine again. "I'll cook dinner as thanks."

"And I would like that," I said, only realizing that I still had his arm linked with mine. I let it go and nodded. "I'll come by around four o'clock?"

"Perfect." He glanced back at his house. "Did you . . . did you want to come in? For a drink or a . . ."

Oh god.

Oh holy shit.

"I really do," I whispered.

His smile, his blush, just perfection.

I was going to hate myself for this . . .

"But," I began.

His smile died as realization dawned. "Oh. There's a but. Of course. I didn't mean anything else. Just a drink. It's fine. I should go . . ." He took a step back. "I shouldn't have . . ."

"No, Rob, wait. It's not like that. I want to. I really do."

He waved me off and laughed, looking anywhere but at me, walking backward. "It's fine. Tomorrow is . . . you don't have to come by. I mean, I can hang some lights, probably terribly, but that's okay—"

"Rob, please." God, I'd ruined our perfect night. I'd ruined the mood, and possibly any chance . . . "I want to."

He climbed his porch steps and put his hand up in a stop gesture. "It's okay. No need."

Fuck.

"I'll be here at four," I said. "To help with the Christmas lights."

But it was too late. He'd unlocked his door and disappeared inside, the porch light turning off a second later.

I stood there in the dark, wondering what the ever-loving fuck I'd just done.

Chapter Seven

ROB

"WHAT DO you mean he said no?"

Hamish kind of yelled it, making a few of the kids in the center all stop and look over at where me, Gunter, and Hamish were standing by the pamphlet rack.

I'd brought in some more health pamphlets from the clinic and surprised myself by how easily I spilled my troubles.

I spoke in a much lower tone. "He said no," I repeated. "He walked me home, I asked him if he wanted to come in, and he said no."

They both stared at me. Gunter with sincerity. Hamish with possible anger? "The hell is wrong with him?"

Yep. Anger.

"He's allowed to say no." I shrugged. "I was so embarrassed. He tried to explain, I think. I don't know. I was too horrified to hear it. I ran away."

Hamish shoved the pamphlets into the rack, came over to me, and took my hand. "That man is into you. He spent the entire night looking at you, and like Shakira said, the eyes don't lie."

"That was hips. Hips don't lie," Gunter said.

Hamish wasn't deterred. "Someone said the eyes don't lie. Who isn't important. What *is* important is that man lied through his perfect teeth last night when he said no. He wants you. Everyone could see that. We all saw that, didn't we?" He looked at Gunter for back up.

Gunter nodded and shrugged. "We thought so."

"I thought so," I admitted. "We talked and laughed the whole way home. He was so sweet. He held my arm as we walked, and he was so sweet. I thought . . ." I sighed. "I misread everything, obviously. I'm clearly out of practice."

"You got no rizz," one girl said. She was making herself a hot drink, was no more than fifteen years old, had green-and-blue hair, pink eye shadow, and dark lips. "Or he got no rizz."

Hamish and I both stared at her. "I don't know what that means," Hamish said, then he looked at me. "I don't know what that means."

I shrugged. "Don't look at me. I have no clue."

"Charisma," Gunter explained. "It means you got no charisma, or you lack the ability to charm or woo someone."

Now both me and Hamish stared at Gunter. "Oh my god," Hamish murmured, horrified. "How do you know that? How do I not know that?"

Gunter shrugged. "I had to get familiar. With the lingo."

The girl rolled her eyes and half smiled. "We don't

expect you to know. You were born in the nineteen hundreds."

Jesus.

Hamish clutched at his chest. "Ow." Then he turned to Gunter, exasperated. "The nineteen hundreds? What is . . . how is . . . ? Oh my god." He gawped at the girl and gestured to his clothes. "I'm still cool. And on-trend. These jeans are a Japanese brand, I'll have you know. I . . . I don't know how to say it, but look at this label. A queer-owned Japanese brand." He turned around to show her the label.

"That's okay," Gunter said, stopping Hamish before he could show her the label on the backside of his jeans.

On his backside.

The girl laughed and sipped her hot chocolate, which just seemed to exasperate Hamish even more.

"Nineteen hundreds," he mumbled to Gunter, as if he wanted Gunter to punish the poor girl.

I chuckled. "Yes, we folks from the nineteen hundreds have no rizz," I said to her. "It's fine."

She clearly liked that she'd rattled us oldies a little. "If you wanna rizz your man, you need less cheugy and more BDE."

Hamish and I stared at her. "I don't know what any of that means," Hamish whispered.

"Ah, no," Gunter said, intervening. "No BDE in here. Thanks, Evie. But we can take it from here. All good."

"Just sayin'," she said, going back to her table. She looked at me. "Make him earn it."

Oh, dear god.

Hamish put his hand to his forehead. "I think I need to sit down."

I kind of laughed because I had no idea what just happened. Except that I was officially uncool and old.

Hamish took Gunter's arm. "What the hell is BDE?"

"Big dick energy," he whispered.

Oh my.

"Oh my god," I mumbled.

Gunter sighed. "It just means you need to act cool, like you're in control. Play hard to get."

"Make him earn it," I repeated what Evie had said. Now it made sense.

Hamish was still spiraling, his hand to his forehead, expression horrified. "Nineteen hundreds. I'm from the nineteen hundreds."

I chuckled. "Damn."

Gunter nodded slowly. "Oh yeah. They keep you humble."

"I'm still cool," Hamish said. His hand was now pressed to his sternum, his expression indignant. "I'm still young and hip. I could hang with the kids."

"Okay, first of all," Gunter whispered, "don't let them hear you say words like cool and hip. They'll eat you alive. Secondly, don't show weakness. Don't let them see your fear." He shook his head grimly. "And I can tell you with my whole heart, Hamish, that we think we're young and hip, and we think we're cool and can hang with the cool kids, but I'm telling you. Five minutes with these guys and you will know—in no uncertain terms—that we are, in fact, neither young, hip, nor cool. We are very much almost forty years old, relics from the nineteen hundreds, and cringe."

Hamish's hand was now in a campy defense pose across his chest and he let out a wail of despair.

Gunter gestured to him. "My point exactly."

All I could do was laugh. These guys were so great.

"Do you need a minute?" Gunter asked Hamish. He nodded, seemingly unable to speak.

Gunter then smiled at me. "Coffee?"

"Sounds great."

I HAD MOST of my Christmas lights up on the front of my house by three o'clock. Well, correction. Clay did most of the work on the ladder while Hamish directed, and I just did what I was told.

I'd asked Soren to help and he'd said he would after four o'clock, but I assumed that was no longer on the table after last night, and Hamish was adamant that I should show him I could do it without his help.

Apparently, Soren turning me down offended Hamish more than me.

I was still in the embarrassed and rejected stage. Hamish had moved straight into anger and said I should use the BDE that Evie had suggested and hang my own damned Christmas lights.

Prove I didn't need him.

Except I did need a ladder, and when Hamish had asked Ren where he kept their ladder, Ren had urged—more like insisted—that Clay do the ladder climbing.

Clay, who just happened to be in the hardware store at the time, understood the assignment and agreed.

Hamish wanted the house done before four, so should Soren turn up, he'd know he missed his chance.

That was probably a little more catty than my MO, but Hamish could be convincing when he wanted to be. Or maybe pushy was the right word.

Either way, by three o'clock, it was done. I had icicle lights hanging from the gutters and soft colored Christmas lights across my porch.

"I love it. Thank you both so much," I said. I couldn't believe they'd both taken time out of their day for me. It was a kindness and generosity I wasn't used to. "I really do appreciate the help."

Clay folded his ladder and slid it onto his truck. "No problem at all. It's what we do."

Hamish stood beside me in my small front yard, looking up at my house. "It's just so cute, and it's all done before a certain someone gets home."

No sooner had he said that than a certain someone came running around Clay's truck.

He was wearing his firefighter long pants and a white T-shirt with the fire brigade emblem on his right pec. He was panting, as if he'd run here from the station.

He seemed to notice the newly installed Christmas lights before he noticed Hamish and Clay. "Hey," he said to me, ignoring them. "I had to come see you. I'm so freaking sorry. I've been useless all day, and Doug threatened to fire me if I didn't come sort myself out. Rob, I need you to know how sorry I am. I should have said yes last night. I've been kicking myself ever since. I just didn't want to rush you, and I didn't want you to regret anything, should we move too fast. I think you're kinda great and I was getting too far ahead of myself, and I swear if you could please give me one more chance. You have to know, next time you ask me if I want to come in, I'm saying hell fucking yes. And you don't have to ask me any time soon. Just whenever you're ready again is okay with me. I'll wait. As long as it takes. I'm sorry, Rob. I really am."

I wasn't sure what to say.

I wasn't even sure I could speak.

But then Hamish, who was still standing there holding an empty Christmas lights box, made a weird, strangled sound. We both looked at him. "Ask him," Hamish hissed at me. Then he pointed at Soren while staring at me. "Ask him!"

I might have panicked. "Do you know what rizz is?"

Soren blinked. "Uh . . . what?"

"Not that," Hamish said, so very disappointed. "Oh my god. Ask him!"

Clay was laughing by his truck.

I had to ignore everyone and concentrate on Soren . . . in his too-tight firefighter T-shirt. "Do you . . . would you like to . . . ?"

Soren strode over to me, determined, and took my face in his hands. "Yes," he said, then crashed his lips to mine.

Warm, soft lips, the hint of stubble, the heat of his palms on my cheeks made me melt into him.

Oh my . . .

Then a very high-pitched keening sounded nearby, which I realized was Hamish. I broke the kiss and glanced over at him, slightly concerned for his well-being, Soren keeping me close with his hand now burning into my neck.

Hamish had his hands to his face, doing a little skippity dance. "Now *that* is BDE." But then Clay came over and dragged him away. "I want to watch," he tried.

"See ya, guys," Clay said with a wave as he basically threw Hamish into the cab of his truck.

"Thank you, again, for your help," I called out.

Hamish had to roll the old-fashioned window down, which took considerable effort, if his enthusiasm was any gauge. "You're welcome. I want details!"

The truck rumbled to life and Hamish had to roll the window back up as they reversed out of my driveway. Soren and I watched them leave, and then it was just us and a lot to talk about.

I turned to him, and, keeping his hand on my neck, he said, "I really am sorry. And I'm sorry I wasn't here to help you put up the Christmas lights. Or that you felt I shouldn't be the one to help. I'm sorry."

"Hamish said I should do it before you got here. If you were still coming here . . . I wasn't sure," I whispered. "I'm sorry about last night. You said no and I panicked. I was embarrassed."

He swiped his thumb along my jaw before he reached for my hand instead. "I was an idiot. We had such a good night at dinner with all the guys and I kept thinking that's what you need. That community, that group of great friends. You didn't need me coming on too strong. You just moved here, and you said you were burned out, and I wanted to give you time."

I smiled at him. "You did a lot of thinking for me."

He made a sad face, his eyes full of sincerity. "I'm sorry. I should have asked and not assumed. Believe me, I've been an ass at work all day. Doug told me to leave, to come and fix this or set the record straight . . . I don't even know. I barely slept. I just wanted to make this right."

He made it right, all right. My gaze dropped to his lips and I had to make myself look back at his eyes. "You did. And I'm pretty sure you made Hamish's day. The whole group probably knows already."

He chuckled. "He said something about BDE . . ."

I snorted. "He did."

And he wasn't wrong.

Soren fought a smile. "Do you know what BDE is?"

I nodded, embarrassed. "I do now. I also know that I'm neither young nor hip, and the lingo of today's youth is lost on my aforementioned too-old self. I was also told I have no rizz."

He barked out a laugh. "Who have you been speaking to?"

"A nice young girl at the youth center was imparting her wisdom on me. If I'm going to help out there, I'll need the Urban Dictionary. Is there an app for that?"

"I have no idea." Soren chuckled then looked over at the Christmas lights. "I am sorry about the lights. I wanted to help you."

"I still have to decorate inside," I whispered, fully aware that it sounded like the invitation it was. "I have a tree now as well, thanks to Clay. If you wanted to help me—"

"Yes. If you think I'm saying no again, you're out of your mind." His eyes scanned my face, drawing down to my lips. "I really want to kiss you again, and we probably shouldn't be outside for that. Mr. Ling across the road is no doubt watching us right now. I mean, he's a real sweet old guy and he loves some gossip, but he might not appreciate just how obscenely I'm going to kiss you."

Oh shit.

My blood flushed hot and my skin prickled all over.

"Obscenely, huh?" Suddenly breathless, I glanced across the street, and I couldn't see anyone peeking through windows or anything. But Soren was right. "We definitely should take this inside."

I'd never wanted anything more.

My stomach was full of butterflies. My legs felt like Jell-O as I climbed the front steps and held the door open for him.

"I should take my boots off," he murmured, bending over inside the door and pulling at his laces. I got a fabulous view of his trapezius and his latissimus dorsi as he did this, and I almost forgot my own shoes. Which were much easier than his, thankfully.

"Uh, can I get you a drink?" I asked.

He stood up straight and dropped his second boot to the floor, his eyes burning into mine. "No thanks."

He looked at my lips and took a step closer.

"Can I get you anything?" I whispered, not capable of speaking normally, apparently. "I'm trying to remember my manners."

He shook his head and touched his index finger to my chest, then dragged it up to my chin. "And I'm trying to forget mine."

My breath caught, and my knees almost buckled. He lifted my chin, tilted his face, and pressed his body to mine, commanding and crowding me in the very best way. His lips were so close to mine, almost touching.

Almost.

My heart hammered, my lungs needed air . . .

"Can I kiss you?" he asked, his eyes dazed.

"I think I'll die if you don't."

He smirked as his lips met mine. But then his hands cupped my face, my neck, as he tilted my head and deepened the kiss.

His lips opened mine, his tongue slid into my mouth, and I moaned.

I'd never moaned like that in my life.

He grunted in the back of his throat and kissed me deeper, his body now pressing against me. My hands found his waist, his back, and the feel of his body . . .

Muscular and hard in all the right places . . .

Oh my.

I broke the kiss, for air and some mental clarity. "Damn."

He chuckled, his lips swollen and wet, his eyes dark. And the way he looked at me . . . like he wanted to devour me.

"You shouldn't look at me like that," I murmured, my voice rough.

"How am I looking at you?"

He knew damned well.

"In a way that isn't conducive to abstinence."

He laughed and shook his head. "You're so fucking sexy," he said. "Is abstinence something you're striving for?"

I was still a little dazed by the fact he'd just called me sexy . . . "Uh, no. Not really. I don't know . . . without making it awkward, and I'm still on a high from the way you kissed me just now. You were very correct, by the way. Mr. Ling did not need to bear witness to that."

"Was it obscene enough for you? Because I can do better. I was trying to be polite."

I barked out a laugh. "Polite. Huh."

He smirked like the devil himself, but when he took my hand, he interlocked our fingers and was serious again. "You said you were unsure about the abstinence comment and didn't want to make it awkward. Unsure about what? Rest assured, Rob, there's no need for it to be awkward here."

I laughed again and had to remind myself that I was older than him. I was the serious, professional medical practitioner, and there wasn't any reason for me to be awkward. Despite how I'm certain my cheeks burned red, I didn't have any reason to be embarrassed.

"I'm not practicing abstinence," I began. It was easier for me to take a medical approach. "I think we would need to discuss boundaries and expectations before I comment further on the matter of sexual activity."

He seemed slightly amused. "Okay. Sure. Should we sit down?" He gestured to the sofa.

"Good idea." I led him to the couch, still holding his hand. God, even holding hands felt good. He waited for me to get my thoughts in order. "It's nothing really, and I've probably set up this entire conversation wrong."

"It's fine, Rob. If sex isn't something you're comfortable with, it's okay. You can tell me."

"No, it's . . . I'm very comfortable with it. I was just hoping to maybe not have this conversation until our second date, at least. And I don't want you to think I'm reading way too much into this. As in waaaaaay too much."

"Okay," he said.

God, now I'd made it into a big deal.

I sighed and decided to just get it over with. "You mentioned abstinence, which is not what I'm aiming for here. Believe me. I've felt more in that regard in the last four days than I have in years. But before when you were kissing me, I thought if I don't stop this right now, I was about to ask you to take me to bed. Like now, Soren. And I don't know if that's what I want for us. Just yet, that is. Which is why it's getting awkward, because here I am thinking about the longevity of us when we haven't really established anything between us at all."

Soren blinked.

So I kept rambling. "And I don't want it to sound like I'm saving myself or anything—I think we both know that ship sailed a long time ago—"

He smiled at that.

Christ, stop talking, Robinson.

"I do this when I'm nervous, I'm sorry. What I'm trying to say is, depending on how we see this relationship developing and what each of us want from it, is concurrently relative to how soon we have sex."

He pressed his lips together to stop from smiling. "I see."

I pulled my hand from his and wiped my palms on my thighs. "See? There's the awkward I was trying to avoid."

"Let me get this straight," he said. "You want to have sex with me but you need to know how I feel about you first?"

I wanted to bury my face in my hands but what he'd said was right. In a nutshell.

"Well, that makes me sound like a virginal teenager whose boyfriend wants to go all the way. Which I'm not, honestly, I just have reasons . . ." I groaned, because this had far exceeded awkward, and I held up two fingers. "First reason is that I'm new to town and I'm a doctor. I can't be falling into bed with the first hot stranger who looks at me twice. That's not professional, and quite frankly, the people of Hartbridge deserve someone who will be a little more upstanding than that. Secondly, if we're just going to be fuck buddies, if that's all you want, then that's fine, but we need to set some boundaries and rules. We each have jobs to think about and reputations within the community that we need to consider. It would have to be secret, and we might have to, I don't know, take a panel of fencing out in our backyards so you can sneak over without Mr. Ling seeing."

Smiling, he took my hand again. "Okay, so," he began.

"You can see now why I told you it was awkward. Asking if you want to date or just be fuck buddies before I invite you to my bed. It's the definition of awkward and I can now see why Evie said I had no rizz."

He laughed but now held my hand in both of his. "I want to date you," he said. "I think you're kinda great, and I want to get to know you better. I would hope that sex is something we could explore, if and when you're comfortable. The points you made were valid, and I can appreciate you needing to know where I stood before we went any further." He glanced back over to the front door. "Because that kiss was hot as hell."

I laughed, relieved and happy. So freaking happy. "It was hot. I think that's why I panicked. Because I was like two seconds away from taking you to my room, but then it would have made things complicated because we hadn't talked. Just because I haven't had sex in a really long time shouldn't be the leading factor in decision-making."

Soren bit his bottom lip. "A really long time, huh?"

"Like forever, in gay terms. Maybe two years?"

He seemed surprised by this. "Oh. I see. But you were busy, working crazy hours."

"And hitting up gay bars or terrible apps really are not my style. I like meeting people the old-fashioned way."

"Like going out into your front yard to yell at them in your flamingo pajamas."

"Exactly." I nodded. "And just so you know, I'm still going to be setting those on fire."

His eyes lit up. "A fire, huh?"

"Yes. It will be a ceremonial burning. A bonfire, even."

"Ooh. You'll need a permit for that. And that's lucky, because I just happen to be a firefighter. But I will prohibit the burning of those. Any other pajamas are fine."

I chuckled, but of course then I just had to look at the Hartbridge Fire Department logo on his T-shirt. "Will you wear your firefighter uniform?"

Soren laughed, his eyes wide. "You like it, huh?"

I rolled my eyes. "You're so hot and you know it."

His eyes met mine, amused, and he shrugged. "Still nice to be told though."

"Okay, yes, I find your uniform appealing," I admitted. "Though, full disclosure, I've never found any particular uniform attractive so I'm almost certain it's *you* in that uniform. Or . . . maybe just you in anything you wear, basically."

His smile was flirty, his eyes sparkled, and he licked the corner of his mouth. It made my breath catch, which of course made him grin. "Full disclosure," he said. "I've never found anyone older than me attractive, never looked twice at any doctor or intellectual type—"

"Great."

He chuckled. "But you. One look at you and I was a goner."

"It was the flamingo pajamas, wasn't it?"

"One hundred percent." He laughed, but then he studied my eyes for a heart-stopping moment. "But you, Robinson, there's something about you. I want to date you. I want to cook you dinner and make you laugh. I want to see you smile because, damn, it trips a circuit in my brain. And I want to kiss you again. Though full, *full* disclosure, now that I've kissed you once—"

"Twice, actually."

"Sorry. Now that I've kissed you twice, I want to kiss you all the damn time. I'm happy to wait until you're ready for more. I just want to spend time with you. I wasn't kidding when I said I wanted to give you the time you needed. I don't want to rush this. I want to get it right."

Well, damn.

I had some difficulty speaking for a few seconds. "I'd like that," I finally managed. "Dating. Kissing all the damn time sounds kinda great to me too. And for what it's worth, I've not been with anyone younger than me . . . that I know of." I made a face. "Certainly never dated anyone younger." I put my hand to my chest. "But to be fair, I gave up eight years of my life for medical school, so we're basically the same age."

He laughed and threaded our fingers, looking at our hands on his knee. "I'm glad we talked, and I'm glad we're on the same page."

"Me too."

"And I know it's early days, and honestly, as tempting as

the offer of fuck buddies is, like sex right now—because believe me, I'm tempted, and I'm sure my dick hates me right now—but I really want romance. And I know that sounds sappy and stupid, but dinner dates and flowers for no reason, and all that sweet stuff. I want that too." He worried his bottom lip with his teeth. "I see how the guys are with each other—the smiles and the looks—and I want that. Sounds kinda lame, right?"

"No. Not at all. It's not lame to want to feel appreciated and wanted."

His eyes met mine. "Thank you for saying that. I swear, Chucky thinks I'm so desperate for love that I'd take anyone."

I recoiled at that. "Oh." Because that was . . . that was . . .

Soren grabbed my hand tighter, his eyes wide. "No, not you. I mean before you. He used to say I was such a sucker for love that I was gonna fall head over heels for the first guy who looked at me twice."

"And that's not true?"

"No. You looked at me once. You actually came stomping across your yard to yell at me, holding your coffee cup with your hair all messed up—"

"Please don't say wearing those damned pajamas."

He chuckled. "They're burned into my memory."

I smiled at him. "Romance, huh?"

He shrugged. "Well, yeah. Do you not want me to sweep you off your feet? Make you coffee, make you smile. Bring you flowers."

"For me? I thought you wanted those things."

"Well, I'm not opposed, but I meant for you. That's

what I like to do; I like to spoil my partner and look after them. Some guys find it too much, and I might get carried away."

"I don't want to come home to a thousand red roses."

He snorted. "I wish I could afford that, but no. I'm more of a one single rose kind of guy."

"One rose is completely acceptable. But I won't come home to find my pet bunny in a boiler on the stove, will I?"

He looked positively horrified. "Who the hell have you dated? Ted Bundy?"

"It's from a movie."

"Jesus Christ."

"Yeah, it wasn't my favorite film."

"Okay, so no, that's a hard, hard pass. But maybe some dinner on the stove sometimes. Though it'll probably be vegetarian after the bunny visual."

I laughed. "I like vegetarian. I make a mean chickpea curry. Well, I used to. I haven't made it in a long time."

"Then I would love to try it sometime."

I glanced back at the kitchen. "I was going to cook you dinner tonight, but then I was certain you wouldn't be coming over so I didn't plan ahead, sorry."

"It's fine." He checked his watch. "It's still early."

"Want to help me cook something?"

He grinned. "Yes." Then he gave a nod to the Christmas tree. "Did you still want to decorate—"

"Yes. I would like that very much."

He leaned over and gave me a soft peck on the lips. "Thank you. I'm glad we talked about all this."

"Same. And we're on the same page . . ." I cringed. "Dating, yes?"

He looked so damn happy. "Dating. If we have dinner tonight, will this be our first official date? Or technically our third date? If we don't include last night, because it was a whole group of us at dinner, then maybe our second date? Just for the sake of clarity, should someone ask."

I pretended to consider this, but really, my mind kept going back to one thing. "Well, I'm not sure we should count last night. It was a group dinner, which was lovely, by the way, but then I went ahead and asked you if you wanted to come back to my place, and it all went downhill and I spent the entire night under my covers, pretending everything was fine. Which would make this date number two, in which case, making out is an acceptable way to close out the evening. After dinner and Christmas tree decorating, that is. If you'd be so obliged?"

He grinned at me. "Oh, I am so obliged. Date number two it is."

But then his gaze dropped to my lips and he slow blinked, and my stomach swooped and my blood seemed to surge to a certain part of my body.

Because I wanted him. I wanted him in ways I hadn't wanted anything.

I shot up off the couch. "Okay, dinner. Yes, dinner first. Well, we should start dinner. Before we . . . do other things."

He smirked, clearly aware of the effect he had on me. I hurried to the kitchen and opened the fridge. "Uh, I have steak. And vegetables to steam. Or we can bake them if you'd prefer. I've been appreciating the time to cook more this week than I have in years." I slid the tray of steaks out, but when I turned around, Soren was closer than I'd expected. "Oh."

His hand went to my arm. "You okay?"

"Yes. Just nervous. Which is ridiculous. I'm thirty-six years old. I'm a doctor, for Pete's sake."

He took the steaks from my hand and slid them onto the counter. "You're human," he murmured, "who's been too busy for years."

I swallowed hard. That was all true. But damn . . . I pressed my hand to my stomach, trying to quell the jitters.

"Belly full of butterflies?" he said, his voice low and his eyes full of heat. He took the hand from my stomach and lifted it to his lips, softly kissing my knuckles. "Steamed vegetables sound great."

I was so enraptured by him, so dazed, it took me a second to catch up. "Huh? Oh, vegetables. Yes. Dinner."

He smiled in a way that did my stomach no favors. Or my lungs. And he knew it because his tongue licked the corner of his mouth again, teasing me.

My whole body was on edge. My heart was hammering. My dick . . . well, it was interested too.

"You know," I said breathlessly. "I think we miscounted. I'm fairly sure this is date number three. Actually, I'm certain it is."

He stepped in close, his body pushing me gently backward so my ass hit the kitchen counter. He was pressed against me, his nose brushing mine, and I could barely remember to breathe. "You wanted to take it slow," he murmured, his voice hot on my ear.

"I was a fool," I breathed.

He smiled and nudged his nose to mine again, his eyes drawing up to meet mine. Full of fire.

So fucking hot.

My body thrummed, and he had to feel how turned on I was. I could certainly feel his . . .

"I'm going to kiss you," he whispered.

"Please."

He leaned harder against me and slid his mouth over mine, slow and controlling.

So much self-control.

I wanted to tear at his clothes, grip his face, and devour him, but he was leading this. He was in command and so, so fucking hot.

His mouth, his tongue, sliding against mine, deep and devouring. Then his arms slid around my back, warm and strong, holding me.

My body moved of its own volition. I lifted my leg without thought, hitching it over his hip. My hands found his neck, his hair, and I tilted my head so he could give me more of his tongue.

I groaned and rolled my hips and he put his hands to my face and broke the kiss. He stepped back, making my leg fall, and I had to steady myself. He closed his eyes and took a deep breath. "Holy fuck," he panted. "If we don't stop, I'm not sure I'll be able to."

"I'm not sure I want to," I replied, again, without thinking. That seemed to be happening a lot around him . . .

His gaze met mine, his last thread of self-control visible. "Rob."

"I know what I said. And I'm sorry for the mixed signals. But, Jesus Christ, you're so fucking hot." I shook my head. "Sorry about the language. I don't normally cuss. There seems to be a distinct brain-to-body disconnect when I'm around you."

He chuckled and let out a sigh. He had himself back under control now, I could tell. And I was disappointed, but I understood.

"It's okay," I said. "It's just all so new for me. I can't even remember the last time someone touched me in a non-sexual way, so my brain is drinking down dopamine like a college kid on a beer bong, and my body . . . phew! Well, my body is, uh . . ." I adjusted my now-aching dick. "Well, yeah. It's not opposed to the attention."

He chuckled but his smile became a little tortured. "That's why I need to slow down. I have to do this right even if it kills me." He looked down at my crotch and groaned as he turned away, and with his hand to his forehead, he let out a laugh. "And it's gonna kill me."

"Why do you *have* to do this right?" I asked. He'd made it sound like a chore.

"Because you said it yourself. It's been a while since someone touched you in a non-sexual way." He put his hand to my face, and I couldn't help it. I leaned into the touch and closed my eyes.

And I realized I'd proven his point.

I was touch-starved, and I was craving it.

"I want to show you all the little things. The soft touches, the intimacy."

"The romance," I added, remembering what he'd said before, and he nodded.

"We'll get to the good part," he said. "I know we will. And it's gonna be so good. I will make it so good for you, Robinson. I promise. But it will be a whole-body experience. Not a hand job in your kitchen."

Holy hell.

My blood burned at his words, but it was different than before. Not desire, not the need for physical touch. Something else. Something better, deeper.

"I was actually thinking more of a blow job," I joked, rolling my eyes.

He groaned out a laugh. "That visual isn't helping."

I put my hands on his shoulders and made him stand at arm's length. "You being too close to me isn't helping. You looking at me isn't helping, and the way you lick the corner of your mouth really, really isn't helping."

He laughed and deliberately faced the wall. "Is that better?"

"Not really. Your side profile is just as hot."

He turned his back to me. "How's that?"

My eyes went straight to his ass. "So much better."

He laughed again and turned around with his hands up. "Okay. So if we're having steak and steamed vegetables for dinner, it will take fifteen minutes, max. Let's decorate your Christmas tree."

"That's not a euphemism for sex by chance, is it?"

He laughed as he walked into the lounge room. "No. Now stop it. Or we will do the euphemism. How long has your tree been settling?"

I followed him in and stood beside him, both of us staring at the tree. "Uh, he dropped it off this afternoon."

"Hm. You probably should give it a bit more time."

"Oh."

"We could decorate it tomorrow?" he said with a shrug. "I'll finish around four, if that suits you? I mean, you can totally do it yourself any time tomorrow without me; I didn't mean to imply you had to wait."

A thrill ran through me. "That would definitely be date number three."

His eyes darted to mine and he knew exactly what I meant. "It would be, yes. Date four, by some standards."

I had to chew on the inside of my lip so I didn't smile too wide. "Hm. Dinner and wine and . . ."

"And I'd like to say second base but I'm pretty sure once we get past first, we're just gonna blow right past second into third and probably a home run."

"Not if you use a baseball analogy we won't be."

He laughed. "Not a fan?"

"Terrible. Not the sport, just the analogy." I grinned at him, glad we could get past any awkwardness and still be joking with each other. I went to the table and slid the box toward me. "Should we see what other amazing Christmas decorations the Home Mart had?"

Soren stood beside me and opened the lid to the box, only when he did, he sliced his finger. "Ow." He instinctively put his finger in his mouth. "Paper cut."

I pulled out a seat. "Sit down. I'll grab my kit." I came back from the bathroom with my small med kit. It held no more than acetaminophen, bandages, tweezers, cotton swabs, some saline, and alcohol wipes.

"You don't have to do that," Soren said. "It's really fine. Just a paper cut."

I sat next to him, our knees touching, and I took his hand. "It might get infected."

He pulled his hand away. "But if you treat me, I'll technically be your patient. Then there will be no euphemisms, no baseball analogies."

I rolled my eyes and took his hand again. "You're not my patient." I inspected the sliced finger, took an alcohol wipe, and he hissed when I cleaned it.

I lifted his finger to my lips and blew on it, and it made him smile.

I opened a bandage. "Paper cuts, which are such a small nuisance infliction, hurt so much because of the damaged nerve endings in the epidermis, setting off mechanical nociceptors."

He snorted. "Interesting."

I wrapped the bandage around his finger. "And those nociceptors let loose a flurry of electrical signals that travel through your nerve fibers and into the spinal cord. Then nerve cells in the spinal cord relay those signals to the brain."

"I happen to find your intelligence a huge turn on," he said. "Just so you know."

"Is that right?"

"Yep. And you know I do have extensive first aid and emergency training, and I'm sure you forgot something."

I looked at his finger—at his measly paper-cut-bandaged finger. "Is that so?"

"Mm." Then he lifted his bandaged finger and pouted. "You need to blow on it twice. It's the second time, that's the key."

I laughed, the humor and warmth in his eyes making my heart thump. But I took his hand and gently blew on his finger again. "Better?"

His gaze lingered with something I couldn't quite read. "So much better."

Chapter Eight

SOREN

I WALKED INTO WORK, Doug took one look at me, then another. "You look happier."

I grinned at him. Hell, I don't think I'd stopped yet. "Much happier. Sorry about yesterday."

He rolled his eyes. "I take it from that stupid smile there won't be a repeat of yesterday."

"Not if I can help it."

Chucky clapped me on the back. "Finally got some, huh?"

I shoved him. "No, actually. And it's not like that. We're . . . dating. Like dinner and talking and hanging Christmas decorations."

Chuck made a face. "Oh god."

"He cooked me dinner. I kissed him goodnight and went home."

Both Chuck and Doug stared at me. I wasn't telling them that I kissed Rob until he almost came in his pants, or that I had to go home and jerk off last night *and* this morning.

They were both still staring. "What? It's true."

"You're a fucking goner, already," Chuck said. "I can't believe you didn't score. You, of all people."

I snorted. "We're . . . seeing if it could be something special. And I think it could be. He is . . ." I shook my head slowly, "boy, is he something special."

Doug groaned and headed for his office. "I need coffee for this."

I looked at Chuck, because I knew he'd get this, and I was excited. I needed to tell someone. "When we're together, it's like a damn powder keg. Like the air's electric or something. I've never felt anything like it. When we do eventually . . ." I searched for an appropriate word.

"Fuck?"

I nodded because, well, yeah. That.

"It's gonna be so fucking amazing. I just know it." I shook my head, still not really believing it. "Can you believe it? He's older than me. He's a doctor, for fuck's sake. Like, he's so smart."

"You read books," he said, as if that was a barometer on intellectualism.

"Yeah, but he's *smart* smart. He's a doctor. And he's so fucking sexy."

Doug came back with his coffee mug in his hand. "Oh good. We're still talking about this."

"Give me something to do, boss," I said, "or I'll be talking about him all day."

"Yes," Chuck agreed. "Please. Make him do something. I thought yesterday was bad."

"I have a list," Doug said flatly. "It's on the roster wall, if either of you ever cared to look at it."

I headed into the break room, and I heard Doug behind me. "You too. Go look with him."

"What did I do?" Chuck cried.

A second later, Chucky clipped me over the back of my head. "'S'your fault."

I was in too good a mood to care. Even mopping the floors until they shined and cleaning every surface did little to kill my mood. Between regular equipment maintenance, and a safety inspection of two local businesses and the paperwork, my day was a dream. I had scheduled training, some weight training with hoses, tanks, ax and shovels, generators, full medic kits, power tools, that kind of thing.

We even had a call from Shirley Cassel on Oak Lane because her neighbor across the road, Mr. Jim Pavel, who was a sprightly ninety-one-year-old, had decided to check his gutters before it snowed too much.

So Shirley made him a coffee in the safety of his kitchen while Chuck and I cleaned out his gutters. I told him we'd book it in earlier in the year next time so he wouldn't have to worry. I even brought some more wood inside for him.

All in a day's work.

I freaking loved my job.

Then, at about ten minutes to four o'clock—not that I was clock-watching, waiting for my shift to end—I just happened to be out in front of the fire hall when I happened to see a familiar figure crossing the street just up from me.

His smile made my knees weak.

"Hey," I said, checking my watch. "I was just thinking about you."

"I'm just heading home," Rob said. "It's almost four.

Someone said he was stopping by. I have a Christmas tree that *really* needs decorating."

Yeah, there was definitely innuendo in that.

"Oh, I'm definitely gonna decorate your tree."

That came out way filthier than I'd intended, but he blushed so it was worth it.

"You been at the youth center again today?" I asked.

"Yes. Being schooled by a bunch of teenagers is my new reality check. If I ever think for one second that I'm cool, or perhaps holding my own for someone my age, they'll shoot that down pretty quick."

I chuckled. "Brutal."

He smiled, easy and relaxed. It was a good look on him. "You were right about helping Gunter. I've enjoyed it."

"And you still have more days off."

"I know. It's bizarre. I don't actually know what I'm going to do tomorrow. I have the entire day with zero plans. It's unheard of."

"Tomorrow? I just might happen to have tomorrow off. I could take you out for a ride on Harley, if you want."

"On your motorcycle?" He looked at me, horrified, but there was a flash of excitement too. "I've never been on a motorcycle before and I don't have the appropriate clothing."

"I have a spare helmet, and any long pants and boots will do. You don't have to have leathers."

He absolutely looked me up and down. "Will you be wearing leathers?"

I laughed. "For safety purposes, yes."

He made a face. "I'll think about it."

"About riding the bike, or about me wearing the leathers?"

His cheeks went red, but he tried to play it cool and cleared his throat. "It's not like that. I could quote statistical data on the importance of protective leathers relating directly to the survivability of motorcycle accidents."

"Hm-mm."

He was absolutely going to ride with me, and the idea of that, of him sitting behind me, his arms around my waist . . . it made me so damn happy.

And that I now had a reason to see him again tomorrow.

"Did you want to leave the Christmas tree decorating until tomorrow? We'd have more time—"

"No," he said quickly. "I really do need my tree decorated." There was that euphemism again. "Now that I've been thinking about it, I really would like that."

I laughed and checked my watch again. "I will be at your place in . . . ten minutes. Should I change first, or is this okay?" I gestured to my uniform.

His gaze drew down my front, from my chest to my boots, before he looked back to my face. "That is more than okay."

Damn.

But then the siren at work blared, red light flashing. I spun to face it.

Fuck.

"I have to go," I said quickly. "Gonna need a raincheck. I'm sorry."

He looked over at the fire hall, worried, waved me off. "Don't be sorry. Go, go."

I turned and ran into the hall. "Fire alarm at the retirement home," Chuck said, pulling on his gear. I raced to match him, when Doug came around, fully dressed, and lifted himself into the truck. We hauled ass behind him and were on the road in under ten seconds.

Rob was still standing, right where I'd left him, watching. His hands stuffed into his pockets, his cheeks and nose turning red. I smiled at him, hoping he could see me.

Chuck whacked my arm. "Head in the game."

Shit.

I straightened up, because dammit, he was right. "What do we know?"

IT WASN'T a fire at the nursing home, just the fire alarm. But the alarm required a full evacuation, and when dealing with the elderly, it was never easy, or fast.

Everyone was fine though, thankfully.

We needed to check the fire alarm and why it tripped. Doug deemed it was an electrical fault and then that became a whole other issue.

Colson was there helping the police, talking to the residents and making sure they were okay and looked after. There was no emergency, safety or medical, so he was mostly being cheeky and making them smile, which was all part of the job.

He came over when he had a minute. "How's it looking?"

"Circuit's fried," Chuck said.

"Lucky it didn't start an actual fire," Colson noted.

I nodded. "Doug's called the electrician. But we have a long list of procedures to check off."

Chuck rolled his eyes. "He's just pissed because he's supposed to be getting lucky."

I gave him a shove. "Supposed to be on a date." Then I looked at Colson. "A date."

"Ah," he said with a smile. "And how is the good doctor?"

"He's . . ." Where to start?

"Oh, please don't," Chuck said. "Please don't get him going. He hasn't shut up about him since Rob asked him to you-know-what and Soren here had a brain fart and said no. Then there was the meltdown—"

Colson looked at me. "Wait, what? You said no?"

"It wasn't like that," I began. "I was trying to treat him properly, if you know what I mean."

Colson stared at me as if I'd spoken in tongues. "Just so you know, treating him properly might mean *treating him properly*, if you know what I mean."

Chuck laughed. "He learned this lesson, yes. And we all had to suffer."

I sighed and ignored their bullshit. "Anyway, we talked and discussed all the things, and we got past that."

Chuck huffed. "Short version is they're *dating*—" He used air quotes. "And tonight was supposed to be the night. But now he's here, and we're suffering because of this. Again."

Colson clearly found this funny but he raised an eyebrow at me. "Dating, huh? Sounds official."

"It is," I replied.

"He's a nice guy," Colson said, smiling at me. "I'm happy for you."

"Thanks. Same. He's . . . kinda great."

"Captain?" Doug called me from the door.

I gave Colson a clap on the arm as a goodbye, followed Doug, and got back to work.

It was after eight when we got back to the fire hall and then we had to run through the typical unpacking of gear and equipment. Even though we hadn't used any of it, it was still standard procedure to be 100% ready for next time. Doug had once said it wasn't standard procedure, it was critical procedure, and well, he wasn't wrong.

Standard, critical, whatever.

It simply meant it was closer to nine when we called it a day. And I had every intention of going straight home. I didn't want to bother Rob, given the hour, but his porch light was still on, and there was faint light coming from behind his blinds in his living room.

So, standing in front of his house, I shot him a text.

Still up?

A second later, he replied.

Yes. How was your night? Everyone okay?

The way his first concern was if people were okay made me smile. Instead of replying, I walked up his porch steps and rapped gently on the door.

A second later, the door opened and he stood there in

comfy sweats, a book in his hand, and a slow spreading smile on his face. "Oh, hey."

"Hey."

"Everything okay?" He looked me over and opened the door wider. "Come in."

His house was warm. The only light was a lamp beside the couch where he'd obviously been reading. "Sorry I'm late." I smiled at the still-bare Christmas tree. "You uh, you didn't decorate your tree."

His smile was more of a sultry smirk, his gaze drinking me in. "I could have taken care of it myself, but I've been doing things solo for a while now, and when you offered to lend a hand . . ."

Well, damn.

He just about set my nerves on fire.

"A hand, huh?"

He pulled his bottom lip in between his teeth, then sucked back a breath. "Can I get you something to drink? To eat? You would have missed dinner."

Before I could decline, my stomach answered for me with a growl. I shrugged. "Sorry. You mentioned food."

He laughed and gently touched my arm. "Take your boots off, get comfortable. I'll reheat you something."

Lord, have mercy.

The second we saw each other, the electricity between us sparked. As soon as I was near him, there was so much static in the air, I could feel it buzzing on my skin. Sexual attraction an undercurrent just waiting for ignition.

I'd never known anything like it.

I'd seen guys I was attracted to before, sure. And I'd had

times when things got hot real fast, usually on a dance floor a few beers deep or with a random Grindr find.

But nothing like this. Nothing even close.

Something was definitely gonna happen tonight, and my whole body was buzzing.

I got my boots off and hung up my coat just in time to hear the microwave beep. Rob was putting a plate on the counter when I joined him in the kitchen. "So the fire," he said. "Everyone okay?"

"No fire. The fire alarm tripped at the nursing home. Everyone was fine. Well, Colson was busy."

Rob looked at me, mildly confused. "No fire is a good thing, yes?"

"Very. But protocol states if the fire alarm goes off, they have to evacuate. Which is good, but there were forty elderly, somewhat ambulant, and very confused people we needed to deal with. Colson was there, he did most of the wrangling."

Rob's face softened. "Come and sit at the table so you can eat."

We carried the plate and silverware to the table. I sat and had shoveled two mouthfuls of vegetable pasta in before Rob came back with two glasses of water. "This is delicious, thank you."

"You're welcome. Do you miss dinner often?"

"We can miss any meal if duty calls. But it's fine. No big deal. I do appreciate this though. Did you make this?" I was sure he did because it was so fresh; nothing store bought could come close.

"I did. Dare I say it, I enjoyed cooking. I have all this

time, which I still am not used to, obviously. And I say that while you worked a fourteen-hour day. I'm sorry."

I swallowed my mouthful and shook my head. "Don't apologize. You deserve some time off." I stabbed some zucchini with my fork. "Still don't think you'll get bored?"

"Bored?" he scoffed out a laugh. "I volunteered at the center, I cooked dinner, I read a book. A fiction book, for fun. I haven't done that since high school. And I was thinking I should start making a list of any home improvements that will need to be done come springtime."

"Can you do home improvements?"

"Oh, heavens no," he laughed. "I said I'll make the list. Then I'll call the appropriate contractors."

I chuckled as I ate.

Rob seemed happy to talk as I finished my plate. "I lived in an apartment before. High-rise, new, fully maintained. I never had to worry about anything. But this little house is older and I should do regular upkeep. Or so Hamish said. And he's married to Ren, who would most definitely know."

I snorted. "He would."

"So will I ever get bored?" he mused. "While I can't see the future, and everything is always subject to change, I can't see myself getting bored anytime soon. Gunter said there's always something in town to volunteer for. Community projects, festivals, and committees, fundraisers, etcetera, and I love the idea of it."

"Which part?"

"All of it. I wanted to find a sense of community, and I think I found that here. I really like the guys. Gunter is so nice, and Hamish is funny without even trying." He smiled at me. "Thank you for introducing me to them."

"You're welcome. I'm glad you like it here."

His smile became a sigh. "I'm kind of waiting for the other shoe to drop. Or the ax to fall. Or whatever the cliché saying is these days."

"You should ask the kids at the center for what the new lingo is."

"Oh god, no, they already think I'm cringe. Because cringe is an adjective these days, apparently."

That made me laugh. "Did you point that out to them? Because that's probably why they might have used it. You know, for context."

He laughed and knocked his knee to mine. "Your age is closer to mine than theirs, so you need to be on my side. And no, I do know better than to critique the grammar of teenagers, especially when there's a pack of them."

"A pack?"

He shrugged. "I'm not sure what the collective noun would be. The word pack depicts an elevated status on the food chain and the ability to pick my confidence clean down to the bone."

I chuckled as I finished the last of the pasta. "Savage."

"Exactly. Maybe they could be a savage of teens."

He was funny. "I don't think they're that bad."

"No, they're a great group of kids, actually. They like having somewhere to hang out. It's a space just for them. Gunter's doing a really good job."

I studied him for a moment. The sincerity, the softness in his eyes. He really did enjoy helping others, being sympathetic and attuned to those in need, and that was something I really needed in a partner.

And damn, I could listen to him talk all day.

"I used to treat teenagers, back in Seattle. The usual horrible things: drugs, assaults, abuse. And it's easy to get complacent, to get systematically prejudiced into thinking all teenagers are lazy and ungrateful, you know, as the older generations would have us believe. But that's simply not true. These kids are passionate about a lot of things. They care about the environment, about equality and equity, and they don't stand for intolerance. They're just silenced in a world built and run by adults and governments who don't listen to them, and they're frustrated. They're going to get left a world that's unsustainable, financially, environmentally, and be expected to fix everything . . ." He shook his head. "Sorry. I didn't mean to rant. I get a bit preachy."

I turned to face him, our knees interlocked, and I took his hand. "Don't apologize. I like that you're passionate about it."

He smiled, embarrassed, his cheeks pink.

"I haven't been passionate about anything in so long." He shrugged. "But I want to look at youth programs and training programs and—"

I leaned forward and kissed him.

I don't know what made me do it. I just had to kiss him right then, mid-sentence. He was so fucking attractive, I couldn't stop myself.

"Oh," he whispered. "Are you trying to tell me to shut up?"

I shook my head. "Hell no. I could listen to you talk

about this all day. I just . . . you're so fucking hot when you talk like this."

His cheeks burned red. "Like what?"

"Like it's something you believe in. Something you feel strongly about. I mean, you're hot when you're not talking too, but right now?" I let out a low breath. "So fucking sexy."

He scoffed, as if that was the most absurd thing he'd ever heard.

"I should have asked you first," I whispered. "If I could kiss you. Sorry."

"Oh, don't be sorry," he murmured, his blush creeping down his neck.

Christ, that shouldn't be so hot.

All I could do was stare. Taking in the line of his neck, his jaw, his perfectly pink lips.

"Soren," he whispered, making me look at his eyes. His eyes were dark and full of desire. "Ask me again."

The air crackled between us, instantly electric.

Oh, hell yes.

"May I kiss you, Robinson?" I put my hand to his jaw, running my thumb over the stubble on his chin, then the softness of his bottom lip. "I wanna kiss you so fucking bad."

He made a grunting sound before he nodded. "Yes, please."

I pulled his face to mine, crashing our mouths together. Open lips, tongues colliding, sparks ignited in my bones, my blood ran hot all over.

I thrust my tongue into his mouth and he took it, sucking and groaning, and my god . . . my dick was aching with need. I wouldn't be going home to get rid of it tonight.

This was going to end here, with him. One way or another . . . We were both too riled up, too hot, too fast.

I'd never wanted anyone so much, so badly as I wanted him.

I held his face and tilted his head so I could devour him, and he let me. He grunted and slid forward on his seat, and when that wasn't close enough, he tried to straddle me, but the table was in the way.

I wasn't having that.

I stood up, brought him to his feet with me, still kissing him, still holding his face, still feeding him my tongue. I walked him backward to the sofa and lowered him onto it, laying him down, me on top of him.

He felt heavenly underneath me, and even better when he opened his legs. Muscular and warm, his mouth hot, his erection hard against mine.

Divine.

He opened his legs wider, and his hands went to my ass, rocking into me as our tongues tangled and tasted.

He broke the kiss with a groan, arching his back and giving me his neck. I licked and sucked, scraped my teeth, trying to ignore how hard we were. And while I could probably come like this, I needed to touch him, feel him.

I pulled back so I could meet his gaze. His eyes were dazed, his lips wet and swollen. "Fuck," I breathed. "I want to make you come."

His cock twitched against mine and his breath stuttered. "Oh. Please. And you too."

I pushed up and went to my knees, and he fumbled

with the button and fly of my work pants. I slid my hand under the elastic of his sweats at the same time he freed my aching dick. I held my weight off him with my left hand and slid my right around his length at the same time he wrapped his hand around mine.

"Fuck," I hissed, trying to resist driving into his fist.

"Oh god," he breathed. "I'm not gonna last."

Then his eyes rolled back, and he thrust into my hand. I dared to look down, and holy shit. His thick pink cockhead was slipping through my hold, the slit leaking precome with every pass.

Rob was too far gone, and his hand seemed to stall on my dick, so I took both our cocks in my fist and jacked us both off. The hot slide was so intense, hard as steel, soft as silk, and so fucking good.

"Oh," he bit out, his eyes wild. "Soren, I . . . oh fuuuu-uck . . . I'm so close."

I could feel him swell and pulse, my own cock aching for release. The slick slide of our shafts, the bump of our frenulums an exquisite torture.

Then his hands were up under my shirt, and he rubbed my nipples, making me hiss. My dick throbbed and he drove up into my fist as he tweaked my nipples, rolling and pinching. The pleasure shot straight to my balls, making me groan. His back arched up, neck straining as he came, his cock spurting come onto his chest.

The sight of him, the sounds he made, the smell of his sex, and it felt as if my orgasm ripped through my bones. I came so hard. So fucking hard. I think my brain disengaged, reality swam in and out, and when I came to, my fingers were digging into the arm of the couch and my come was painted over the top of his.

Fuck.

"Wow," Rob murmured, panting.

Smirking.

I barely remembered to let go of our cocks, making us both shudder. I almost collapsed on top of him and managed to stop myself, but my head hung heavy.

I was wiped out.

Rob put his hands to my face and leaned up to kiss me. "That was incredible."

"Hmm," I said, slow blinking. "Still have no brain activity."

He laughed, making our bodies tremble, but then my arm began to strain and I didn't want to smear the mess between us. I leaned up off him and somehow managed to get to my feet.

I think I swayed.

Rob caught me. "Whoa there. You okay?"

He was so close and my gaze drew down to his lips, and now that I knew what he tasted like, I didn't want anything else. I leaned in and kissed him. "You taste like heaven."

He barked out a laugh. "Okay, you're still not okay." He took my hand and led me to the bathroom. "Come with me."

He leaned me against the vanity then. With his feet in between mine, he pulled off his shirt. Watching him wipe our come off his body was one of the hottest things I'd ever seen.

He was lean and fit. Not a gym junkie, but it was plain to see he looked after himself. He had dark chest hair that, much like the hair on his head and in his scruff, was peppered with gray.

"Fuck, you're so hot," I breathed, skimming my fingers through the hair on his pec. I was so used to the fitness freaks who waxed and oiled that I'd forgotten chest hair even existed. "Oh, I really like this."

He tossed the soiled shirt into the hamper, and he watched me thread my fingers through his chest hair as if he was trying to see if I was being serious.

Like he wasn't a walking sex god. Jesus Christ. How could this man doubt himself?

I snaked my hand up his chest to his neck and pulled his chin between my thumb and forefinger so I could kiss him. "You're the sexiest man I've ever been with. Please never wear a shirt again."

He chuckled at that. "Pretty sure there are rules for doctors to be dressed."

I looked down at his hairy chest, drawing my gaze slowly up to his face, taking in every inch of him. "Hm, that's a damn shame." I slid my hands around his lower back and pulled his hips to mine. "Okay, maybe just be shirtless for me."

Rob hummed a humored sound, smiling. "I think you may be suffering from sleep-deprivation and impaired cognitive function."

"I don't think there was any impaired function about what we just did on your couch. That was hot as hell."

His cheeks flushed pink. "It was . . . unexpected."

"Unexpected? Pretty sure we both expected something to happen. Well, hoped. Maybe expected was the wrong word. I definitely hoped something would happen."

"Same," he said softly. "I'm glad you texted me."

"I saw your light on. I'm sorry we never decorated your tree."

He smirked. "Oh, the actual tree, and not the innuendo tree decorating?"

"We made a start on the innuendo tree. Still plenty of decorating to do yet."

He laughed and his hands felt far too comfortable around my back. "Tomorrow, we can maybe do the real tree. If you want?"

"I want. And maybe more of the innuendo tree decorating as well. And you said you'd come for a ride on Harley with me."

He made a cute face. "Ugh. I'm having regrets."

"It'll be fun. But I should go. It is late and . . ." and then I remembered. "Ugh."

Of course he was concerned. "What is it?"

"Ah nothing." I pouted and gave him my puppy dog eyes, whining to get what I wanted. "It's just so cold outside and your house is nice and warm."

"You could stay here," he said, smiling. "My house *is* warm, and my bed is too. You can sleep here. You're almost dead on your feet."

"Because that orgasm blew my brains out. I've never come so hard in my life."

Rob was stunned for a second, but then he laughed and took my hand again. This time he led me to his bedroom. He flicked on the lights, dimming them nicely. "Considering said orgasm and what we did on the couch, sharing a bed for the purpose of sleep is nothing."

"Purpose of sleep?" I waggled my eyebrows at him.

"Why, what else does one do in a bed? Whatever are you implying, doctor? I'll have you know, I am a man of chaste integrity."

He gave me a playful nudge with his elbow. "Oh please. I just had to wipe your chaste integrity off my stomach."

I laughed, pleased that we could joke like this. "Okay, I'll stay. Thank you." There was no way I was saying no to that offer. "But only if you promise to keep your hands to yourself."

I made a show of pulling off my sweater and shirt in one go, and of course his gaze went to my shoulders, my chest, my abs. I rubbed my hand over my six-pack for good measure, and he let out a slow shuddering breath.

"You didn't promise," I murmured. Then I undid my pants and let them slide down my legs.

He very deliberately didn't look down. "I'll go and turn the lights off," he said, his voice hoarse.

I grinned as he walked out. He absolutely liked what he saw, and to be fair, most guys did. I was ripped. My job required fitness, and I liked to look good. I spent hours in the gym for this body.

But I liked that he liked it.

The fact that Rob found me attractive made something warm unfurl in my belly. Kinda made my heart thump funny too.

I folded my pants, shirt, and sweater over the chair in his room, took off my socks, but kept my underwear on. Guessing he slept closest to the door, I went to the far side of the bed and was just pulling the covers down when he appeared in the doorway.

He seemed shocked or stunned, his gaze raking down my body.

I stood there in my briefs, which might have been the problem. "Is this okay? I normally sleep naked."

He looked up at the ceiling and sighed. "Oh god."

Oh yeah. He liked it a lot.

"If you'd rather I sleep in pajamas, I'll need to borrow some—" Then I remembered. "Oh, can I have the flamingo pj's? Pretty please? Just the bottoms."

He stared at me then, probably trying to determine if I was serious, which I absolutely was. "Did you just say *pretty please?*"

"With a cherry on top."

He sighed but went to his dresser and pulled out the familiar long pants. He tossed them to me. "Will you stop talking about them now?"

"Absolutely not."

I pulled them on and they fit surprisingly well. Well-worn and soft. Yeah, he was never throwing these out.

Happy, I climbed into bed, pulling the covers up and staying very much on my side. I folded my hands under my face and grinned as he rolled his eyes and switched off the lights.

He got into bed, staying very much on *his* side.

"Now," I said seriously, "please respect my chaste integrity and stay on your side. No touching, no wandering hands. Definitely no cuddling, and one hundred percent absolutely no blow jobs."

He chuckled, his smile lighting up the darkened room. "I'll try to remember."

I was ridiculously happy. Giddy, even.

"Night, Robinson."

His gaze cut to mine. "Night, Soren."

I WOKE up with my arm under Rob's neck, my other arm around his chest. My front plastered to his back, my leg hitched over his, and my erection pressed snug against his ass.

So much for no cuddling. Granted, I hadn't said anything about spooning or grinding. My dick was very happy where it was right now. It most certainly didn't want me to move.

But move, I should.

I peeled myself off him, missing his warmth already. I couldn't pull my arm out from underneath him without waking him so I rolled onto my back instead. At least I wasn't a few layers of fabric away from near fucking him.

But then he stirred, and rolled over, now using my chest as a pillow. He mumbled, slid his hand over my chest, his thigh over my leg. Was that his dick on my hip?

Yep. Pretty sure it was.

And then he froze, clearly awake now.

"Morning," I said, my voice husky. "I think you broke the no-cuddling rule." He immediately pulled back, but with my arm around his shoulder, I held him to me. "Nah, you're here now. Might as well stay."

He was quiet for a second, settling back in with his hand on my chest. But he did move his hips back so his morning wood was no longer poking me. "I was having the best dream," he mumbled. "Best sleep too."

"Best dream, huh? Wanna talk about it?"

He snorted. "Absolutely not."

I might have whined. "But they're the best kinds."

He sighed and we fell into a contented silence. I rubbed his arm and his breathing got deeper. I wasn't sure if he fell asleep again or just dozed, but there was no way I was risking waking him.

This was perfection.

I'd known this man for a week. We'd officially been dating for one day, and here I was waking up in his bed, with him in my arms.

Too soon? Probably.

But my god, it felt right.

This was what I'd longed for. Not some crazy fantasies about mega-rich playboys, or muscle men, or younger guys looking for a daddy-figure to rail them.

What my heart *should* have been looking for was a guy who was older than me. Not some young gym-bro, but a doctor, no less. Intelligent, funny, with a sexy natural body, who just wanted a simpler, quieter life.

Because if perfect for me was a person, I was beginning to think it was Robinson O'Reilly.

Waking up on my day off work with this man in my arms was something I could so easily get used to.

I had no idea what time it was, and I didn't care. I wanted to stay in bed with him all day. Except he'd said yes to going out for a ride on my bike with me this morning and that was what my real dreams were made of.

I smiled at the ceiling and rested my eyes. I was happy.

So freaking happy.

And hungry, and I needed to piss.

But I still wasn't moving.

"I can hear your stomach," Rob said. "I think it's searching for food."

I chuckled. "You should hear what my bladder is saying."

He laughed and rolled onto his back. "I'll make a start on breakfast." He rolled out of bed and stood up, and I didn't miss the tented sleep pants, and he didn't miss me looking at it. "Don't blame me. It's your fault," he said as he walked out.

I laughed and waited for him to use the bathroom first before my turn, and yeah, I had the same problem. The flamingo pajamas did nothing to hide my morning wood, though a piss and a splash of cold water on my face helped a little.

I found him in the kitchen at the coffee machine. Christ, he was so sexy. Gray sweatpants, shirtless, stubbled chin, hairy chest. And my efforts to stop the tenting of my pants was in vain.

"How do you like it?"

"Oh, I like it exactly like this," I murmured.

He looked at me, so I very pointedly looked him up and down. I was not ashamed for finding him so damn hot. He was a fox. Hell, I even loved the hint of gray in his hair.

"I meant your coffee," he said, turning back to the machine.

I could see his cheeks were red, as was the tip of his ears. I had to bite back a groan because damn.

Just fucking damn.

"Black is fine," I replied. Then, taking pity on my

aching dick, I sat at one of the two stools at his small kitchen counter. It was such a cute place. The layout was almost identical to my house, probably built in the same year by the same builder. Most houses in this street were. But his was bright and cheerful, and dare I say it, maybe decorated by someone with more style than the person who chose and installed my kitchen and the paint color.

Or maybe it was the man standing in front of me offering me coffee.

Certainly made for a cheerier start to my day.

"Thank you," I said, taking the mug. It smelled like the good stuff too.

"You're welcome." He sipped his own. "Now, breakfast. Scrambled eggs on toast sound okay?"

"Sounds perfect. Need me to do anything?"

He smiled behind his coffee. "Just sitting there is more than enough."

His words went straight to my heart, sending a jolt of warmth through me. I stuck out the leg of my flamingo pants. "It's the pajamas, right? I told you, they're hot. There's no resisting a man in these."

He chuckled, his eyes crinkling at the corners as he smiled at me. "Today's my last day off. Back to work tomorrow."

"We better make the most of it then."

"Doing what?" he asked, his voice low.

Christ.

I cleared my throat. Damn, at this rate we were never going to leave the bedroom. "We need to do your Christmas tree. That's very important. Then maybe we can take my bike and grab lunch somewhere while the weather's good. The sun's shining, so that's a start."

"Sounds great."

"And then this afternoon I have to do very boring things like groceries and laundry."

"Ugh. Reality."

"Unfortunately."

He took the eggs out of the fridge. "Then I should get started on breakfast."

SCRAMBLED eggs on toast had never tasted so good. He swore it was the real butter and fresh bread, but I was pretty sure it was the cook.

I did put my shirt on, and unfortunately, Rob did too. He clearly liked my fire department shirt though so it wasn't a total loss.

And then we decorated his tree.

Literally.

He had the red and green baubles and Christmas lights from the Home Mart, and it was a pretty decent job, even if I did say so myself.

The best part for me though was how we talked while we did it. He told me how he'd decorate the tree when he was a kid. How he'd loved the holidays, and how his mom always made a big deal of it, even if they'd never had much money. Then when he was sixteen, she'd gotten ill. Had been ill for some time apparently, just never complained.

Cancer took her when he was eighteen, in his final year of high school.

And there began his desire to do medicine. To help people. To treat and heal people. She'd told him to follow his dreams and do what made his heart happy.

And medicine had made him happy. But the hours and the bureaucracy had almost killed him.

And now he was here.

It wasn't a particularly happy story, but he smiled when he spoke of his mom; the memories happy ones, obviously.

He had an older sister who lived in Seattle. He had two nieces he didn't see as often as he should have. He sent them gifts and they FaceTimed when they could.

He really had given up so much of his life for his work.

I told him about my family. My parents, my brother. About my childhood in Canada. How I'd loved playing hockey but blew out my knee in high school so that was the end of that. I told him I never had any inclination for college, how I'd considered joining the police but chose the fire department instead.

I'd done a few years in Calgary but then went through a two-week wildfire training course in Missoula, and I'd liked it here so much, I decided to stay.

I told Rob the truth. I'd needed a change of scenery. I'd needed to get out of my hometown and spread my wings. I hadn't gone too far, but it was far enough away for a new start, close enough to get home in a hurry if I ever needed to.

He was just so easy to talk to. He thought about his word-choice, he was a great listener, and he had that calm and patient energy that doctors seemed to have.

And his body.

Damn.

Even in his sweatpants and a T-shirt, he turned me on. Maybe it was *because* of the sweatpants and T-shirt. That casual, homebody vibe that I wanted to put my arms around, that I wanted to hold, maybe snuggle up on the couch with and watch a movie.

That I wanted to do obscene things to.

"You okay?" Rob asked. "You zoned out there for a bit."

"Oh, just thinking," I said.

"About?"

About taking you back to bed. Right now. And not leaving all damn day.

I realized then I was holding the last bauble. I held it out for him. "That you should put this last one on the tree, then turn the Christmas lights on."

He put the bauble on, then pressed the button for the lights. They were the type with different settings, and he chose a slow twinkling type. Gentle, just like him.

The tree looked . . . "Perfect," I said.

He'd also put a small Christmassy center piece on his table and draped some garland across the window.

He looked around at it all, then made a face. "It's very . . . Christmassy."

I laughed and, doing what I'd wanted to do earlier, stood behind him and put my arms around him. I rested my chin on his shoulder. "It looks great."

"I guess I'm not used to it," he said softly.

"The first Christmas you've celebrated in a while should be special," I said, giving him a squeeze. Which was not a good idea because my dick was very on board with the proximity.

I dropped my arms and took a step back. "I should go home, take a shower, and get a few things done before we go for a ride. We need to take full advantage of the sunshine." I headed to his room before I could change my mind and pounce on him again. "Just gotta grab my clothes."

It also helped that I could walk out holding my clothes in front of my semi-hard dick. "See you in about an hour?" I said as I got to his front door. I shoved my feet into my boots, no socks, and gave him a bright smile. "Just come over, okay?"

"Oh, okay," he said. "Ahh, you're still wearing my pajama pants."

I looked down at the flamingos. "Yeah, I'll wash them. I promise not to steal them." I straightened up. "Unless you want me to take them off right here. Mr. Ling might jump to some foregone conclusions if he sees me leaving your house in my underwear."

He laughed. "Is there a back gate?"

"No, but we should seriously consider putting one in."

Rob's smile was so sweet, I almost couldn't leave. "God, I do not want to leave, just so you know," I admitted. "This is me using all my willpower to leave before I take you back to bed."

He barked out a surprised laugh. "Oh."

"Yeah. God, you turn me on so much." I rolled my eyes and groaned at myself for saying that out loud. "Yes. Leaving now. Making myself walk out the door like a good boy." I got the door open and stepped out into the brisk morning. "This is me leaving. Going home to have a very cold shower."

That wasn't true. I was going home to jerk off in the shower but I didn't think I should tell him that.

He chuckled from the door. "See you in one hour."

Chapter Nine

ROB

Oh boy, oh boy.

Soren.

Soren was amazing. Blisteringly hot, sugar sweet and, god help me, well endowed.

He was also thoughtful and kind. And he had manners when he ate, which, believe me, I'd seen men who didn't. He even cleaned up after breakfast. Said that was the rule if I'd cooked.

It'd been an incredible night.

I was so bummed when he'd had to work instead of coming over. But I understood that. Lord, did I understand that. But then he'd come by as soon as he could, as eager to see me as I was to see him.

As soon as he'd walked through the door last night, the undeniable chemistry was there. The sexual tension crackling between us. From zero to scorching in an instant.

I wanted to jump him the second he walked through the door, and I was surprised we made it through him eating a late dinner. We didn't get much further than that though, before we ended up on the couch, frotting, grinding to orgasm.

Like teenagers. It felt reckless and wicked, too worked up to take it to the bedroom.

I hadn't been that desperate since I was eighteen years old. Hell, I almost came from him kissing me. Before we had our pants undone.

Then I'd asked him to stay and I woke up with my head on his chest.

His glorious, well-defined, muscular chest. And his arm around me, and his warmth, and strength. His scent.

It had been so long since I'd woken up with a man. Hell, since I'd even been with a guy or had any kind of physical contact. Even sleeping next to him was comforting, and I can't remember ever sleeping so soundly.

So safely.

Because I hadn't ever felt so safe with anyone. I hadn't had any man touch me in months and even then, it was just a quick and terrible exchange.

But Soren's strong arms, and his big hands were like nothing I'd ever felt before. I was about to initiate another round of sex when I remembered that he wanted to take things slow, that we both did, and proceed with caution, so I jumped out of bed and suggested breakfast instead.

And then he had to go be completely perfect and help me decorate my Christmas tree. Oh, I was enamored already. And this sexy, younger, so-damn-fine man wanted me.

Me?

He kept saying I turned him on, and that was pretty evident by his prominent erection. And that he had to make himself leave because he wanted to take me back to bed.

The crazy part? I'd have let him.

I'd have fallen back into bed in a heartbeat. I'd have begged him to take me any way he wanted because, sweet mother of mercy, I wanted it too.

I wanted him inside me. I could just imagine his huge cock pushing into me, and if I thought about it, pictured it, I could almost feel it. I ached for it.

But we had a bike ride to get through first.

Admittedly, I was not a fan of motorcycles. But from the second I'd laid eyes on him on that very first day, the way he straddled it, the way he smirked at me . . . I wasn't so opposed.

And the way his whole face lit up when he'd offered and I'd said yes?

Totally worth it.

So, after a shower, I put on my jeans and my boots, pulled on my jacket, and a minute later I was knocking on his front door.

He opened the door and almost stole my breath.

He looked freshly showered, wore black leather riding pants and a black T-shirt that was just tight enough.

"Wow. Those pants are . . ." *Don't say that out loud.* "Is all black a biker thing? Was there a dress code?" I looked down at my very boring blue jeans and green sweater. "Because I missed the memo."

He laughed. "You like the pants, huh?"

"Well, obviously, yes. Because . . ." I couldn't help but look at them again. They looked a bit like jeans but different, and they were snug. I mean *snug*. "Damn. I would go home and get changed but I have nothing that comes even close."

"You look great. Come in, come in. I just need to make sure this fire is built before we go, if that's okay?"

"Yeah, of course."

He went to the fireplace and knelt down in front of it, giving me a wonderful view of how those pants stretched across his ass and thighs, and he carefully placed a bigger piece of wood on the fire. "It was dead cold so it was a good opportunity to clean it out and build a new one, ready to be lit when I get home."

Oh right. The fire. Not the pants.

Concentrate, Rob. Jeez.

"I didn't think a firefighter would have a wood fire in his house," I mused. "Not that I'd given it much thought before, but you know, fire safety and all that."

"Wood fires are fine," he said. "If they're properly maintained and have the correct grills and guards, of course. Most house fires start with an electrical fault or appliance. Dryers are common. Electric blankets, phone chargers are a big one too." Then he snorted. "Sorry. Don't mind the fire safety spiel that comes out every so often."

I smiled. "It's fine. I have a similar spiel about preventable diseases."

He chuckled, stood up, closed the door to the fireplace, adjusted the damper, and put the grill in front of it. "Are you ready for your first ride on a Harley Davidson?" His excitement was contagious.

"Uhhhh, yes?"

He came over to me and squeezed my arm. "You'll be completely fine. I'm a safe rider, and we won't go too far.

I'll take you for a scenic tour; then we can grab some lunch. How does that sound?"

"Good. I think. I *am* nervous," I admitted, though he could surely tell. "But I'm also excited."

He took my hand. "Me too." Then he led me through his kitchen to his laundry and mudroom, and if I thought my house was tidy, his was meticulous. Not one single thing out of place or even a speck of dust, that I could see, anyway. As he pulled on his riding boots in the mudroom, I noticed even the towels on the shelf were folded and stacked with military precision, his detergents neat enough for hospital surgical standards.

"Your house is very tidy," I noted.

He laughed as he did up the second boot. "It's my training. Fire hall requirements. I spend more time in any given day cleaning that place than doing anything else. All fire halls are the same."

"Fire hall. I haven't heard them be called that in a long time. I notice you say it a lot. Is that an industry thing for you to call it a fire hall instead of a station?"

"Nope. It's a Canadian thing. Well, it is where I'm from anyway. But people know what I'm talking about when I say it."

And then, as if he wasn't already hot enough in all black and boots, he had to go put on a leather jacket. This was a riding jacket. Still insanely cool, but it was built for safety, should the rider meet the road.

And he was so dang hot it made my heart race.

"Well, I'm really glad that doesn't make you ten times sexier," I joked. "I'd hate to be distracted."

He laughed and straightened my very uncool, sensible

jacket. "If you enjoy today and think it might be something you want to do again, we'll get you a proper jacket. Maybe some leather pants."

"Me? In leather pants?"

He lifted his knee and tapped it. "Kevlar fabric. Kinda cool, huh?"

"Well, yes. The doctor in me, who has tended far too many motorcycle riders in the emergency department, fully approves. But how come you get the cool Kevlar pants, and I get leathers?"

He grinned without shame. "Because then I get to see you in leather pants."

I walked right into that. It made me blush, and Soren let out a pained sound. My eyes met his and he put his hand to my face, thumbing across my cheek. "This color. It fucking kills me."

Oh.

Of course, I blushed a whole lot harder.

His nostrils flared and he did that thing where instead of leaning in to kiss me, he pushed forward with his whole body, so not only did his lips meet mine but his body did too.

It was a little bit domineering and a whole lot of hot.

My breath caught. My heart thumped so hard it almost hurt. His lips, his body, his hands . . . I wanted more. Needed it.

And then he pulled back with a frustrated groan. "We're going out on the bike," he mumbled. "This is me doing the right thing. I'm not going to take you to bed. I'm taking you out on the bike. It's going to be fun." He took a step back. "Which is why I'm all the way over here."

I couldn't help it. I laughed, dazed and happy. "It's kinda crazy, huh? This." I gestured between us. "Phew."

He nodded. "Glad it's not just me."

"It's really not just you."

He stared at me, then shook his head and whined as he went to the back door and held it open. "This is me doing the right thing again. Leaving the house and being a gentleman."

I laughed and went out onto his back deck. The fact he wanted me, that he felt this undeniable sexual energy between us too, it was such a heady feeling.

I felt giddy.

I felt . . . happier than I'd felt in a long, long time.

His bike was out of the shed, two helmets on the seat, and . . . oh, dear god, I'm getting on a motorbike.

My nerves were starting to feel a lot like anxiety and regret.

"Um," I said. "I'm not sure about this."

Soren picked up one of the helmets and stood in front of me. "If you hate it or don't feel safe, just tap my leg and I'll bring you straight back. But just try it."

The fact he acknowledged my fear and gave me an easy out was reassuring. The fact he wanted me to at least try was the least I could do.

I nodded. "Okay."

His grin made my already-pounding heart squeeze. He pecked my lips before putting the helmet on me and fixing the strap. He checked it for size and fit. "How does that feel?"

I wobbled my head and it didn't move around. "Fine."

He gave me a quick rundown of the bike, like where to

put my feet and where to watch for the heat of the exhaust, then put his own helmet on, completing the whole hot-as-hell look. He slid his leg over the bike, straddling it, and it did visceral things to my body.

He patted the seat behind him. "You gonna get on or just stare at me all day?"

I stepped closer. "It's not my fault you look so hot right now. My brain stops working." He laughed and put down the visor on my helmet. I slid my leg over, sitting right behind him. As in, right behind him. Flush against his ass, my thighs on the outside of his. "Oh."

He took my hands and pulled me closer, my palms on his flat stomach. "Hold onto me."

Well, this was certainly cozy.

But then he turned the key and pressed a button by his throttle. The bike started but it didn't sound like a Harley . . .

"It's just the starter," he said, loud enough for me to hear.

Then he pressed another button, and the bike rumbled to life. There was a reason they called Harley's a chopper—they sounded just like one.

Despite the nerves and anxiety, I was smiling.

It was thrilling! And I couldn't believe I was actually doing this. That this was my life now. Just a few weeks ago, I was a burned-out zombie, ready to walk away.

Now I was on a Harley Davidson-riding date with a firefighter who was so far out of my league, who for some strange reason, wanted to be with me.

Soren looked down, checking my feet were on the right pegs, tapped my hands on his belly, and rode us out of his driveway. It was barely at a walking pace, very safe, but the thrill it gave me . . .

What a rush.

He took us down toward Main Street and turned left, going past the clinic and the fire station, and I wondered why I'd been so scared of this . . .

It was the best feeling. Exhilarating and fun.

I couldn't even remember the last time I'd done something purely for the enjoyment of it.

Soren took us out on Ponderosa Road. Snow blanketed the ground, though it wasn't banked up yet. He drove at a reasonable speed, much slower, I imagined, than he'd have gone without me.

As we passed some fields and a magnificent house below the mountains up on the left, he pointed to the sign on the gate.

Arabella Bed & Breakfast.

Was that Jayden and Cass's bed and breakfast? Maybe that was why Soren had pointed it out.

It was a beautiful place, but then again, everything here seemed to be next level. Even the small, quaint houses in town—like mine and Soren's—were simply lovely.

We passed some ranches, and the farther we went out, as we wound through the mountains, the tall snow-covered trees enveloped the road, and this was something out of a fairy tale. Tree-covered mountains on one side, river on the other.

I was smiling so hard the helmet was hurting my face.

Then Soren pointed up ahead and I saw an old sign to a scenic lookout. He slowed down and we pulled off the road and came to a stop.

I climbed off the bike, my legs still vibrating, and took off my helmet as Soren cut the engine. The silence was stark but then I registered other sounds: birds and running water.

Soren pulled his helmet off and swung his leg over. "So," he said. "You're smiling. Did you like it?"

I was so excited I could barely stand still. "Loved it. It's so . . . freeing! And this place." I looked up at the tree-covered mountain and then out to the view. "It's breathtaking. Is that a waterfall I can hear?"

He nodded towards the railing on the far side of the rest stop. "Go take a look."

I walked over and sure enough, down below was the river and a small waterfall, mostly frozen now, before the river snaked its way along tree-covered banks.

Soren was soon beside me. "Pretty cool, huh?"

"Cool?" I was dumbfounded. "Soren, this is amazing. And it's twenty-five minutes from Hartbridge. The mountains, the trees, the water. I cannot believe that this . . ."

I wasn't sure what I was about to say or if I should say it out loud.

"You can't believe that this what?"

"That this is my life. That I'm doing this. That I'm here. With you on that bike." I shook my head. "Where I can feel the sun on my face, and the air is so crisp and clean it's like a rush of oxygen."

Soren smiled at me, squinting one eye from the sun. "I'm glad you're here."

"Here right now? Or here in Hartbridge?"

"Both."

"Me too. I wish I'd come here five years ago."

He put his hand to his heart. "But then I wouldn't have been here."

I pretended to be struck in the chest. "Ahh, okay then maybe two years ago."

"That's better. Five years ago, you'd have been fighting Hamish for Ren."

I laughed at that. "Not likely."

"What? Ren's a great guy."

"Oh, my issue wasn't with Ren. Could you imagine anyone fighting Hamish? I bet he fights dirty."

Soren chuckled and leaned his ass against the railing. "You'd have been out of luck anyway. Those two are watertight."

"Ah, yes. They told me about the Hartbridge Christmas Cupid thing," I said. "They all swear by it, you know. Like they had absolutely no say in who they fell in love with."

Soren nodded slowly. "Oh yeah. I know all about it. I was here last year and got to see it in action with Colson and Braithe."

"Do you believe it?" I asked. "Do you think it's actually true? I mean, it sounds ridiculous, and at first, I thought they were joking."

Soren's eyes met mine for a second before he turned and looked out over the river, at the water, the trees, the snow. "I didn't. I mean, I never used to. It sounded crazy, right?"

That sounded very past tense . . .

"Never used to?"

He cut me another glance before he looked away again, chewing on his bottom lip. "Now I'm not so sure. I mean, it always sounded so absurd to me, the way they talked about it." He turned to face me, his eyes imploring, his smile nervous. "But then you turned up."

But then you turned up.

"Me?"

"Yes, you. Who else?" He laughed. "You turned up at the beginning of December. That's the way it plays out, apparently. As for having no say in it, I don't believe that for one second. I could say no if I wanted to. You could too." His eyes never left mine, but they swam with honesty and a little fear. "But I don't want to."

Holy shit.

I had to swallow so I could speak. "I don't want to say no either."

He beamed a smile at me. "I want to see where this goes. And I'm trying not to get ahead of myself, Rob, because it's been like one week, which is just crazy, but I think we could have something here."

Holy, holy shit.

I wasn't sure what to say. I wasn't even sure I could speak. "Wow."

"You don't need to reciprocate," he added quickly. "I just wanted you to know that I think you're great and I really like being with you—"

"I do too," I blurted out. My hammering heart seemed to kickstart my mouth. "I think we could have something here too. And it is crazy, because it's been one week. And everything in my life has changed so much. For the better. All of it. And that includes you. I like spending time with you as well, and the energy between us, the tension, it's off the charts and nothing I've ever experienced before. God, I wish I hadn't have said that. But you feel it too, right? I'm not imagining that. You have to keep reminding yourself to be a gentleman so . . ."

Soren threw his head back and laughed, then took my face in his hands and planted a kiss on my lips. "Fuck yes, I feel it too. You know I do. And I still want to try and pace it out so we don't crash and burn, ya know? Dating and romance is fun, right? I just want us to establish a solid base. Too many times it just fizzes out because once the sex subsides there's nothing else, and I don't want that for us."

Everything he said made perfect sense, and it was a rational approach. It proved to me, along with communication, that he really did want to see how far we could take this.

"It's been so long since I've dated anyone," I admitted. "Like years. I just never had the time for any kind of commitment, so I might not be any good at this. But I'm willing to try."

That had to be the important part, right?

"Just be you."

Oh damn. He really was so freaking perfect.

I slid my hand along his jaw and kissed him softly. "Thank you for bringing me here and for making me get on your bike with you. I really wasn't sure and I can't believe I would have missed this. I can't believe the feeling." I put my hand to my heart. "It's exhilarating and the scenery is so amazing. I mean, look at this place! I think we should do this more often. If that's okay. Like once a week or something."

Soren's smile was warm and, oh man, it made my stomach swoop. "I'd really like that," he whispered.

"You okay?"

He laughed and took a deep breath in. "Oh yeah. I'm okay. Kinda can't believe this is my life now either."

"You've lived here for two years," I said . . . then I caught on to what he meant. "Oh. Bringing someone out here on your bike?"

He took my hand, playing with my fingers. "Not just anyone. You, Rob. Bringing you out here. Dating, spending time with you." He studied my face then, groaning up at the sky. "The way you blush is gonna be the end of me, I swear to god."

I laughed, embarrassed, putting my hands to my cheeks. "I'm not blushing. It's cold. It's one hundred percent not blush. Did you know that erubescence is a physical reaction to a psychological trigger, as in an emotional response. Embarrassment, joy, but also anger and even sexual stimulation, and I don't know why I just gave you the medical breakdown of that. Seems to be a new nervous trigger but only when I'm around you."

Soren laughed. "Are you angry?"

"Not at all. But *now* I am leaning more to the embarrassed side of the diagnosis."

He gently thumbed my jaw, his gaze following its wake. "It's the damnedest thing. And you said sexual stimulation, right? I didn't mishear that."

I opened my mouth and promptly shut it again, certain my face was now bright red. "I have no recollection of that."

Soren chuckled and pulled me in for a hug. Nothing else, just a warm embrace that soothed something in me. I wrapped my arms around his waist, under his jacket, and held onto him, never wanting to let go.

He was warm and so comforting, I melted into him.

How was a hug so soothing and healing, I'd never know. Probably the serotonin boost—

Just shut up and enjoy it.

It's human contact, the feeling of being wanted and safe. Comfort and empathy. That's what it is. Something you haven't had in forever. Something you haven't let yourself have in forever.

I buried my face against his neck and inhaled the scent of him. Addictive, irrational, but so addictive. I never wanted to let go. If I kept my eyes closed, I could actually fall asleep . . .

"We should go," Soren whispered.

I had to force my eyes open and make myself release him and step back. "We should," I agreed.

He pulled his gloves out of his pocket and tugged them on. "This is me being a gentleman again," he said. "Trying very hard to do the right thing."

It made me chuckle. "Your strength of will knows no bounds."

He laughed, but it was a tortured sound. "It's not without pain, I can assure you."

I almost felt bad as I followed him back to the bike, but the confidence it gave me was something I hadn't felt in a long time either.

He helped me with my helmet again. "Want some lunch at the diner?" he asked.

It was a bit early for lunch, but I remembered he'd said he had some chores to do this afternoon, and I didn't want to cut our date off early. Spending another hour with him, even at the diner, was more than fine with me. "Sounds great."

When we were back on the bike, Soren took my arms and tightened my hold on him. My front was glued to his back, including my crotch against his ass. I was no expert at these things, but I was fairly sure I didn't have to be *that* close. He patted my arm, as if telling me I should stay like that—as if I'd ever move when I got to touch him like that—and he began the ride home.

It was no less breathtaking on the return trip. The sunlight was filtered through the trees, the snow glinting perfectly. There was hardly any traffic and it could have just been us in the entire world for what it felt like.

It was perfect.

We rode into Hartbridge, Soren slowing down well under the limit. We passed the fire station, the clinic, went past the bridge, and he slowed to a stop at the diner, and reversed us in.

I reluctantly let go of him and climbed off the bike, took my helmet off, and handed it to him. He removed his helmet and swung his leg over, running his hand through his hair.

God, he's so hot.

And there, on the sidewalk, I almost told him to take me home. Take me home and do whatever he wanted with me. The level of desire I had for him . . . it felt like he'd taken my libido and given it a good shake.

Sex had never been a priority for me. Merely just a physical release. Granted, I'd never had the time or many options. Just a quick hook up and, even then, that was only every few months.

Now I could barely think of anything else.

"You okay?" Soren asked. He was standing near the

door to the diner, clearly wondering why I wasn't following.

"Oh, yes," I said quickly, ever so grateful he couldn't read my mind. "Sorry."

He held the door for me and the delicious aromas hit me as soon as I stepped inside. Okay, so maybe I was hungry for . . . food.

And hungry for Soren and for what you want him to do to you.

I cleared my throat, silently telling my inner voice to shut up, and slid into a booth. Soren sat opposite me, pulling his gloves off, and then his jacket. Which was almost a shame, until I got a visual reminder of how tight his T-shirt was.

Lord, help me.

My dick was starting to thicken, which was obscene. I was in a public place. Where families and the elderly were—thankfully the diner wasn't busy yet—but still, my patients from the clinic could see me.

I needed to think about other things.

Like the menu.

Yes, the menu. "What looks good?" I asked.

"You know," Soren said, "I might have the beef and stout pie."

"That sounds pretty good," I agreed. I hadn't even read the menu. I didn't particularly care what I ate, as long as it was fast and we could get back to my place, stat.

A woman who looked a lot like Lucille Ball came to the table. "Can I get you boys some coffee?"

"Ah, Crystal, yes please," Soren said. Then he checked with me. "Is that okay?"

"Perfect," I said, giving her a smile.

"Ah, you're the new doc in town, right?" she asked.

"I am, yes. Rob O'Reilly."

"Nice to meetcha," she said. "Crystal's my name." She pointed her pen to her name tag. "Been out for a ride, I see." She nodded to Soren's bike out front.

"Lovely day for it," I replied with a smile.

"Would you like more time to look over the menu?"

"Oh no," Soren said. "We'll have two of the stout pies, please."

"Ah, Jayden's outdone himself with those. Very popular."

I'm sure that was a great story but I'd really appreciate it if you could please hurry with our order because I really need Soren to take me home and rail me, thanks.

My inner voice was getting impatient. And rude, apparently.

And then, because the universe was set on torturing me, Hamish came in. Well, more like burst in through the doors and, spotting us, sidled up to our table.

"I'm supposed to be working right now, but I told Ren I was getting us coffee—"

"Two of the usual, love?" Crystal asked.

He nodded. "Yes, please."

She disappeared and Hamish looked at me and smirked. "So, I just happened to be looking out the window when I saw Soren's motorbike pull up, and lo and behold, who should be on it with him?"

My face burned. "Ah, yes. Lo and behold."

Soren chuckled. "And you just had to come over."

"Absolutely," Hamish said. His attention drew back to

me. "I'm going to need all the details. Will you be at the youth center tomorrow, perhaps?"

I bit back a smile. "Ah, no, actually. I'm working for the next three days."

Hamish looked stricken before he pursed his lips and nodded. "Okay, we need a group chat."

"Hamish, dear," Crystal called out. "Your coffees."

He took the two takeout cups from the counter and gave us a parting, excited smile. "Have fun," he said, before breezing out the front doors.

I cleared my throat. "So glad that wasn't awkward or embarrassing."

Soren laughed. "He's going to need details."

"Oh, believe me, he's not getting details."

Crystal slid our coffees in front of us. "Oh, Hamish is a real hoot, isn't he?" She didn't wait for an answer before she went back behind the counter. "Pies'll be out in one sec."

I smiled at my coffee, taking a moment to consider the last few minutes. "So, does everyone know everyone's business in this town?"

"Pretty much." Soren nodded slowly. "Especially when it's a newcomer to town and he's the new doctor. And especially when he's a handsome, eligible bachelor. I'm sure there were some lovely single folks who were hopeful of catching his eye."

I smiled at him, meeting his gaze. "They can be disappointed."

He cracked a grin. "Yes, they can."

Crystal put two plates in front of us, with two of the most delicious looking, golden brown flakey pies, and even a scoop of mashed potatoes. "Enjoy, boys," she said.

"Wow." I cut into the pie to let some steam out. "This was a great choice."

And it was absolutely delicious.

As was the man sitting across from me.

He cleared his throat and it made me realize I'd been caught staring. When my gaze met his, his eyes were dark. "You keep looking at me like that," he whispered, his voice low and rough. "You shouldn't look at me like that, Robinson."

Holy hell.

My whole body flushed hot at his tone, his words. The way he said my first name. And the heat in his eyes.

I couldn't find the words to say or the ability to say them, though I'm sure the color of my face said it all.

He let out a low breath. "Jesus. That makes being a gentleman very hard." He shifted in his seat and squinted uncomfortably. "You're freaking killing me."

"About that," I managed, my voice just above a whisper. "You being a gentleman. It's very gallant, and I appreciate the restraint. But . . ."

"But what?"

"I don't want you to be a gentleman anymore."

His gaze cut to mine, understanding exactly what I meant. I nodded anyway, in case he needed confirmation.

His nostrils flared. "Let's go," he said, pulling out his wallet and throwing some twenties on the table. He slid out of the booth, grabbing his jacket on the way.

I scrambled to catch up, saying thanks to Crystal as we hurried out the door. He had his jacket on and his leg over the bike in a flash. We fixed our helmets and he started the bike, barely waiting for me to wrap my arms around him before we were driving down Main Street.

He pulled into his driveway and cut the engine, and the silence again was so freaking loud.

Because now there was nothing to fill the void. Nothing but us and what I'd told him I wanted to do.

My legs were a little wobbly with anticipation when I finally got off the bike. I took my helmet off and couldn't make eye contact with him. Had I really been so shameless just two minutes ago?

Where was that courage now?

"Tell me," Soren said, his helmet on the bike seat. "Yes or no."

I nodded.

He groaned and lifted my chin with his finger. "You need to say the word, Rob. I have to hear it, and you have to mean it."

My body was just about to combust, shame and courage be damned. My body was in charge now. I looked him right in the eye. "Yes. Take me to bed."

He took my hand and led me inside, not even stopping in the mudroom for our boots. He took me down the short hall, into his room, and stopped before the bed.

He was breathing hard, his chest heaving, and he cupped my face in his hands. "Tell me what you want and I'll do it. Anything. I'll do anything you want."

God help me.

My belly swooped, warmth pooling low and curling, my balls drawing down. I'd never had anyone ask me so brazenly, and instead of freezing up and letting him decide, I went with the truth. "I know I should say something like fellatio or another mutual hand job. The frotting was out of this world, but Soren, I really want you to fuck me."

His jaw clenched and his nostrils flared again, his breath shuddering as if testing his self-control. But then he pulled my face to his and kissed me, opened my mouth, and delved his tongue in deep.

My knees almost buckled.

Without breaking the kiss, he clawed at my jacket, tossing it to the floor, my shirt swiftly joining it.

I was honestly a bit reluctant to rid him of his jacket. He looked so damned hot in it, but it met the floor too, and we only stopped kissing long enough for me to pull his shirt off.

He unbuttoned my jeans, then stopped. "Get on the bed," he ordered, his lips wet and swollen, his eyes black fire.

I'd have done anything he asked if he looked at me like that.

I sat on the bed and scooted back a bit. He grabbed my boot and undid the laces, quickly pulling it off my foot.

And all I could do was watch, as he stood before me, shirtless, the body of a god, and the bulge . . . in those pants . . .

Fucking hell.

When he had my second boot off, he wasted no time in pulling my jeans off me. I pulled my briefs down and he stood there, watching, almost panting. "You are so fucking hot," he breathed, his eyes drinking in every inch of me.

It was such a rush knowing he liked what he saw.

He lifted his foot to the bed, pulling at his laces, giving me a fantastic view of his body, the way his shoulders and traps worked, and those damn pants. He filled them as if they'd been tailor-made just for him.

Then he did his second boot, and my hand found its way to my cock, giving it a lazy stroke as I watched.

"Ah, your pants," I murmured.

He undid the button and managed to get the fly undone over his erection.

"Shame they can't stay on," I whispered.

He gave me a filthy smirk as he pushed his pants down. "Maybe next time, but not for this." He kicked his pants off, wearing just his briefs, which did very little to conceal his cock.

"Oh my god," I breathed. My belly tightened, knowing where that big dick was about to go.

Lord, I needed it.

Yes, you do.

You need it both slow and deep, and fast and hard, for as long as he can give it.

"I really do," I mumbled.

"You really what?" Soren asked.

Shit. I'd just said that out loud. "I really need you," I said. "And while I'd normally be down for long bouts of foreplay and games, taking our time and drawing it out, I think this time needs to be—" *Slow and deep, fast and hard?* "No games."

Soren went to his bedside, tore into a new box of condoms, and threw a foil packet and a bottle of lube onto the bed beside me.

Anticipation burned deep, my cock twitching.

"No games, huh?" he asked, smiling salaciously as he finally peeled off his briefs. His cock sprang free, full and rock-hard. Easily seven and a half inches, and thick. So thick, and absolutely fucking glorious.

I needed it in me so bad my hips flexed instinctively. I stroked myself, precome beading at the tip.

Soren knelt on the bed and collected the condom. "You getting desperate, huh?"

"I've needed it since the second I laid eyes on you," I admitted. Not caring one bit about my pride or shame.

"And I wanted to do our first time right," he said. "Take my time, take you to heights you've never been."

Oh, damn.

My cock throbbed and I groaned. Of course he saw, and he smiled. He was kneeling on the bed, his rigid cock jutting out. He still hadn't put the condom on, and he still wasn't inside me.

I snatched up the lube and smearing two of my fingers, I raised my knee and slipped my fingers over my taint, smearing the lube.

"What are you doing?" Soren asked.

I thought it was pretty obvious. "You weren't being fast enough." I pushed my fingertip inside my ass and began to work it in deeper.

"Yeah, I don't think so," he said. Then, he took my leg and my hip and somehow flipped me over. I let out a surprised grunt, but then he was between my thighs and pressing against me. He leaned down and whispered gruffly into my ear, "That's my job. I will look after you. I will make sure you're ready."

Before I could get my brain into gear, before I could form any words, he gripped my hips and dragged me closer until my thighs were over his; my cock free to stroke, my ass open.

Now, I'd never been particularly passive in bed, but he was one hundred percent in control of me, and it was so fucking hot.

I heard the rip of foil and felt the brush of his hands and his cock as he rolled the condom on.

Oh hell yes.

Here we go.

Then the feel of lube pouring down my crack, his thumb smearing and circling before slipping into me, working me, stretching me. Then his thumb was gone, replaced by two fingers, and I was stroking myself, rocking back on his hand.

"I need more," I pleaded. "I need your cock. Bury it in me, please." I was begging and didn't even care. Shameless, desperate. "Now, Soren."

He chuckled, a low throaty sound, as he fixed my hips to how he wanted them, pressed my shoulders down, and drove me forward. He pinned me with his weight, his cock at my hole, and he slowly, oh so slowly pushed into me.

I regretted my urgency. For those first few seconds of the breach, until the pop of relief as his cockhead slid in. I breathed through it, the sting soon subsiding as he moved, and I relaxed into the gentle push and pull of his hips.

He trembled above me with restraint, his lips at my shoulder. "Oh fuck," he said, his voice strained. "You feel so good." Then he slid one arm underneath my shoulder, across my chest, and his other hand raked through my hair, pulling on the strands as he pushed all the way in.

"Oh god," I squeaked, as he hit the wall inside me.

"Hmm," he moaned, his forehead pressed to the back of my head, to my neck. His lips, teeth and tongue sending shivers through me, his hot breath, his grunts and moans as he began to thrust.

Heaven.

I was in heaven.

"God, that's good," I rasped. "Oh yeah, just like that. Fuck yes."

His arm around me tightened, his hand in my hair pulled harder as he thrust slower, deeper.

His thick cock filled me so completely, his arm held me, his face in my neck, lips kissing and sucking. I'd never felt so convincingly owned.

He had complete control, dominating my body, and I loved it.

It was so hot, so good.

Soren groaned out a pained sound, thrusting harder, faster. "I can't stop," he bit out between thrusts. "God, Robinson. You're so fucking tight."

I loved the way he said my first name.

His forehead pressed against the side of my head as he tried to hold back, as he tried to stave off his orgasm. He thrust into me once more, upwards, driving into me. He cried out. "Fuck, please. I can't stop. I need to come so bad."

Lord, have mercy.

Soren grunted and his grip on me tightened as he fucked me. Pulling almost all the way out just to push back into me, his glorious cock harder and thicker.

I yelped and groaned at the severity, at his thick cock buried to the hilt inside me. But he never let go of me, he just gripped me harder, held me tighter, and impaled me deeper. His hand in my hair slid down to my mouth, covering it, silencing my moans of pleasure.

"I'm gonna come," he ground out as he drove into me one more time.

I raised my hips to meet him and spread my legs. "God yes, please. Need to feel it," I urged him.

He slammed into me one last time before driving me upwards on the bed, his cock impaling me as he held my shoulder for leverage. He came with a gasping roar in my ear, his cock swelling inside me.

I felt the pulse of his cock, shooting his load into the condom. And he groaned and shuddered with each spurt. "Holy fuck," he gasped, driving up into me one final time, gripping me so tight. "Oh god."

It felt divine.

Everything about it was divine. His power, his body, the way he pinned me down and held me. His strong arms, murmured sweet nothings, and soft moans.

Everything about him was perfect.

He stayed on top of me, inside me, until he caught his breath, then slowly pulled out of me. I missed his cock already; my body bereft of where he'd been.

I wanted him to stay inside me.

He pressed his forehead onto my spine and collapsed on top of me again, his breath hot on my skin. "Are you okay?"

"I'm so good right now," I replied, stretching my back, my shoulders, relishing the ache in my muscles. And my ass. I was very likely going to be sore tomorrow, but I still wanted to go another round. I wanted him to do that to me every day, for hours. I chuckled. "Good lord, I need more of that."

He kissed my spine, then rolled me over onto my back. He kissed my sternum, then ran his nose through the hair on my chest. He sucked on my nipple, making me hiss and buck my hips.

He smiled like the devil, looking up at me through his lashes, then moved down lower, and lower, until he reached my cock. "Oh, I haven't forgotten," he murmured. "I'm going to make you come now, if that's okay?"

I chuckled and relaxed, looking up at the ceiling, waiting . . . and waiting.

"Rob," he said.

I lifted my head to look at him, confused.

He was lying between my legs, his face at my cock. I could feel his hot breath on my balls. "You didn't answer me," he said, half smiling. Then he licked a hot stripe up the length of my shaft. "Want me to make you come?"

My breath hitched; my whole body shuddered. "Fuck yes," I said, fisting the base of my cock, holding it up for him, offering.

Begging.

"Suck it," I hissed.

So out of character for me. I was never this brazen, this demanding. But with him? I needed him in ways I'd never known. In ways I didn't understand.

He grinned as he sank his mouth over the tip, licking the slit, the frenulum, then sucking me down.

It damn near brought my hips off the bed, and I cried out. My orgasm rushed to the surface, so fast, so hard.

I tried to back down and pull away, but Soren gripped

my hips and held me still as he devoured me. He sucked and tongued my cock, tugged on my balls, and with my freshly fucked ass, I had no hope of holding on.

I came so hard. So, *so* hard. My orgasm ripped through me, decimating my bones, my mind. My whole body surged as I shot my load down his throat. He drank it, swallowing every drop until I was wrecked and convulsing.

Unable to speak. Unable to think.

Floating on an incredible high. Ecstasy, like nothing I'd ever felt.

Soren collapsed on the bed beside me with a laugh. I lifted my hand, my arm so heavy. I still couldn't speak. Hell, I could barely blink. Another tremor racked through me and I groaned.

Soren laughed again, lifted my hand to his lips, and kissed my knuckles. "So," he said. "That was possibly the best sex of my life."

I laughed, still not sure I could speak. Then Soren pulled me into his arms, pulled the blankets over us, and I slept like the dead.

My ass was sore the next day, but I didn't regret it. Hell, if Soren walked through my office door right this second, I'd let him rail me again.

On my desk.

God, on the floor if he wanted to. Anywhere he wanted, any way he wanted me.

We'd fallen asleep in his bed for an hour, and I'd woken up to him tracing gentle circles on my back. We showered together and he made me coffee, never more than a step away. Always touching, pressing soft kisses to my back, my shoulder, my neck, my lips.

He was a touchy-feely lover, and while I was very new to that, I loved it. Couldn't get enough of it.

He was gentle, caring, attentive. In the bedroom was a different matter. He was totally dominating and in charge but still tender. The way he held me and kissed my shoulder while he nailed me was a juxtaposition I couldn't get out of my head.

Was having a bit of trouble getting the blow job out of my head too . . .

"Doctor O'Reilly," Katie said from the door. "You have a visitor. Captain De Silva. He's not a patient here. He doesn't have an appointment."

Captain De Silva. Oh, I liked the sound of that.

My stomach swooped, excitement tingled through my veins. "That's fine, Katie. I'll see him. Send him in."

Soren, dressed in black jeans and a dark gray sweater, appeared in my door, smiling and sexy as hell. He had his hand behind his back and produced a rose. A single red rose.

"For you," he said.

My heart thumped and my grin became a laugh. "Really? For me?"

He nodded and stepped inside. "Of course. You have to accept it because the appointment's been made at the florist to have my kidney removed to pay for it. Do you know how expensive these are at this time of year?"

I stood up, unable to stop smiling. "Then I accept it."

He handed it over as if it were some kind of declaration in itself. Heck, maybe it was. "How are you . . . feeling?"

I ignored the heat in my face. "Can unequivocally confirm that I'm more than fine. Best I've felt in years, to be honest."

His eyes danced and he chewed on his bottom lip. "Glad to hear that."

We heard the clinic door open, and Katie greeted my first patient. Soren nodded. "I should go," he murmured. "I have to do all the things I didn't get done yesterday afternoon."

Because we'd been unable to stop touching each other, even just wrapped up in each other in his kitchen, fully dressed. Or later, cuddling on the couch while he insisted we watch the Christmas movie channel on TV . . . but that had turned into more kissing than cuddling, until I'd *made* myself go home when it was dark enough so Mr. Ling wouldn't see me doing the walk of shame.

The memory made me smile, but then I remembered that I would hardly see him this week. "You start night shift tonight?"

He nodded. "Sorry."

"Don't be sorry. I understand shift work. Anyway, we'll make up for it."

He raised an eyebrow, his smile becoming a grin. "I'll text you."

I nodded. "Okay."

He stood there for a beat, and we just stared at each other. My heart was now hammering, nearing tachycardia levels, I was almost certain. He nodded as if he understood. "I'll see you soon."

He left, and I had to put my hand to my heart and do some controlled breathing—and rein in my stupid smile—before my first appointment.

I put the rose on the bookcase behind me and went about my day.

I had a full day of appointments, ranging from an infected big toenail to a possible fractured hand, baby check-ups, elderly medication consults, and repeat prescriptions.

It was easy and incredibly rewarding to take five minutes to chat with each patient. To be reminded that patients are people and not just a number or an insurance statistic.

I was home early enough to make dinner and settle on my sofa with my book. I even turned the Christmas tree lights on and the lights at the front of my house. It was the most festive I'd ever been, in my adult life, at least. And something so simple as having a Christmas tree made me smile.

So did the few texts from Soren, and the ones I'd replied with. It was all so fun and flirty, a little bit dirty, but damn, that made me smile too.

I was the most relaxed I'd ever been.

And happy. But mostly I was sated. Not just my body, but my heart too.

I was, possibly for the first time in my life, content.

The next day I got a text from Hamish. He'd organized a small gathering for dinner at the pizzeria. I was certain he just wanted details, and given I had no other plans other than a few more chapters of my book, I agreed.

Plus, I really did like these guys.

And getting to actually hang out after work with friends over pizza sounded pretty damn great.

It was snowing, so I drove the short distance to Main Street, hurried inside, and pulled my beanie off as I walked inside. I'd not been in the pizzeria before and I was immediately transported back to my childhood in the old Pizza Huts. The décor, the smell. I loved it already.

Gunter and Braithe were in a booth so I made my way over. "Hey," I said. "How amazing is this place?"

Braithe laughed. "Right?"

"Pizza Hut, circa 1985," Gunter said.

"Exactly," I agreed.

Braithe made a face. "Wasn't alive then."

Gunter nudged him. "Oh, shush."

I chuckled just as Hamish arrived. He slid in next to me, taking his beanie and gloves off, ignoring the others and smirking right at me.

Yep.

This was going to be an interrogation.

"Sooo," he began.

"No details," I said, putting my hands up.

He sighed dramatically, then spoke to Braithe and Gunter. "Good evening," he said cheerfully. "What a wonderful night for some delicious pizza and some details on the newest Hartbridge Christmas Cupid victim."

I laughed. "Victim?"

The three of them laughed and nodded. It was absurd.

"I do not kiss and tell," I declared.

Hamish met my gaze. "But there's been kissing."

"Oh, yes."

"And? There's more, I can tell."

"We…"

"Oh my god, you got railed," Hamish said. "It was after the bike ride, wasn't it? Because that was hot as fuck."

I didn't have to answer because my face betrayed me with a searing blush.

"Oh my god," Hamish said. Thank god no one was paying us any attention because he was loud. "Spill the deets."

"I already said, I don't kiss and tell."

"Yes, but there's a difference between kiss and tell and getting railed and telling us," Braithe said.

"I don't do either," I said. They all stared at me, and I relented a smile. "I'm not saying anything . . . except . . ." I had their complete attention and this whole meeting was all so ridiculous. "Except, nothing. No details."

"Bike ride?" Gunter asked.

Hamish tapped the table in front of the other two, as if he had the gossip of the century. "Oh, yes. The other day I just happened to be at the store, working very hard, staring out the window, when who should I see pull up on his big sexy Harley Davidson motorbike but Soren. And *whoooo* should be on the bike *with* him but our very good doctor here."

Gunter and Braithe both smiled at me. "Really?" Braithe asked. "Doubling. You had to hold on to him and everything?"

Hamish nudged me with his elbow, his smile very knowing. "Oh, I think they're well past the holding onto him stage. You can say you don't kiss and tell, but your face gives you away."

My face flamed and I hoped the red décor and lights made it unnoticeable.

Hamish's little wiggle-dance in the seat told me otherwise. "I knew it."

I had to tell them something. There was no point in denying it, and if anyone here understood the absurdity of it all, it'd be these guys.

"We're dating," I admitted.

Braithe did a little clap. "Oooh, yay!"

Gunter just smiled warmly at me. "I'm happy for you."

"It's this town," Hamish said. "I keep telling y'all."

"Y'all?" Braithe asked in his slightly affronted English accent. "Did you just say y'all?"

Hamish grimaced. "It's terrible. I've been binge-watching the Atlanta Housewives. And I miss Jayden. He's been working so much lately, I'm losing my Australianisms."

"He's working tonight?" Gunter asked.

Hamish nodded. "They have a lot to get organized with the B&B. Christmas is always so hectic for him and Cass. And the diner of course. Those are two busy boys."

A waitress came over and took our order. We agreed on two pizzas for us to share. "And can I order one to go, but when we're ready to leave?" I asked.

"Sure thing."

She went on her way and the others were all looking at me, so I explained, "Soren's on the late shift. I'll take them a pizza later."

"Oh, that would be why he wasn't at the fire safety talk at the school today," Braithe said. "It was Doug and Raf."

I wasn't too sure what that meant . . .

"Mmm," Hamish buzzed. "So . . . just *how is* dating the sexy firefighter going?"

Braithe sighed. "It's easier just to give in, Rob. Tell him something. It keeps his pervy heart happy."

I sighed. "It's going . . . great?" I shrugged. "But I keep waiting for the shoe to drop, ya know? He's funny and sweet and romantic, and . . ."

God. I couldn't say it.

"And?" Hamish asked, hanging on every word. "And what?"

"And . . ."

"Really hot in bed?" Hamish prompted quietly. "I mean, he's a firefighter. It's gotta be smoking hot, right? On fire, even?"

"Those puns are terrible." I laughed, embarrassed. "But not exactly untrue." I fanned my face. "Holy hell. Like nothing I've ever had."

They laughed and Hamish gave my forearm a squeeze. "This is what I'm here for."

Gunter studied me for a long few seconds. "But you're worried about how fast it's moving, and you don't know if it's real or just lust, and it scares the hell out of you."

It wasn't a question, but oh boy, he'd nailed it.

I conceded a nod. "I've, uh, I've been alone a long time. My whole life was work, work, work. So this is all such a change of pace for me, and everything is perfect. So perfect."

"Too perfect?" Braithe added.

"Like something out of a Hallmark Christmas movie?" Hamish asked.

Yeah. They got it.

I nodded. "Yes. And I have professional obligations to this town, so I need to be mindful of that."

"Is he your patient?" Hamish asked.

"No. He's not on our books."

"Then it's a non-issue." He patted my arm again. "And as for the whirlwind, crazy-fast falling-in-love thing, we all questioned it when it happened to us."

Both Braithe and Gunter nodded again.

"It's this town," Hamish said with a sigh. "Where better to meet your perfect man than in a perfect town at the perfect time of year, huh?"

That made me smile.

"Just see where it goes," Braithe said. "Don't fight it. If falling in love is the worst thing that happens, how bad could it be?"

Our pizzas arrived and we ate a few slices in silence before talk turned to Braithe's school Christmas play and Gunter's youth center, and by the time we were done, I felt so much better.

The laughs and the friendships were a big part of that. But also voicing my concerns over this crazy whirlwind romance with Soren too. Acknowledging, to myself at least, that I already had feelings for him but it was normal to be scared and excited at the same time.

Was it a silly Christmas Cupid thing?

My rational brain said no, but my heart was saying maybe . . . maybe it wasn't as silly as I thought.

I took the pizza box and the four of us walked outside. It was still snowing, just flurries and dustings, but the way it all looked by the streetlights and the Christmas lights in shop windows and on awnings, it really was like something out of a Hallmark movie.

We each said our goodbyes, and I stood there for a second taking it all in. How utterly serene it was. And pretty. And how even something as simple as waving goodbye to friends before I took a pizza to my boyfriend at work was just so surreal, I couldn't believe it.

You just called him your boyfriend.

You said boyfriend. Like he's your boyfriend, but he's not. Not yet, anyway.

"I know. Shut up," I grumbled to myself, fully aware I was now talking out loud to myself.

But the voice in my head was, thankfully, silent as I carefully walked to my car. I drove the short block to the fire station, and taking the pizza, I walked to the door. The rolling door was down, so I wasn't even sure he was here, but I rang the buzzer anyway.

Suddenly feeling very foolish, I regretted not texting first. Would he mind me bringing him food? Was this out of line? Would his colleagues tease him?

Oh god. Did they even know about me?

This was bad.

Before I could turn and leave, the door opened and a man who was not Soren stood there in coveralls and a beanie. "Uh . . ." He said, confused. Then he did a double take. "Hey, Captain? Soren!"

"Yeah," a familiar voice called out from somewhere. A few seconds later, Soren appeared. He was wearing his coveralls and beanie, and his huge firefighter coat, looking a dozen kinds of incredible.

He broke out into a grin. "Hey."

"I'm not interrupting, am I?" I cringed. "I was just having pizza with the guys and thought you might like some."

The other guy's face lit up. "That's for us?"

Well, Soren, but yes. "Sure."

He took the box like a kid who just got a candy bar, and he began walking backward to what looked like an office or break room. "You got two minutes before this is gone."

Then it was just Soren and me. The fire engine was parked just a few feet away, there were ladders and gear, but the place was immaculate. But Soren . . . he was smiling at me in a way that made my heart two sizes too big.

He took my hand and pulled me into the fire station, and cupping my face, he pressed his lips to mine. Clearly he didn't care who saw, and neither did I.

But then, without a word, he took my hand in his, wrapped his other arm around my waist, and he began to lead us in a waltz. Slow and ridiculously romantic, all I could do was laugh. He kissed the side of my head before he spun me out and under his arm, bringing me back in for a soft kiss.

And yeah, those feelings I'd thought about earlier tonight, that I'd tried to ignore, that I was too scared to name?

There was no ignoring them now.

Chapter Ten

SOREN

He brought me pizza.

And that might be nothing to anyone else, but it meant the world to me.

Because it wasn't just pizza. It meant that he was thinking of me. That I was on his mind, that he was considerate and thoughtful, and he went out of his way for me.

He might have only been just down the road, but that wasn't the point. He could've very well had just gone home. I wouldn't have even known he'd been out for pizza.

But he didn't.

He'd ordered it with me in mind and hand-delivered it. Even driving and walking in the snow, which I knew he didn't love. And for me, the guy who had dreamed of having someone in his life to look after and be looked after by, well, this was a gesture I'd never forget.

And damn, he'd looked so uncertain when he was standing at the door. And incredibly gorgeous.

As soon as Chuck relieved him of the pizza, I had to do

something that expressed how insanely happy I was in that moment. Which apparently was dancing in the fire hall.

I was kinda glad it was just Chuck and me, not because I cared what anyone else thought, but holy hell, the ribbing they'd give me for weeks would be relentless.

Chuck was too busy feeding his face with pizza to even notice.

So I danced with Rob. Because he made me so fucking happy. And my god, the way he laughed, the way he smiled.

The way he kissed me when he left. It was so soft and sweet it was almost indecent.

It did crazy things to my heart.

"Go and enjoy your pizza," he said. "While it's hot."

"What's left of it," I said. "Tomorrow's your last day this week?"

He nodded. "Yeah. Working three days a week is . . . a lot to get used to."

"Good," I replied. "Then tomorrow night when I finish work, I'll come to your place. You'll need your first day off to sleep it off."

His pupils blew out and his cheeks grew pink. "Oh." He swallowed hard. "Okay."

I watched him as he walked to his car. He managed not to slip and slide, and only when his car turned the corner did I close the door and go inside.

Chuck gave me his shit-eating grin with his mouth full of pizza. "You are in so deep already." He nodded to the door. "I saw you dancing."

I fell into my seat with a sigh that ended with a groan. "He is so . . ." I let my head fall back with a groan. "Perfect. I can't explain it."

Chuck pushed the pizza box toward me. "Eat it before it gets cold. And no one is perfect. If you believe that, you're setting yourself up for heartbreak, my friend."

"He's not perfect, obviously." I shrugged as I bit into a slice. Because Chuck was right. No one was *perfect*. "But I dunno, Chucky. I'm thinking he's perfect for me."

Chuck looked at me and shook his head with a long sigh. "I'm happy for you, bro. I know you've been wanting someone of your own for a while now. I hope it works out. I really do. I mean, he brought you a pizza. A whole-ass pizza." Then he shrugged. "If you decide he's not as perfect as you thought, put a good word in for me."

I shoved him so hard he almost fell off his chair. "Fuck off." Chuck was as straight as an arrow and in a long-term relationship with a great girl, whom he absolutely adored, despite his best efforts to act blasé. "Your girlfriend might have something to say about that."

"She's never brought me a pizza at work."

I nudged him this time, finishing off the rest of the slice of pizza. "You get lazy in the bedroom, you ain't getting no pizza. Do them so thoroughly they can't form words for ten minutes and you're getting pizza. Trust me."

Chuck cracked up laughing and I bit into a fresh slice— it was so damn good—but then a call came in and we were on our feet and out the door in a flash.

WORKING shifts wasn't all bad, and it'd been a part of my job forever. I was used to it. What I wasn't used to was wishing I kept similar hours to a certain someone or wishing he was in my bed sound asleep when I finally got home, that I could crawl in beside him, cuddle up to his warm body, and fall asleep with him in my arms.

It was early hours of the morning when Chuck and I'd finally clocked out. My house was dark and my bed incredibly empty and cold. I was exhausted but couldn't sleep. Knowing Rob was just next door, so close but yet so far.

But I didn't have to wish that tonight, because I'd told him I was coming to his house straight after work, no matter what time it was. I'd also implied it was just as well he wasn't working the day after as he'd need to sleep in the following morning.

To say that I was looking forward to it was an understatement.

I arrived at work, smiling when I saw Rob's car at the clinic across the street. He was right there, again, yet so far.

I wouldn't disturb him at work. His was an important job involving the private lives of people in town. And I only had to get through one shift.

One shift, then I'd be in that man's bed, with him in my arms and preferably with him underneath me. Naked, with me nailing him to the mattress.

Our first time together had been magical.

It was an intensity I wasn't quite prepared for. Which, given the build-up, I shouldn't have been surprised. But being inside him, holding him while I impaled him, hearing how his breath hitched, how he moaned, pleaded . . .

Utter perfection.

Today was going to be a long day. And long it was . . . Time dragged, every minute on the clock, and my anticipation ticked up a notch. Keeping busy didn't even help much.

Chuck kept laughing at me, and the last time he caught me checking the damn clock on the wall, he clipped me upside the head. "Stop it. You're making me antsy."

"Can't help it," I grumbled. "If you had plans for hours of sex, you'd be watching the clock too."

"Hours?" He squinted at me, then shook his head. "Really?"

"And this is why you don't get pizza hand-delivered to work. You need to up your game, bro. Worship that woman's body, wring her out, good and thorough. Make it all about her."

"Hey, I know what I'm doing. How is this even a conversation we're having right now?"

"Have you ever hand-delivered pizza to her work?"

"Well . . . no. Have you?"

"I hand-delivered him a single red rose," I said proudly. "At his work, three days ago. You should have seen his smile."

He gave me a disappointed shake of his head. "You're making me look bad. Come on, man."

I laughed. "It doesn't have to be a red rose or anything expensive. Google how to make a paper flower. Hell, buy a packet of her favorite cookies from the store and make her a hot chocolate." I looked him dead in the eye. "Or hand-deliver pizza to her work."

He sighed. "Fine."

"And then worship her body for hours—"

He shoved me. "Shut the fuck up."

I laughed, then looked at the clock. It had moved all of three minutes.

Goddammit.

It was after midnight by the time I got to Rob's place. He'd left the front porch light on, a warm light welcoming me, and that made me smile. Whereas my house looked dark and cold, lonely, and the metaphor of this contrast was not lost on me.

I opened the screen door and before I could try the door handle, the door opened inward. Rob stood there in his long pajamas and slippers—home comfort personified—and he smiled. "Hey."

I stepped inside, collected him in an embrace, and kissed him. "You look so good," I murmured.

He laughed, surprised. "I was almost asleep in my chair."

My heart knocked against my ribs. "You stayed up for me?"

"Of course."

Man, that made me so freaking happy. I kissed him softly. "Thank you."

"It's only midnight. If you were finishing at three, it'd be a different story."

"I had visions of sneaking into your house and crawling into your bed. You'd be asleep and all cozy and warm, and I'd snuggle in close, pull you into my arms . . ."

"You envisioned all that?"

"Many times. It played out a dozen different ways."

Grinning, he pushed my coat off my shoulders. "Only a dozen, huh?" Then he pulled my toque off my head and began undoing my belt. "Should I go climb into bed and wait? Or do you need help getting undressed?"

I groaned, so turned on, so desperate. I fumbled and fought with the laces on my boots, and he laughed, hanging my coat on the rack. I tried to slow down, but then I saw his pajama pants were nicely tented, and yeah, slowing down wasn't going to happen.

I all but yanked my boots off, tossed them by the door, took his face in my hands, and kissed him, hard.

He laughed and was smiling, until I plundered my tongue into his mouth. He grunted, the sound sending a jolt through me, and he walked us backward toward the hall. We bumped into the doorway and I couldn't resist pressing him hard against the wall as I fucked his mouth with my tongue.

He whined and lifted one leg up. I gripped his ass and ground our erections together through our clothes.

So fucking desperate.

We weren't going to make it to bed at this rate.

I broke the kiss. "Bed. Now."

His lips were swollen, his eyes dark. Chest heaving, cock straining, he walked to his room. Sultry, inviting.

Holy hell. I was gonna fuck that smirk right off his face.

His bedroom was dark, the bed made. He ripped back the covers, then stripped off his clothes and knelt on the bed. He glanced at me over his shoulder, then at the bedside where he'd put lube and condoms. He put a hand to his naked ass, rubbing the cheek. "Do your worst, Soren."

My dick throbbed painfully, my whole-body electric with anticipation and need.

This wasn't just desire. This was pure need. Like I needed oxygen to breathe, I needed to be inside him.

I pulled off my sweater and shirt in one go and stepped out of my pants and briefs. I took the lube first and poured it down his ass crack, thumbing it into his hole. Then a finger, then two. No preamble, no games.

Still on his knees at the edge of the bed, his back arched and he whined. I put my free hand to his throat, fucking him with my other fingers, and whispered into the back of his neck, "Oh, Robinson. I have no words."

He groaned, pushing back onto me. He stroked himself and it was so fucking hot knowing he was as desperate as me. "Oh god, please. I need it."

I pulled my fingers out of him, rolled a condom down my cock, and lubed up. I followed him onto the bed, pushing him down face first and holding him down with my body, my cock nestled between his ass cheeks. "Is this how you want it?"

"Oh god, yes. Please." His voice was strung tight. "Just do it. I'm ready. I need it."

I positioned myself at his entrance, pushing in just a fraction, testing his hole. "You been thinking about this all day, huh?"

"Yes."

"You wanting my cock buried inside you, is that what you want?"

"Soren, please."

God, hearing him beg for it almost ended me.

I pushed into him, torturously slow, all the way to the

hilt. He clawed at his bedsheets, trying to find purchase, his back arched, and he moaned like the devil.

But he took me. All of me. I was up to my balls in him. So deep, so hot. I lay down on top of him and kept still, giving him a moment to adjust, to breathe.

I scraped my teeth along his shoulder. "That what you wanted?"

He panted and groaned. "Yes."

I ran my hand over the back of his head, lightly pulling his hair as I kissed the back of his neck. "You're so fucking sexy like this. Taking every inch of me, waiting up for me. Waiting for me to fuck you."

He grunted and rolled his hips. "Need you to move, Soren. Do something."

Do something?

I half-pulled out and pushed back in, all the way. "Like that?"

He cried out. "Yes. Please."

So I did it again, and he groaned out a pitiful sound, a gruff keening noise. And the more I did it, the more guttural he sounded.

He loved it.

Getting dicked like this.

He lifted his hips and widened his legs, and I drove into him, slow and deep. He felt so good, so fucking good. Hot and tight, as if he was made just for me.

He slipped his hand underneath his hip and began to stroke himself, and I wasn't having that.

I pulled out of him and flipped him over, spreading his thighs wide and pushing his knees up so I could just sink right back in. I fell forward onto my left hand, my eyes on his as I wrapped my right hand around his cock.

"This what you wanted?" I asked, working him slowly, kissing him, pulling his bottom lip in between my teeth.

"Oh god, yes," he hissed. His eyes went wide, his hands flailed until they found my chest.

He tweaked my nipple and it sent jolts of pleasure straight to my dick. "Fuck," I ground out as I thrust into him, hard and sharp.

He yelped but he did it again, earning him another hard and sharp flex of my hips. His eyes went wide with surprise, his mouth open. "Fuck, right there," he cried. "Oh fuck. There."

Then he kept flicking my nipples wanting more and more, and I realized what was happening. The change of position, the surprised look of ecstasy on his face, how his cock jerked in my hand.

I was hitting his prostate.

So I held him right there and rammed into him, jerking him at the same time. It was unforgiving, without restraint, and so fucking hot.

Then his whole body went rigid, his thighs trembled, and his ass clenched hard around me as his orgasm took hold.

He groaned, teeth clenched, hands shaking, and shot his load onto his stomach.

It was too much, too good, his body squeezing my cock as he shuddered, milking me, milking my orgasm from my balls. I drove into him one last time, as deep as I could go, and pumped my load into the condom.

My world went dark and quiet, spinning in utter bliss. I

came back to reality with Rob's hands cupping my face, and I allowed myself to collapse on him.

He lowered his legs to the mattress, expelling me from inside him. We both shuddered but he made a pained sound. "You okay?" I asked quickly.

"Sensitive," he said, then his whole body tremored, jerking, and he laughed. "God help me. Whatever that was . . ."

I snorted, collecting him in my arms and pulling the covers over us. I'd deal with the mess and the condom later. He needed to be held first. "That was amazing," I whispered, kissing the side of his head. "That's what that was."

He shuddered and shivered again. "No, I mean . . . Uh. Whatever that was. I've never . . ."

"A prostate orgasm?"

He grunted out a laugh, shuddering again. "I've heard they're good."

Smiling, I kissed his temple, his forehead, his eyelids, then his lips. "I had plans to do you slowly tonight, but I think that was better."

"So good," he mumbled. "Slow next time." He was heavy in my arms, as if sleep was dragging him under.

I gave him a long squeeze, breathing in the scent of us. "Go to sleep."

He was already out, and I lay there for a second, watching him in the darkened room, his face a pale outline. His closed eyelids, dark lashes, the Cupid's bow of his top lip.

So thoroughly had and so sated.

So beautiful.

So mine.

I knew it was too early to be thinking long term and to

be feeling such emotions. I always did fall hard and fast. I loved with my whole heart, right or wrong, and I refused to think of that as a flaw.

And I refused to think it was anything other than fate that brought our paths together. There was no way of ever knowing if we had a few months of this or forever. And watching him sleep, peaceful and perfect, I didn't care how long I had with him, how long we lasted. I'd take every second I could get.

I was falling in love with him.

And I refused to think that was a bad thing either. I wouldn't be sorry for it.

I needed to get us cleaned up, but when I tried to move my arm from underneath him, he fussed and clung to me, and sound asleep, he mumbled my name. "Soren."

My heart expanded, soaring and full. I exchanged my arm from under his neck with a kiss to his cheek. "Just gonna clean you up," I murmured.

He mumbled something else I couldn't make out, his eyelids never opening, but his lips curled up in a smile.

Oh yeah, I was falling for him. Absolutely no doubt about it.

I pulled the blankets up for him and kissed his lips before getting out of bed. I discarded the condom in his bathroom wastebasket, found a washcloth, ran it under hot water, and went back into the bedroom.

I cleaned up his stomach and chest, then mine from where it had smeared, and I climbed back into bed.

As soon as I was beside him, he snuggled right in and I held him tight. I closed my eyes, thanking all my lucky stars for bringing this man into my life.

Then I thanked fate, and for good measure—and just in case—I thanked that Christmas Cupid too.

I DON'T KNOW which of us woke first. We both stirred, wrapped around each other. Warm, comfortable, sleepy. "Morning," I croaked.

"Hmm."

"You feel okay?" I rubbed his back, then slid my hand down to his ass, gently rubbing a circle on his ass cheek with my thumb. "Kinda worked you over hard last night. If you're sore . . ."

He stretched his back and clenched his butt cheeks. "Hm. A little. S'not bad though. Not sore enough to not want to do it again."

I chuckled. "Maybe we should give your perfect ass a rest."

He whined and when I pulled back to look at his face, yes, he was pouting. Laughing, I tucked his face into my neck for a tight hug. "I have no clue what time it is, but maybe we could snooze for a little while yet."

"Sounds good," he mumbled.

"Do you have any plans for today?" I asked. "Any time you need to be up by? I'd say from the light behind your blinds it's about eight."

Rob sighed. "Nothing. The only thing I planned on doing this morning was you." He froze, then snorted out a laugh. "I didn't mean it to sound like that and I was going to correct it, but I'm just gonna leave it as it is."

I rubbed his back, and we lay there in silence, dozing. I

heard sounds of life outside: cars, someone calling their dog, even a phone ringing somewhere across the street. And normally I was up by now, even when I had worked the late shift.

But today, I wasn't getting out of this bed or out of Rob's arms for anything or anyone.

Until my phone rang anyway. I groaned, rolling over, wondering where my phone even was. It wasn't on the bedside table, so I peered over the side of the bed, where our clothes were still a crumpled mess on the floor. My phone was in the pocket of my work pants.

Ugh. I had to get up.

"Goddammit," I grumbled, as I left Rob to collect my phone.

"No," Rob said, trying to keep hold of me. "You're nice and warm."

"Sorry. Gotta check my phone. It could be work. If it is, I'll have to go."

I found my phone underneath my pants and checked the screen for the missed call. I sighed with relief. Rob was now propped up on his elbow looking at me, sleep rumpled and super cute. "Was it work?"

I turned the screen around to show him. "Just my mom."

"Oh. Is everything okay?"

I shrugged. "She's probably calling to tell me that my great aunt's third cousin twice removed's niece has had a baby. I'll text her." I thumbed out a quick text, sounding it out as I did. "Will . . . call . . . you . . . later." Then I saw the battery icon. "Ah. I forgot to charge my phone. Can I borrow—"

I looked at Rob, and he was staring—and I mean staring—at my crotch. At my very naked half-mast dick to be more precise.

I resisted the urge to cover up and gave it a little wiggle instead. "Do you like what you see?"

He was still staring, and it took him a moment before he looked at my face. "Oh, huh?"

It made me laugh. "I asked if you like what you see, but I'm pretty sure I know the answer."

"Hmm. I mean, damn," he murmured. "You're so hot. Not just your cock." He waved his hand up and down. "The whole package, honestly." His gaze dropped back down to my cock, and he licked his lips. "I wouldn't mind tasting that."

Of course my cock liked the sound of that.

His tongue slowly swiped across his top lip. "Come over here," he beckoned. "Feed it to me."

Now, I had every intention of suggesting a shower first. Granted, I had cleaned myself up last night, but then he said that?

Feed it to me?

I was on that bed, on my knees in front of his face before he'd barely had time to smile.

He licked the underside of my cockhead, then looked up at me while he took me into his mouth.

"Oh fuck," I breathed. Every nerve ending in my body fired ecstasy and bliss to my balls. His mouth was warm and wet, his tongue swirling.

I was going to come so fast.

From zero to one hundred in a heartbeat. Every fucking time.

And then he used his hands. One on my shaft, one cupping my balls, pumping, pulling, teasing.

"Oh, Rob," I murmured. "Fuck yes."

I braced one hand on the wall, the other on the back of his head, grasping at his hair as he worked me over. I tried to think of other things. I tried to concentrate on nothing but the sensation, the pleasure.

But then I made the mistake of looking down.

His lips around my shaft, my cock sliding in and out, and his eyes . . . his glazed-over fuck-me eyes. Sultry, alluring, sexy.

Mine.

He smiled as he took me in and my grip on his hair tightened as I fought the urge to fuck his mouth. I groaned at the effort it took not to ram into his throat.

"Suck it," I hissed. "Take it."

He closed his eyes and took me into his throat, and that was it. I couldn't fight it. I didn't want to. I wanted to give it all to him. He swallowed around me, sucking my orgasm to the surface. My cock pulsed in his throat, shooting my load in heavenly spurts. He moaned and swallowed again, sending shudders through me.

I leaned against the wall, letting my body succumb to the ecstasy rolling through me. I had to unclench my fist from his hair, and he pulled back, licking me clean as my spent cock slipped from his mouth.

Tremors racked through me, spasms of aftershocks, and I slumped on the pillows with a strained groan. "Fuck," I panted. "Fucking hell."

Rob laughed, then in a move I was not suspecting, he smacked my ass. "I'm making you breakfast."

I wanted to wrap my arms around him, doze in the afterglow, but he was rolling out of bed. I heard him take a piss and wash his hands, then a moment later, I heard the coffee machine beep awake.

Damn.

I considered getting up, but my bones were Jell-O. I ran my hand down my body, giving my dick a palm, and I shuddered and jerked at the sensitivity.

Christ, he'd ruined me.

I was useless to do anything but laugh.

A few moments later, I heard cupboards opening and a pot clanging, so I made myself get out of bed. I pulled on my briefs and work pants but left the shirt off. I relieved myself, washed my hands and face, and found him in the kitchen at the counter, wearing a dark gray robe, whisking eggs in a bowl.

Never had a man looked so sexy.

I walked up behind him, wrapped my arms around his waist, and pressed my face into the soft fabric at the back of his neck. "You're so fucking sexy."

He laughed as he kept whisking. "Scrambled eggs okay?"

"Mmm," I mumbled. "Perfect. Need me to do anything?"

"No, I got it." Then he shrugged. "I like looking after you."

I snorted. "You just did. You gave me the best morning wake-up blow job in the history of blow jobs."

"It was my pleasure."

"Pretty sure it was mine. And I didn't get to return the favor."

He stopped whisking. "You don't have to. I did it because I wanted it, not because I wanted you to do it to me."

"And now," I murmured, kissing the top of his shoulder. "What if I wanted it?"

His shoulders rose with his intake of breath, but he didn't say anything.

"If I were to turn you around right now," I said, undoing the belt of his robe. "And sink to my knees."

He made a noise in the back of his throat. "Yes?"

"And suck your cock right here in the kitchen. Would you like that?"

He turned around then, his robe open, his eyes dark, and his cock half-hard.

"Hm," I said with a smirk. "I take it that's a yes. And you naked under that robe is my new favorite thing," I said as I slowly went to my knees in front of him.

I took him straight into my mouth, earning me a strangled cry. I pinned him to the kitchen counter and worked him over without mercy. Hands, tongue, lips, sucking the come from his balls.

He came with a cry, his hands in my hair, his body clenching, trembling. And when he'd had enough, I stood up, collecting him in my arms. He was heavy, panting, and we stood there for I don't know how long.

Just holding each other, arms wrapped around each other, our faces resting on each other's shoulders.

Embracing what this was. How we felt. Even if we weren't ready to name it yet or ready to admit it or say it out loud, there in his kitchen, we felt it.

I knew he did. I had no doubt.

He couldn't cling to me like he did and not have feelings.

But then the coffee machine beeped, turning itself off because we'd neglected it. He pulled back first, and I cupped his face and pressed my lips to his forehead. "I'll make the coffee," I said.

He nodded, smiling shyly, his cheeks pink. "And . . . I don't even remember what I was doing."

I chuckled. "Nice to know your brain goes offline too, after having your brains blown."

He snorted. "I'm sure there's been research done on the correlation to intense pleasure effects on the cerebral cortex and the hippocampus."

I laughed at that. "And the frontal lobe. Or wherever the ability to form words comes from. At least in complete sentences because you leave me unable to do anything other than blink and breathe."

Rob smiled as he heated the frying pan, and we made our breakfast of eggs and toast and fresh coffee in a companionable silence. Moving around each other in his kitchen so naturally. Not for one second did it feel awkward or forced.

It was the most natural thing in the world.

We ate at his small dining table by the front window, looking out to the quiet street. Snow on the ground, on roofs, trees made it all so serene.

I could get used to this. So easily. So damn easily could I get used to waking up with Rob, making a lazy breakfast, eating next to each other.

The blow jobs were a bonus. But the comfort, the contentment of sharing this with him, was what made my heart so happy.

My phone beeped in his bedroom and I remembered I told my mother I'd call her. "Ugh, better get that," I said, disappearing into his room. I took my phone off the charger and saw the text was from my mom. I saw the words *nothing urgent* in the first line and decided it'd just be easier to get it over with.

I hit Call and went back to the dining table. Rob was still sitting there in his sexy-as-hell robe, his legs crossed, reading a news article on his phone.

Mom answered on the second ring. "Oh hello, love," she said. "I didn't wake you, did I? I never know which week of shift work you're up to."

"No, it's fine, Mom. How is everything?"

Rob looked up then, smiling at me.

"Oh, everything up here is fine. I was just calling to see how you were. You keeping well, love? Taking care of yourself, I hope."

I smiled at Rob and rubbed my foot on his when I replied. "Oh, I'm keeping very well. Taking very good care of myself, Mom."

He grinned, ducking his face, but then he took our plates and cups and let me finish my phone call. By the time I said goodbye and promised I'd call her for Christmas, Rob came back with two fresh cups of coffee.

I slid my phone onto the table. "Oh, thank you."

He sat down, eyes smiling behind his coffee cup. "Everything well back home? And your great aunt's third cousin twice removed niece's newborn doing okay?"

I chuckled. "Everything's fine. She just wanted to check that I was taking care of myself."

"I heard."

I had to rein my smile in a bit. "I gave her the PG-rated version of just how well I'm being taken care of."

Rob's smile and the way his cheeks flushed pink was the sexiest damn thing I'd ever seen. I couldn't take my eyes off him. It was almost funny to me now that I'd never once thought of a man older than me as sexy when this man was everything—every single thing—I could ever want in a partner.

I needed to change the topic or at least stop looking at him so I didn't do something stupid like tell him I was falling in love with him.

Because I was sure that'd bring it all to a screeching halt. I just had to enjoy it for what it was, for where it was up to. I didn't want to rush anything, didn't want to miss a minute of this path we were on.

"Do you have plans for today?" I asked before sipping my coffee.

"I told Gunter I'd stop in. I have an idea I want to put to him. I don't know if it's feasible, or even possible. But it can't hurt to throw some ideas around."

"What idea is that?"

He made a face. "Well, small towns are hard for teenagers, right? It's a great place to grow up, don't get me wrong, but there are limited opportunities for experience. Most of these kids will be moving after school, to the bigger cities for work or college, and so I was thinking, wouldn't it be good if we could provide hands-on experience to help them find work? Barista, waiting tables, food service, that kind of thing. The kinds of jobs city kids have on almost every block, or huge malls. Hartbridge doesn't have that. But there's no reason why we couldn't foster that experience for these kids so they can walk into a coffee shop or retail store and say they have some experience. Hell, even office work, reception skills, classes on how to do budgets and fill in tenant lease agreements, but also on how to manage responsible social media practices because prospective employers look at that now. It's hard out there these days. Different from how it was when we were that age—" He grimaced at me. "Sorry. When *I* was that age."

I chuckled as I stood up, took his face in both hands, and smacked a kiss on his lips. Hearing how passionate he was about helping kids and making this community a better place made me happy. "I think that's an amazing idea."

He grinned. "You do?"

I nodded. "Hell, yes."

"I thought Gunter might like it too. We could use his center to run classes on certain days or afternoons. Get qualified trainers to come in so these kids have a qualification certificate at the end of it. Maybe even get the high school involved? I'm not sure. I was just reading up on requirements in Montana, but I would assume there's more to it than meets the eye." He gave me a shy smile. "I thought it was worth looking into."

"Definitely." Then I thought . . . "I could come down with you. Before work. I'll need to go home and get showered and dressed, of course."

He looked down at my still naked chest. "Or not."

I snorted. "Pretty sure Doug would not approve."

Rob sighed. "Shame."

"Would that be okay?" I asked. "If I came with you. I'd understand if you want to keep that part of your life separate from me."

He was clearly confused. "Separate?"

"Yeah. That thing where we each keep our own thing. I don't mind. I love that you volunteer at the center. I didn't want to encroach on your thing. Know what I mean?"

"Not really. Of course you can come with me." Then he gave me a bit of a side-eye. "Do you have a thing that's just your thing?"

I snorted. "No. I have work. I work out. Go to Vern's Bar a few times a month with the boys to watch a game. I go fishing. Nothing that's just my thing."

He snorted. "Fishing? That is something that will definitely be something you do without me."

That made me laugh. I remembered he'd mentioned it before. "Not a fan?"

"Never been. And it's funny you should mention that," he said. "When I handed in my resignation, the chief surgeon begged me not to throw it all away. She was a friend of mine. Had been for years. She offered me a different role in a quieter department, but honestly, I couldn't go back. Not to that hospital, not to the same red tape and the same policies. I told her I needed to leave Seattle." He smiled sadly as he remembered. "I even told her I might look at one of those build-a-school projects in Vietnam or Peru; it was just an errant thought, but god, the idea of actually helping people sounded so damn good. And she said she knew of a small town in Montana that needed a physician three days a week. She said I could go skiing on my days off, fishing in the summer." He grinned at me and shook his head. "Where she got the idea I'd ever spend one minute of my life fishing, I'll never know."

My smile was wide and determined. "Then I'm gonna

take you. In the summer, we can drive out on Ponderosa Road, past where we went the other day. There's a really good spot. Nothing but sunshine in the mountains, the sound of the river, and birds in the trees. It's a special kinda peaceful you have to see to believe."

A smile won out, his eyes shining. "Well, the sunshine, mountains, river, and birds do sound nice. You can do the fishing part. For me, it'll be purely a spectator sport. I'll bring lunch and a book."

"Deal."

He'd just divulged a sliver of his history to me, and while I wanted to know more, I didn't want to push.

I reached out and took his hand, threading our fingers. "I'm glad your friend convinced you to come here," I added. "As rewarding as building a school in Vietnam sounds, helping kids here at the center isn't so bad."

Rob nodded, and the mention of his time in Seattle brought it to the forefront, because I didn't even have to prompt.

"My friend," he continued. "Alaya Ross, chief surgeon. Helluva of a doctor. I hadn't seen her for a couple of months and she took one look at me and," he snorted. "Christ, she thought I'd started taking amphetamines or coke. That's how bad I looked. I guess the people I worked with every day didn't notice the decline, but I hadn't seen Alaya in a while . . ." Then he sighed heavily. "She asked me what was wrong and I finally admitted I was done. I couldn't do it anymore. I was so exhausted I could barely function, and I was running on autopilot. It was either going to kill me or someone else. Exhausted doctors shouldn't make decisions between life and death."

Oh shit. "Did . . . did that happen to you?"

He shook his head. "No. But it was bound to. It was only a matter of time before I overlooked a symptom, made the wrong call, or didn't connect the dots." He shrugged. "It wasn't just the pace, the hours, and the trauma. It was the bureaucracy. I was having anxiety before every shift, during and after every shift. I became a doctor to help people, to save lives, and make people's lives better. And all I found was red tape, bureaucracy, and insurance companies —" He stopped himself. "Being told I couldn't treat someone because a patient couldn't afford it or because their insurance company wouldn't cover it, again and again, just fucking broke me."

I closed my eyes, inhaled deeply, and let it out slowly, trying to calm down. This poor man. This poor beautiful, compassionate man. I just wanted to scoop him up and protect him.

"I'm glad you didn't quit," I said, squeezing his hand. "The world needs more people like you. Not just doctors who care, but people. And I'm really glad you're here, Rob."

He smiled and looked out the window for a bit. "I still can't believe this is my life. It doesn't feel real. It's as if I've stepped into a movie like *The Truman Show*." Then he laughed and turned back to me. "You'd tell me if none of this was real, right?"

He was clearly joking, but I wasn't. "Oh, it's real. It's all real." Everything. The town. Him, me. Us. How I felt about him . . .

I kissed him again, softer this time, my free hand to his cheek. "I'm so fucking glad you're here."

He closed his eyes and lowered his forehead to the side of my face. "Me too."

We stayed like that for a long moment, me still holding his hand, his head now resting against my neck. Until I pulled his chair closer, our legs tangled, so I could hold him better.

We didn't seem to need words.

He was very nearly straddling me, and I could have so easily pulled him onto me so I could feel him against me. I considered it, because I was only half-dressed, and his robe was barely covering anything. But this wasn't sexual.

It was so much more than that.

I kissed the side of his head. "Thank you for sharing that part of your life with me."

"Do you . . . do you think it makes me . . . ?" He shook his head and sat back, but I was quick to take both his hands.

I looked him dead in the eye. "Do I think it makes you compassionate and caring? Yes. Do I think it makes you a better doctor and a wonderful human being? Yes."

His eyes grew a little glassy, and he nodded, a sad smile on his face.

"Do I think you're amazing? Do I think you're kind, and funny, and actually really kinda perfect? Yes." Sure, it might be premature to be saying this, but knowing he had one lick of self-doubt just fucking killed me. "Do I think I'm the luckiest guy on the planet right now? Absolutely. Hartbridge is lucky to have you. I'm lucky to have you. And I'm glad you made the decision to leave your old job. You deserve to be happy, Rob. Do what makes you happy. Do what feeds your soul."

His eyes were teary, but he laughed and nodded. "Thank you. I like that: do whatever feeds my soul. It's a great motto to live by."

"Absolutely."

"I think being here might do that. In this cute little town, in my cute little house." His cheeks flushed pink. "And you."

God, how hearing him say that made my heart sing.

"And me." I kissed him softly, loving the revealing robe and his naked body underneath, but this was the problem I'd wanted to avoid. I knew once we started having sex, we'd want to do nothing else, and the equally if not more important part of getting a relationship right was communication and spending quality time together outside the bedroom.

So then, of course, he had to move himself closer, his thigh over mine, and he kissed me. Soft, open mouthed with a hint of tongue. I knew where this was going. And my body was certainly on board . . .

But my heart and my head told me to pump the brakes.

I put my finger to Rob's lips, stopping the kiss. His eyes flashed to mine, and I smiled. "You have no idea how much I want you right now, but we shouldn't."

"Why not?"

"Because you wanted to go to the youth center, and I will need to go to work."

"I can go to the center any time. When you go to work or this afternoon. It's no big deal."

"Rob, it's important to you."

"You're really saying no?"

I laughed, though it was more of a pained groan. "You have no idea how much I want to take you back to bed right now. Like good god, so bad." I risked looking down at where his robe barely covered his crotch, how it opened revealing his hairy chest. "Like, damn . . . Okay, well, maybe we could go later. What time is it?"

He laughed then, a free and happy sound, as he sat back in his chair and straightened his robe. "Your willpower lasted point-two of a second."

"Were you testing me?"

"No, I honestly wasn't. But what you said was right. The center is important. You are too, don't get me wrong, but the center is only open for certain hours of the day where you, my own private firefighter," he pointed the finger to my chest, "will just have to come back here when you finish work tonight."

I grinned at him. "Is that so?"

God, I liked the sound of that.

"Yes," he said seriously. "You cannot let me taste the best sex of my entire life, and then put me on rations."

That made me laugh. "Rations? I'd hardly call everything we've done rations. Four orgasms between us in the last twelve hours. Believe me, coming off a long drought, those numbers are a downpour."

Rob chuckled. "I know, I know. I'm just being greedy. I want more."

"Best sex of your life, huh?"

His eyes met mine, full of humor and honesty. "Hands down, the best. Not even a competition. So yes, tonight I will leave my door unlocked, and you may find me in bed, waiting. Naked. Possibly pre-lubed."

I dropped my head back and groaned. "Okay, so now I'm definitely coming here after work."

His grin sent my heart into a flurry, my body was already looking forward to it.

"Okay then," I declared. "Now all that's organized, I should go home and get showered and dressed for work. What time did you want to leave for the center?"

He checked the time on my phone. "In about an hour?"

"Sounds perfect." I stood up. "I should get dressed first, though. Don't want Mr. Ling to see me leaving your house half-dressed."

Rob glanced out the front window. "We could open the blinds and give him a full show."

I burst out laughing. He was only joking but I still hadn't expected his sense of humor. I went into his room and found my clothes, quickly pulling them on. When I went back out to the living room, Rob had fixed his robe and tied the belt, and he was fixing some pine needles on his Christmas tree.

It still looked incredible, but very empty underneath.

"No presents underneath it yet?" I said, sitting on the sofa to pull on my socks and boots.

He looked at the emptiness under the tree and shook his head. "No. I'll ship my niece's and my sister's gifts. Straight from the store, gift-wrapped option included."

Damn. That was it? He had no one else, and that was kinda sad.

"You better get Katie something," I warned him.

"Oh, yes, you're right." He adjusted one bauble that didn't need adjusting. "And you, I suppose. Are we doing gift exchanges? We should probably clarify to save embarrassment or disappointment. You know. I mean, it's fine if you don't want to but I thought . . ."

I walked over and slid my arms around his waist and whispered into the back of his ear. "Hell yes, we are." Then I kissed his nape. "I'll be back in an hour."

He walked me to the door, smiling so sweetly, his cheeks a delicious pink.

God, it almost made me change my mind and march him straight to his bed.

But no, now I had a plan. But it wasn't something I could do on my own.

As soon as I walked through my front door, I pulled my phone out and scrolled for the number I was looking for and hit Call.

"Hartbridge Hardware, how can I help you?"

"Hamish?" I asked, though I knew that voice and accent was his. "It's Soren."

"Oh, hi. Is everything okay? If you're after Ren—"

"No, I wanted to speak to you, actually. I want to do something for Rob, and I'll need your help."

He was quiet for a second and I swore I could hear him smiling. "I'm listening."

Chapter Eleven

ROB

WALKING into the youth center with Soren felt . . . exciting? Different?

I was strangely nervous, because it felt as if we were making some announcement. To Gunter, and Gunter alone. But still . . . we were arriving together, which meant we'd been together beforehand, and I don't know . . .

It just felt official or something.

"Good morning," Gunter said brightly and a touch conspiratorially.

"Morning," we replied.

Gunter looked between us, smirking. "Good to see you two together at this time of day . . ."

He was absolutely fishing for details, which I had no intention of giving him.

But Soren grinned. "Oh, I was already at Rob's this morning, because I spent the night. You know, all night," he said with a nudge to my elbow. "And anyway, he mentioned coming here and I thought I'd come check it out before I went to work." He looked around. "Great place, by the way."

Gunter was too busy giving me his raised eyebrow. "All night, huh?"

I had no clue what to say to that, and given my face felt as if it were about to burst into flames, I guessed I didn't need to.

"*All* night," Soren said nodding. "And again this morning."

Now it was I who nudged him. "What are you doing?"

Soren laughed and gave me a quick hug. "Oh, come on, I have to tell someone. I'll get to work and Chucky won't want to hear any of it." He looked around again. "And there's no one here. It's just us. And Gunter gets it."

Gunter nodded, grinning at me.

I sighed, embarrassed but unable to stop the giddy feeling in my belly, which of course made it impossible not to smile. This was so ridiculous.

Soren eyed me, proud as punch. The fact he was wearing his firefighter uniform didn't help because he was so freaking hot, and he was looking at me like that . . .

Gunter laughed. "You two are as cute as hell."

"So anyway," I began. "I'm free all day if you need me to do anything."

"Oh, that'd be great," Gunter replied. "I'll never say no. Actually, can you go do a quick count of the health supplies in the bathrooms? That'd be great." He handed me his notepad. "Condoms, sanitary pads, that kind of thing."

"Oh, sure." I gave Soren a smile as I disappeared into the bathrooms and filled out a quick tally of all items, including the toilet paper and hand towels, and when I came back out, Soren and Gunter were standing there, smiling at me.

Yeah. They'd definitely talked about me.

"Everything okay?" I asked.

"Oh, sure," Soren said.

"Of course," Gunter added.

I laughed because they were terrible liars. "Did you have enough time to talk about me, or do you need me to go back in there?"

Soren burst out laughing and threw his arms around me, giving me a rocking side-to-side hug. "You're too damn cute," he said. Then, as if we were alone, he planted a kiss on my lips. "I gotta go. See you tonight? Don't stay up for me. I'll let myself in."

Then he breezed to the door with a wave goodbye.

Damn.

Gunter nudged me. "He's incredibly hot," he murmured. "Jeez. How's it dating a younger man? Fun, isn't it? Clay's younger than me too."

Oh dear lord.

My stupid blush gave me away. "If by fun you mean the hottest, best sex of my life, then yes."

Gunter laughed. "He's down bad for you."

I sighed and waved that comment off, ignoring the thrill that gave me. "It's new."

He put his hand on my arm, his eyes serious. "I'm telling you, Rob. He is *down*."

I rolled my eyes. "You've been hanging out with the kids too much." I gave him back his notepad. "So what did you talk to him about. It was about me, I'm guessing. Do I get any clues?"

He shook his head, smiling, as he collected a box of paper cups. "Nah, it was just about the upcoming fire inspection, that's all."

"Sure it was," I said.

He chuckled. "He did mention you had some ideas for this place to run past me."

Wait. What?

"He did, huh?"

"He meant no harm," Gunter said. "He actually said they were great ideas and how excited you were to sink your teeth into some community projects."

"Ugh," I grumbled. "Sorry, I don't want you to think I'm taking anything over. Because I'm not. I just had some ideas that you'd be in charge of. Should you decide you wanted to go ahead. I'd just be the helper." I shrugged. "I don't even know if it's possible or feasible or what kind of funding we could get . . ."

"I'm always willing to listen," Gunter said.

I took a deep breath and told him my ideas, the same ideas I'd outlaid to Soren earlier. Accredited training for the kids in a bunch of fields, such as retail, working a coffee machine, how to work reception. But also helping kids with their resumés, job applications, subject choice, and college applications.

"Not all kids have the homelife to help them with these basic life skills, like budgeting, rental applications, car loans," I added. "And most of these kids are gonna be leaving Hartbridge in a couple of months, and cities can chew up a small-town kid and spit them out. I just thought if we could start up some classes, even if it's in conjunction with the high school? I don't know how that works, but if we can maybe help them get skills for a job when they go off on their own, they'll have a better chance. You know, I've seen a lot of kids—or young adults, but they're really just kids—and they come through the hospital system for drugs or abuse, and I just can't help but feel that as a society we failed them. They had no one to teach them, no one who showed an ounce of empathy." I shook my head because this went way off track. I sighed. "It probably sounds like a stretch, but from these kids here in Hartbridge to the shit I've seen in my old job, it's not a stretch. It's a real short step. And a simple thing like a few certificates and practical experience just might be the difference between getting a job and sleeping rough." I let my voice trail off. I really hadn't meant to get so dark. "Anyway, it was just an idea. Maybe a little start-up café in the vacant store next door, some tables out front. They'd learn barista skills, how to work a register, how to do staff scheduling. I'm sure there'd be some grants we could apply for. Could be worth looking into . . ."

Gunter's smile was slow spreading. "I love it. I was just saying to Clay not too long ago that the kids in town don't have much opportunity for practical experience." He looked around the center, his eyes were dancing with possibilities. "We could set up a proper coffee machine in here . . . Or maybe a start-up café next door would be better. The real estate agent said it was empty . . . I should look into that. And yeah, the local high school would have a better idea about courses and vocational tests. Maybe they already run some kind of program. I haven't heard the kids talk about it at all. Evie was saying some of the kids travel to Mossley for their weekend jobs because there's not enough jobs for teens here in town. Maybe we could create something? I don't know what, but . . ." He grinned at me. "I really think you could be onto something."

I was so happy I could have just about burst. "Awesome." I clapped my hands together. "Let's look into it."

"I have no doubt there'll be copious amounts of red tape," Gunter said, "but we can only try. Thank you," he added genuinely. "I really appreciate someone caring as much as I do."

Hamish bustled through the door, his cute black fluffy dog under his arm. They were wearing matching pink coats, and I shouldn't have been surprised by that, and yet . . .

"Good morning," he said brightly. "Oh, Rob, I'm glad you're here. I come bearing gifts. Well, okay it's not actual gifts, it's more instructions on the gifts, but you get the gist."

Confused, both Gunter and I waited for him to put the dog on the floor, then he produced some envelopes from his inside coat pocket. He flipped through them and plucked one out. "Gunter, for you and Clay." Then he pulled out another. "Rob, for you and Soren."

Before either of us could ask, he gave Gunter a very pointed look before turning to me. "So Rob, every year, our little group of friends does a bit of a Kris Kringle thing. I put the names in a hat and Ren pulls one out and it goes in your envelope."

I was familiar with how Kris Kringle gift giving worked. "Okay."

Gunter, on the other hand, seemed confused. Until

Hamish gave him another pointed look. "Oh, right. I forgot about it," Gunter said. "Had a lot going on lately."

Hamish gave him a big nod, like he'd done a good job for playing along.

I couldn't help but smile.

Between Soren and Gunter's secret conversation and now this? I had the feeling they were trying to plan something. I wasn't sure. But I went along with it.

"Awesome," I said. "What are the rules?"

"Oh," Hamish said, grabbing my arm. "I'm glad you asked. The rules, yes. Given the somewhat-limited shopping experiences we have here in Hartbridge, I thought this year we could do something different, and the rule is you have to make the gift."

Gunter stared at him. "Make . . . the gift . . ."

"Yes! Something homemade," Hamish said, and he seemed to be making it up as he went along and, at the same time, equally horrified at the words coming out of his own mouth.

I coughed to cover up my laugh. "Okay. So pity the poor person who gets me."

"All hopes for our gift now lay solely on Clay's shoulders," Gunter added. Then he gave a very big fake smile to Hamish. "Gee, thanks, Hamish."

Hamish's smile was more of a grimace, and I chuckled again. "It'll be fun," I said. "Though if there's no budget and we have to use something we have, I'm just trying to think what I could possibly make out of alcohol swabs and tongue depressors."

Gunter snorted and held up some cups from the box. "I

have paper cups." Then he offered me an apologetic shrug. "Maybe Soren can . . . make something."

"Hm," I agreed. I was going to make the comment that he *was* very good with his hands, but I stopped myself. "Maybe."

"Orrrrr," Hamish said, as if we were missing the point completely. "You could make something together. Like a fun little project together. It's a couple thing."

"It's a torture thing," Gunter grumbled.

"Oh shush, it's supposed to be fun and Christmassy," Hamish said. "And the gift exchange will be a week before Christmas at Jayden and Cass's place."

"Are they not busy enough right now?" Gunter asked.

"I know, I know," Hamish said, exasperated. "But that night's free and he said he feels bad for missing our last few dinners. I told him we'll make it potluck. Hope that's okay?" He asked, looking at me.

"Sure. Of course."

"It's just so he doesn't have to cook for ten people on his day off. We'll discuss menu options in the group chat."

I was in the group chat?

Hamish apparently can read minds. Or faces. "I added you already."

"Oh."

"You've been absorbed into the masses," Gunter joked. "It's easier if you don't resist."

I laughed. "Awesome."

He shrugged. "It's mostly harmless, save the occasional inappropriate comments or unsolicited fashion advice. And the Australians and the Brit will sometimes argue amongst themselves about something the rest of us don't understand, like Vegemite or brands of teabags or something. The cooking tips are usually good though, and if you need anything done around the house, one of us will usually be able to help."

I laughed at that. I knew he was only joking but he had no idea just how amazing it sounded. A group of friends—of queer friends—each doing their own thing in this little town but making time for each other, supporting each other, helping each other, and the casual dinners and coffee catch-ups were such a beautiful thing.

And rare.

In my world, in my old life in Seattle, I could only ever dream of finding this.

I went to open the envelope Hamish had given me. "So do we open these—"

"No!" Hamish said. "Not here. It's supposed to be a secret." He collected his dog. "Okay, I have to go find the sexy deputy to give him his envelope." Then he breezed back out the door with no more than a wave of his hand.

Gunter and I looked at each other and laughed. "We do love him," he said, taking the box of cups and sliding it onto the small kitchen counter.

I was almost certain the Kris Kringle idea wasn't a tradition with these guys, and for some reason, I got the feeling it was for me. And that somehow Soren was behind it.

The wide-eyed looks Hamish kept giving Gunter, telling him to go along with it, was pretty obvious. But it was sweet and a fun Christmas idea, so I was happy to go along with it too.

"Speaking of Christmas gifts," I said, following Gunter toward the kitchen. "I need some gift ideas for Soren."

I KEPT my word to Soren.

My front door was unlocked, and knowing he'd be home around midnight, I spent a good while getting myself cleaned out. I put the condoms on the bedside for easy access, then crawled into my bed with a bottle of lube.

Douching was never my favorite thing to do, but the hot, steamy shower helped relax my body and get my mind into that languid state in preparation of what I knew was coming.

I lay on my stomach, one leg bent, and began working the lube over my ass and then inside me. One finger, then two, making myself slippery and open, slow and sensual. I was no stranger to ass play during masturbation. I loved it, so I took my time, enjoying the act itself rather than a means to an end. Getting myself all worked up, turned on, and waiting.

Desperate for what Soren would do to me.

I didn't have to wait long.

I heard his boots on my porch, the front door open and close, the lock sliding closed. "It's just me," he said softly.

I smiled into my pillow.

A few seconds later, he was at my bedroom door. "I'm awake," I murmured. I was more on his side of the bed, laying on my front with my leg bent, hoping he'd get the hint.

He was a smart man.

Or maybe the fact I'd left the bottle of lube on his pillow was a strong clue.

He slid into the bed, his body cool, his hands cold. I startled and shivered at his touch.

"And you're naked," he said.

I slid my hand down my ass crack. "I'm also ready for you—lubed and stretched."

He grunted, his forehead pressed to the back of my neck. "Jesus Christ, Rob."

"I told you I would be—"

He was gone before I could finish speaking. He whipped his briefs off, was on his knees and tearing into a condom in a flash. Then he lay his body down over mine, his cock nestled along my ass crack, his lips at my ear.

"And I told you I'd fuck you just like you wanted."

I groaned out a laugh. "I don't remember you saying—"

He pushed into me, breaching, stretching, then pushed my shoulder flat to the mattress so he could sink in all the way.

Every thick inch of him.

Once he was fully planted inside me, he left his body weight on mine, keeping utterly still. For a few moments, there was only our breathing, his lips at my ear. "Been thinking about you all day," he rasped. "Been thinking about this," he rolled his hips, sending sparks of fire through me.

"Oh god," I breathed. "You feel so . . . your cock . . ."

He rolled his hips again, his cock flexing inside me. Thick, full, and rock-hard. "You wanted this, huh?"

"So bad."

He pulled back a little, sliding in again, pushing deeper, again and again, until he was rolling waves of pleasure through me. An ebb and flow, pushing and pulling, amassing an ocean of ecstasy until the tidal wave broke and I cried out as my orgasm took me under.

I felt his cock swell and pump his seed into the condom as he came. The way his fingers dug into me, the way he roared as his orgasm ripped through him.

Utter bliss.

I was warm all over, my bones embers, a fire in my belly.

I had a vague recollection of him cleaning me up, but I was soon in his arms, wrapped up warm and safe.

And I slept like the dead.

THE NEXT MORNING, I woke up before Soren, and I slipped out of bed and left him to sleep. His job was a physical one, and mental and emotional too. So as much as it pained me to leave this gorgeous man alone in my bed, I kissed his temple and went in search of coffee.

I ached in all the right places, and standing in my kitchen, in my robe and slippers, sipping my coffee, I took stock of how I felt.

My ass wonderfully tender, my shoulders relaxed, my heart happy.

Actually, my heart was more than just happy. It was full and felt too big for my chest. It thumped a wild staccato, sending a buzz through my belly and limbs.

I put it down to the mind-blowing sex, and the giddiness was simply because this was a new and exciting thing.

It couldn't possibly be anything else. It could not be because of that sexy man in my bed; not his body, not his soulful eyes, not his breathtaking smile or the sound of his laughter.

Or the way he looked at me.

Or how he made my whole body feel alive . . .

It was ridiculous to think it could be anything else. Anything more than infatuation. Certainly not anything starting with the letter L.

Love. The word you're looking for is love.

Oh good. You're back.

I never left. I'm you, you idiot. For an intellectual person, you're pretty daft.

I don't love him. I can't. It's too soon for that. It's just . . . new and wonderful, and something I haven't had in my life in . . . well, forever. That's all.

Hm-mm.

Don't give me that tone.

I'm not giving you anything. I am you.

Oh shut up. And keep your opinions to yourself. It's not love. I'm not in love with him.

Anything you say, champ.

. . .

What? No comeback?

Champ?

My inner voice sighed. *Yeah, look, I'm just gonna leave you to get used to the love idea.*

Good.

What?

"I said good."

"Huh?" Soren said behind me. "What's good?"

I jumped, almost spilling my coffee. "Oh. Sorry. The coffee," I lied. "Coffee's good. Want one? I'll make one for you." I went to the machine, and he wrapped his arms around me, giving me a sleepy back hug. "I thought you might want to sleep in."

"Hmmm," he moaned out a sigh.

"Rough night at work?"

"Long," he said, still holding me tight, still pressing his face into my shoulder. "Was exceptionally better when I got here though."

I chuckled. "Glad I could help."

I finished his coffee and, turning in his arms, put it in front of his nose. He inhaled and took it gratefully. I noticed then that he was only wearing his underwear.

"Are you cold?"

He shook his head, sipped his coffee, and sighed. And then he froze and looked down at his junk. "Are you saying I've got shrinkage?"

I burst out laughing. "No." Then I also looked at his junk. "You definitely don't have a shrinkage problem."

He smirked without shame and went back to sipping his coffee.

It gave me a great idea for his Christmas gift though.

"Are you hungry? I'll make you breakfast." I went to the fridge and collected the eggs and milk.

"You don't have to do that," he murmured.

"I like looking after you," I replied, not really meaning to sound so breathy and honest. I also didn't mean to blush. "I mean, I like looking after people."

It was too late. He was already smiling. He leaned against the kitchen counter and watched me as I went about my business, and it was then he noticed the opened envelope with both our names written on it.

Soren and Rob.

"Oh, what's this?" he asked.

"Open it."

He pulled out the small piece of paper. "Colson and Braithe."

"Don't happen to know anything about that, do you?"

He seemed genuinely confused. "About what?"

"About the Kris Kringle gift exchange that Hamish organized. Swore it was some group tradition, though Gunter seemed as surprised as me."

His eyes went wide as it dawned. "Oh. Oh, yes. Right." He swallowed hard. "Uh, yeah. I've heard about it. But I wasn't in on it last year or anything."

I smiled. He was definitely in on it. I put the butter beside him and gave him a kiss on the cheek. "You're a terrible liar. The tips of your ears go pink when you lie."

He tried to lie again and gave up, giving me a smile instead. "I . . . I, yeah. So it's a couple thing, huh?"

Couple thing.

Were we a couple? Dating, yes. We'd established that. But couple seemed next level.

"Mm," I said. "So now we get to handmake a gift for Colson and Braithe."

His gaze went to mine. "Handmake?"

"That was the rule, apparently." Then I laughed. "Don't worry. Hamish looked increasingly horrified as he went along. I guess it's a good thing that none of you can lie convincingly. It's cute."

He sighed. "I just thought it'd be a nice idea," he said gently. "And another gift to go under your tree. I hated seeing it was bare and thought it'd be fun. I also wanted you to see how . . ." He frowned and shrugged. "How well you fit in here. With them, the whole group. I didn't know he was going to make it handmade gifts."

"Pretty sure Hamish didn't know either until he'd said it." I went to Soren, lifted his chin, and kissed him softly. "It was very sweet of you."

My heart squeezed, double tapping my ribs when his eyes met mine. "You're not mad?"

I shook my head. "How could I be?" I kissed him again. "But we need to think of something. We have just over a week to come up with something."

"Oh." His face fell. "I have night duty next week, remember? Three-week rotation. Morning, night, then I stay at the fire hall. We each have to do it, but I'm captain. I get it every three weeks. Someone needs to man the station at all times, and it's—"

"Hey," I whispered. I kept my hand to his cheek. "It's fine. Why are you worried?"

"Because," he murmured, "I won't see you for almost a week. And we have to handmake something for Colson and Braithe, and I won't be here to help." He frowned. "I could make it while I'm at the station all by myself, I guess. Midnight to seven is pretty quiet, but still. I feel bad."

He was just the absolute sweetest.

"It'll be fine. I can do it. I'll think of . . . something. No clue what, but I'll think of something." I sighed, softly kissing his lips one more time. "A whole week, huh?"

He nodded. "Sorry."

"Don't apologize," I said again. "If anyone understands shift work and crazy hours, it's me."

He finally smiled. "Yeah. And then I get five full days off in a row."

"Every month?"

"Yep."

"So, if you can't come by my house at midnight for a whole week, then you get to spend five days making up for it."

He gave me a filthy smirk. "Oh yes."

"I really hope those days line up with my days off," I added. "Then you can do to me over and over what you did to me last night."

He chuckled. "Oh, believe me, I have no problem with that."

I was half tempted to take him back to bed right then and there, or sink to my knees, but decided to feed the man instead.

"Breakfast," I said, turning back to the eggs. "You distract me far too easily. I swear, I've had more sex this last week than I've had in the last three years, and I still want more. It's absurd. I haven't been this horny since I was seventeen years old and found the editorial locker room photo shoot of the all-star hockey team in a sports magazine."

He laughed. "Was that your awakening?"

"Partly. I knew I liked guys before that, and I'd relieved myself of many an erection to the images of guys, but that photo shoot?" I shook my head slowly. "Was the first time I'd really thought about not what I wanted to do with a man but what I wanted *him* to do to *me*." I gave him a smirk over my shoulder. "If you get what I mean."

"Oh, I believe I do, yes. You saw all those jacked-up men and finally imagined what it'd be like to get railed."

I laughed. "Thoroughly."

He chuckled. "My true awakening was high school gym class. Naked guys in the shower. Kinda knew then that I wanted to be the one that does the railing."

I let my head fall back. "And my god, you do it so well."

Soren groaned. "Yeah, we really should change the subject or we can forget breakfast."

I looked at the eggs I was still whisking and, showing a willpower I didn't know I possessed, poured them into the frying pan. Soren made more coffee and toast, and we, at least, made it through eating before I turned him around in his seat at the table and kneeled between his legs.

I sucked him dry, and when he left for work, he insisted I leave the door unlocked again.

Which I did.

And I tried to stay awake for him, but sometime after midnight, I fell asleep and woke up around 3:00 a.m. to him pinned to my back, sound asleep.

The next night he'd planned to make it up to me but he didn't get home until after one. "Sorry," he whispered when I stirred. "Car accident."

I alerted, and all those years of sleeping in a cot at the hospital between emergency shifts kicked in. I sat up, ready to go. "How many occupants? Any injuries? Where are the—"

"Hey," he soothed me, urging me back down. "It's all okay. Two occupants, both taken to Mossley hospital. Just a lot of road clean-up." He shivered. "They were lucky."

Realizing the night he'd had, I put my arms around him

and pulled him to my chest. Hoping he felt the comfort he needed, the security.

Everything I wished I'd had this last decade after terrible nights at work but never had.

I kissed the top of his head. "Go to sleep," I murmured.

He tightened his arms around me and sighed, his breathing evening out soon after.

Yeah, this is definitely not that L-word you've been trying to ignore.

Shut up.

Because it is the L-word, you do know that right? You can tell yourself it's too soon or it's just some teen-like infatuation. But it's not, and you know that, right?

I sighed, then the voice in my head sighed too.

I wanted to tell my subconscious to shut up but there was no point.

Because it was right.

I told you.

Oh, shut up.

It is the L-word. He's asleep in your arms right now and you've never been happier. Go on, say it. It's the L-word.

Fine. It's the L-word.

My subconscious preened.

Yes, you're absolutely right. I do like *him.*

. . .

That's not what I meant and you know it.

It was my turn to preen a little now, and I kissed the top of Soren's head again.

You do know that I am inside your head, right? You can say the word like instead of love, but we both know which you mean.

I'm not answering. I'm going to sleep.

I'm not leaving you alone until you admit that you love him.

...

...

...

...

Fine! I love him. I'm in love with him. He's absolutely the best thing to happen to me. Are you happy now? I've admitted it. Now leave me alone.

My subconscious smiled wryly, knowingly, then nodded to Soren.

Now you gotta tell him.

I was done arguing. I was too tired, too comfortable, and with my arms securely around the man I loved, I drifted off to sleep.

WORK THAT WEEK WAS GREAT. Very conventional, very peaceful. Nothing out of the realm of ordinary, nothing drastically urgent, nothing terrible anyway. Katie kept my appointments structured, all patient files were prepared and organized. And if I wasn't being too full of myself, I'd like to think that my patients were even happy to see me. Given I was so new and given Doctor Humphries had been their physician for most of their lives, I was generally very well received.

They even called me Doctor Rob.

Not Doctor O'Reilly. And it was hard to put into

words what the distinction was, other than acceptance. They saw me as someone who was part of their town.

So yes, work that week was great.

I missed Soren though.

His late nights and my early starts meant less time together, but he had stayed over last night and kept me awake until after one in the morning. And I'd come to work this morning with a sore ass and zero regrets.

But tonight he'd start his graveyard shift, which meant a whole week of not seeing him at all.

Or barely seeing him.

Definitely no midnight thorough dickings, that's for sure.

"Why the long face?" Gunter asked.

We were sitting at the table in the youth center going through information and proposals for the vocation idea I'd put to him, and I must have zoned out.

I snorted. "Am I that obvious?"

"Did you and Soren have a fight?"

I scoffed. "No. Just the opposite, actually. We are . . . we are so good."

He laughed. "Then why the long face?"

I shook my head at myself because this bordered on embarrassing. "He's starting his week of the graveyard shift, where he has to sleep at the fire station. I won't see him as much, that's all. Which is stupid and pitiful, to be honest. And embarrassing."

Gunter laughed. "Sounds fair to me. So you miss him. That's not embarrassing."

"We've been dating for like two weeks," I cried. "I've known him less than three. Three weeks. It's insanity, that's what it is."

Gunter sighed, still smiling. "To hell with sanity. If it feels right, go with it."

I put my hand to my chest. "I'm a man of medicine. I trust science. I trust procedure and—"

"And I hate to break it to you, doc, but your heart can't see or hear, and it certainly can't read. It can only go by feel."

I sighed and possibly pouted.

He nodded as if he understood my internal plight. "And how does it feel?"

I didn't really want to admit this out loud. I hadn't even wanted to admit this to myself, but Gunter was my friend. My closest friend here in Hartbridge, if I was being honest and wanted to put a label on it.

I sighed again, slumping in my chair in defeat. "It feels like . . . love."

Gunter's smile was slow to spread. "I'm happy for you. But most of all I'm happy Hamish isn't here to hear you say that."

I laughed and rolled my eyes, mostly at myself. "You know, I think I can say unequivocally that it has nothing to do with any Hartbridge Cupid thing and a lot to do with Soren and his . . . you know."

He clued in pretty quick. "Oh. His ability to keep you happy," he said, then using his hands, measured a good seven inches apart.

I took his closest hand and moved it out another inch or so. "Yep."

Gunter laughed and laughed, and I buried my face in my hands.

I had no idea how this was my life now, but the truth was, I'd never been happier.

"It's not just that. It's everything. He's intelligent, and caring, and funny. And I know it was his idea about the Kris Kringle thing. He wanted to do something sweet for me."

Gunter gave me a nod. "I had to get the lowdown off Hamish later. It was sweet of him." Then he groaned. "Do you know what you're doing for your couple's gift?"

"No clue."

He grumbled. "Handmade. I could have killed Hamish when he said that."

"To be fair, I don't think Hamish expected Hamish to say that either."

He snorted. "True. But we're running out of days."

"Yeah, I planned on using my week without Soren to get it done."

"You make it sound like he's going off to war."

I barely refrained from wailing. "I know! It's pitiful. I'm pitiful."

Gunter clapped my shoulder. "He lives next door to you, and he works across the road from you. Put dirty little notes in his mailbox or something. So at the end of the week, he'll be banging on your door."

The more I thought about that, the more I had to suppress a smile. "That's . . . that's actually a really good idea."

Just then the door pushed open and the first of the kids came in. Jeez, I didn't realize the time. "Wow, school's out already."

"Hey Mister Z," Evie said to Gunter, the first through the door.

Gunter straightened up all his papers and stood. "Hey Evie." As the others filed in, he gave me an awkward smile, then said, "Hey, I have a question," he began. "It's just something we were thinking about. But you guys have, what, a year left of school?"

They mostly nodded.

"And you'll be looking at colleges or even just moving to get out of town, right?"

They mostly nodded again.

"Well, you're gonna be looking for work and whatnot, so what if we set up a coffee machine in here and get you all experts so you can walk into any coffee shop in any city and say yes, you have experience."

They looked among themselves and it was Evie who answered. "Uh, yeah. That sounds cool." She looked around. "In here?"

"Well, maybe. We don't know. To begin with. But there's an empty store next door, and maybe we could get a proper café set up, with tables. Make it a cool hangout for teenagers, but also staffed by you guys too. That way you get experience across the board. Then you could apply for jobs in retail, at the cinemas, but there's a coffee shop on almost every corner and it's a good place to start."

They were clearly excited about it, and Gunter put his hands up. "Wait up. We're just in the discussing stages, and if it can happen at all, it's a long way off. It might not be up and running before you guys are gone, which would be a shame. But we can at least get the machine in here so you guys can learn that before you go. Proper training, with certificates and everything."

Well, if this was a test group, the response was positive. It just made me more determined to make it into a reality.

I helped Gunter out for a short while, but the last thing a bunch of kids wanted was another adult hanging around, even in the office. I waved them goodbye, donned my coat, gloves, and beanie, and made my way up onto Main Street.

The old-fashioned awnings with Christmas decorations, the small Christmas trees along the shop walls, the snow-covered mountain backdrop . . . it looked surreal.

The way people smiled and said hello to me . . . it felt surreal too.

Maybe it was my good mood or the clean fresh air, but with my newfound inspiration for making little notes for Soren—and after a trip to the Home Mart—I needed to go to the hardware store.

I hadn't been inside the store so I was excited, hoping to see Ren and Hamish in their natural habitat.

The doorbell chimed above my head, the smell of sawdust and lacquer hitting me as soon as I walked in. It reminded me of something like *The Waltons*, just more modern, obviously.

Ren was behind the counter, and he grinned when he saw me. He was cute as hell, wearing his plaid shirt and apron. "Hello there," he said. "Is there something I can help you with, or are you here to see Hamish?"

"Well, both," I said. "I need some supplies for this homemade gift thing I've been roped into."

He put his hands up in surrender. "I know nothing, and I cannot be held accountable for my husband's actions."

Hamish appeared from an office. "He also can't testify against me in a court of law, so." Then he shrugged. "Did I hear you needed supplies?"

"Well, yes. For the Kris Kringle thing that Soren absolutely forced you into organizing."

Hamish looked like he'd sucked a lemon. "Uh, no he didn't."

I laughed. "It's fine. He told me. You're all very bad liars."

Ren put his arm around Hamish, smiling at him fondly. "All you had to say was that it was a ten-dollar limit."

"I know." Hamish winced. "I panicked."

"It's fine. I actually have an idea and I need some supplies. Oh, and this," I said, fishing out my front door key. "I need to get a spare cut. Red or green if possible."

Hamish came and plucked it out of my hand. "To give to anyone in particular."

"No," I squeaked.

Ren laughed and took the key from Hamish but then he looked at me. "Welcome to the terrible liars club."

Hamish laughed and took my arm. "Tell me of these supplies you need."

I took out my phone. "I had to have Google's help I'll have you know. I'm not creative at all and this will probably look terrible, but this is what I need."

He took a quick glance at the screenshot of supplies. "Easy. This way." He led me over to the paint supply section. Acrylics in red, white, and blue, painters tape, foam brushes, and something called Mod Podge. Hamish looked at the supplies he shoved into my arms. "I thought I could guess what you were going to make, but the food-safe sealant is throwing me off. Any clues?"

"No. You'll need to be as horrified as everyone else when they open it."

"I think you mean surprised."

"No. I didn't."

"It won't be that bad," he tried. "But tell me, are you and Soren doing gifts?"

"We are."

He wiggled excitedly. "And? What are you getting him?"

"I'm not telling you. I've seen your face when you try and lie."

He rolled his eyes. "Fair."

"But I have ordered it."

"Things between you are going well?" He raised an eyebrow.

"They are." I still wasn't giving him details. "But he's working graveyard this week so I won't see him."

Hamish made a sad face, but then he corrected it. "Then you just need to go find yourself accidentally in his bed when he gets home."

I laughed. "You know, out of yours and Gunter's suggestions, I think I like yours better."

This clearly pleased him greatly. But then Ren was back, holding up a brand-new red key. "All done."

"Perfect."

I paid for my supplies and Hamish walked me to the door. "I will be in touch with the list of potluck dishes. I know it all sounds like a lot of work, but it'll be fun, I promise. We always have such a good night."

"It sounds great, to be honest. I've been enjoying getting to cook actual meals lately," I replied. "And a Christmas dinner sounds perfect. I'm looking forward to it."

He really had no idea just how much I meant that.

Hamish gave my arm a squeeze. "I'm glad you're here," he said softly.

Okay, so maybe he did know.

I met his gaze and nodded. "Me too."

Chapter Twelve

SOREN

I NORMALLY DIDN'T MIND the graveyard shift. I'd done it so many times, I was used to it. In fact, I didn't mind quiet hours of uninterrupted reading time. When and if there was any emergency, I liked being right freaking there to put out the call.

I'd originally thought a few days apart would do Rob and me some good, but no. I was miserable.

These last three nights were long, lonely, and I kept thinking of Rob being asleep alone in his bed.

Well, the first two weren't so bad, but the last night had damn near killed me.

I missed Rob.

It was pitiful, but I didn't care.

Instead of going home, I walked up and knocked on Rob's door. He opened it, still half-asleep, tying the belt to his robe, and clearly annoyed at being woken up.

Until he saw it was me.

"Everything okay?" he asked.

I stepped inside and collected him in a bear hug,

holding him so tight I almost lifted him off his feet. "It is now," I mumbled into his neck.

And we just hugged. It wasn't sexual, never even looked that way. It was just . . . soul-fixing good.

But the next day, after I'd spent the day sleeping, I found a note had been slid under my front door.

Just a folded piece of note paper. I opened it.

I miss you.
Rob xx

My heart almost burst and I laughed out loud. Then before I left for my shift, I knocked on his door again. It really was so much easier when I finished at midnight and he'd leave the door unlocked . . .

This time he'd opened the door, maybe expecting it to be me, and he laughed when I collected him in a hug and spun him around. I was dressed for work, but I was early.

"Have you eaten?" he asked. "Can I get you any dinner?"

"No," I said, taking hold of his face and kissing him. "I have two hours before Doug comes looking for me."

He grinned. "Two hours, huh?" He pulled me into his room. "We won't need that long."

Oh boy, it was sexual that time.

The next day there was another note.

Text me if you want me to leave my door unlocked.

Rob xx

Oh, hell yes I did.

Leaving early again, I knocked on the door and he called out, "It's open."

He was sitting at his dining table, still in his work clothes, even this late. He smiled at me, but something didn't quite sit right. "Hey," I said gently, closing the door behind me. "Wassup? Everything okay?"

He sighed and held up a large wooden fork. "I'm a reasonably intelligent person, right?"

"Smartest man I know."

"Then perhaps you could explain to me why I cannot, for the life of me, figure this out."

I chuckled, sitting in the seat next to him. "It's a fork. I mean, it's a giant wooden fork, but I'm not sure what you need help with."

Then I noticed the items on the table. Blue painter's tape, three tubes of paint, a paper plate, and some foam brushes. And a giant matching wooden spoon, only this one was painted.

"Did you do that?" I asked.

He pouted. "That one was easy." Then he tapped his phone screen. "This one is not."

On screen was an image of the Union Jack.

"I cannot mark it out with the tape," he said.

"Rob, this is a great idea. For Colson and Braithe, right?"

He nodded again. "Well, at this point, the only good

thing their salad servers are good for tossing is into the trash."

I laughed, then abruptly stopped when Rob cut me a glare. "It's not funny."

It kinda was.

"Rob, this idea is amazing. This one is amazing." I pointed to the spoon. One third of the long handle was blue, and two thirds of it were very neatly painted red and white lines.

"I still need to paint the stars on it," he said, pouting.

He was so stinking cute.

He let out a frustrated snarl. "But this fucking Union Jack!"

"Okay," I said, taking the offending fork from him before he tossed it across the room. There was also a pile of crumpled up blue painter's tape, evidence of his previous failed attempts. He clearly hadn't any practice in wrapping hockey sticks, but I wasn't about to bring that up. "How about I take it with me to work tonight and get it taped up, at least."

"And painted," he added, sulking.

"And painted," I agreed, smiling at him.

He nodded. "I would appreciate that. Actually, Braithe would appreciate it too, I'm sure, given I would mangle his country's flag."

The American flag for Colson and a Union Jack for Braithe. It was so perfect.

"I love this idea," I said, pulling his seat closer to mine so I could kiss him. "I'm sorry I wasn't here to help earlier."

His pout became a smile, and then he blushed, his cheeks a dark pink. God, it did things to me. I ran the back of my fingers across his jaw. "What are you blushing for?"

He chuckled and ducked his head. "I, uh, I . . ." Then his eyes met mine. "I've missed you. Not just in the bedroom." His blush deepened but he never took his eyes from mine. "I've missed you. I want to hear about your week, about your work. If you ordered your parent's gifts yet. If you've been sleeping okay. I want to hear about everything."

Oh, this man . . .

I took his face in my hands and kissed him, chaste and sweet. "I've missed you too. Work's been fine; busy as always but no emergency calls, thankfully. I ordered my folks' present at three a.m. two nights ago. It'll get there next week, just in time for Christmas. And I've been getting some sleep. Nothing like when I sleep next to you though."

"Come here when you finish your shift tomorrow. Sleep in my bed. I'll look after you."

Warmth flooded through me. "Okay. And what about you? What's been going on in your world this week?"

"Work is great." He held up two fingers. "Two people said 'hello, Doctor Rob' to me in the store. Gunter's been making some progress with the café training idea, with permits and whatever, and I think it's turning into a whole thing; the kids love the idea. We have to bring scalloped potatoes and the cranberry sauce for the potluck dinner next week." He made a face. "I had to google the recipe, and I was thinking I'd make a practice one tonight."

I was smiling so hard at him. He looked so happy and it made my heart clench.

"Oh, and I bought Katie's gift," he added. There were

three beautifully wrapped boxes under his tree. "I got her a musical snow globe. It's a whole Christmas scene from *Frozen*, the Disney movie. She has a lunch box with that on it and a sticker on her phone, so I figured it was a safe bet."

"Sounds perfect," I replied. "You are an awesome gift giver. The hand-painted salad servers and a snow globe. It really shows that you put thought into who the gift is for."

He shrugged the compliment off. "Ideas, yes. Actioning, not so much." He frowned again at the salad fork, as if it was its fault.

I squeezed his hand. "It's okay. I'll make it happen." I looked back to the gifts under the tree. "There's two other boxes . . ."

He huffed and rattled my hand a little. "No peeking, mister."

I laughed. "Are they for me?"

"Of course they are." He tried not to smile. "You're gonna love it."

My heart was hammering, my belly all knots and nerves. Even hearing him say the word *love* gave me a thrill and it wasn't even aimed at me.

I was so close to saying something, telling him how I felt, but I didn't want to scare him off or ruin what we had going on. This thing between us was a very good thing, and I'd always been the type to jump in with both feet, falling hard and fast and loving with my whole heart.

That could be too much for some guys, and I didn't want Rob to feel overwhelmed and need to step back.

So I didn't say anything.

Instead, I pulled his legs around so he faced me better,

went to my knees right there at the dining table, undid his fly, and brought him undone.

Afterwards, when he was a sated and smiling lump in his seat, I packed up the craft gear and went to the door. "Oh, and yes, leave your door unlocked," I said, then went to work.

I helped the night crew finish up their chores, said goodbye to them, and locked up the fire hall behind them. I did my checklists and reports, then set about taping the salad fork. Sure, the Union Jack was tricky, but I'd had plenty of practice in taping hockey sticks.

It was never going to be perfect, given the handle was cylindrical, but as long as it was recognizable . . .

And I had hours to get it done.

I didn't want to jinx myself, but it'd been a quiet winter so far. Which was a good thing. Quiet meant safe, and I'd be a happy firefighter if I never had to battle a blaze.

Sure, we'd had a barn fire, a car wreck clean-up, and a false fire alarm, but getting through a winter without fires risking person or property was a good thing.

It just meant for long quiet hours.

Gave me time to get the first coat of red paint on the Union Jack, and it gave me a lot of time to think about Rob. How he'd be sound asleep in his bed.

How I'd be sleeping in his bed at the end of this shift. Counting down the hours, counting down the minutes . . .

And yes, my dick was very eager for me to crawl into his bed. But my heart was even more so.

I was pretty sure I was going to tell him how I felt. It felt inevitable at this point. As if it would explode out of me if I didn't tell him.

The rational part of my brain told me I should wait until after Christmas. In case he didn't reciprocate or if he freaked out, then it wouldn't ruin the holidays. Maybe I could tell him when we counted down to midnight on New Year's Eve . . .

I could tell him I loved him and wanted him to be my boyfriend as the clock ticked down to midnight. At least then I'd know if I was heading into the new year with or without him.

By the time I heard Doug's truck pull up out back, I'd added the blue and the white to the salad server—grateful acrylic paints dried so fast—and I was desperate to leave.

"Morning," Doug said, his usual no-nonsense voice gruff.

"Morning," I replied. "Coffee machine's on for you."

He stopped. "Why can I smell paint?"

I held up my masterpiece. "It's a long story."

He nodded, as if me holding an oversized wooden fork with a Union Jack handle was exactly what he expected me to have, and went to the coffee machine. "Busy night, I see."

"Just how I like it." I picked up the bag of craft supplies. "I know I normally stick around for the boys to get in, but I'd really appreciate it if I could clock out now." They were only five minutes away . . .

Doug's eyes met mine as he stirred his coffee. "Hm-mm. Somewhere more important to be, I take it?"

I grinned at him. "Absolutely." I pulled on my coat and nodded to the whiteboard. "Everything's done. Reports are on your desk. I even filled in the snow report."

He almost smiled, until he remembered to be mad.

"Mm," he grunted at me. Then the big teddy bear softened. "Tell your doctor boyfriend I said hi."

I laughed on my way out the door.

Boyfriend.

Damn, that sounded good.

I couldn't get to Rob's place fast enough. I bounded up the patio steps and, before knocking, thought I'd try the door handle.

It was unlocked.

I let myself in, shed off my coat, toque, and boots, left my clothes on the floor in his bedroom and slid into bed. Quick to sidle up to him, the first thing I noticed was how hot he was, and then . . . "Uh, why is your hair wet?"

He chuckled, stretched his back, and stuck his ass out. "I just had a steaming hot shower."

Oh damn.

"I set my alarm," he murmured. "Was about to start lubing myself but you're early."

Jesus Christ.

All the blood left my brain and filled my dick.

"Oh Rob," I breathed, kissing his spine. "You'll be the death of me."

He hummed when I used my knee to spread his legs. "Good morning, by the way."

I pressed my weight down on him, letting him feel how hard I was already. "This is a great morning."

I was inside him five minutes later. Slow and deep, holding him so tight as I climaxed. I never wanted to leave his body. I never wanted to let him go.

I held him afterwards, our bodies tangled, his heartbeat lulling me to sleep.

❄

I WOKE to the smell of food, smiling when I remembered I was in Rob's bed. I saw his robe hanging on the back of his bedroom door, so I pulled it on and found him in the kitchen at the sink.

I walked straight up to him, wrapped my arms around him, pressed my face into his back, closed my eyes, and sighed.

"Did I wake you? I'm sorry," he said.

"Time is it?" I asked.

"A little after one in the afternoon. You haven't slept enough."

"Nah, s'okay. If I stay up now, I'll sleep tonight."

"Are you hungry? I made that potato thing. It's really good. It's hard for something with potatoes, cream, and cheese to be anything but good, but the carb count is astronomical."

I chuckled. "Sounds good to me."

He dished up some grilled chicken, scalloped potatoes, and steamed green beans, and it was possibly the best thing I'd ever eaten. Granted, I was starving, but wow. "This is so good," I said, trying to refrain from vacuuming it in like a heathen.

And then we spent the entire afternoon on his couch, snuggling under a blanket, watching the Christmas movie channel. It was sappy and sweet, and I dozed off a few times with him tracing patterns on my back and pressing kisses on the top of my head.

The next day he put the clear coat on the salad servers while I shoveled his driveway and mine. Then I helped

Chuck do his. I found myself back in my own house, trying to distract myself, wishing like hell I was with Rob, until I couldn't fucking stand it and went and knocked on his door.

He laughed when he saw me, held the door open for me and closed it behind me. I wasn't even pretending to be anything other than pitiful. "I think my furnace is acting up again—" There was nothing wrong with my furnace, I just needed an excuse. "—and the house is cold, and my bed is lonely. Everything is gray and gloomy over there, and everything here is warm and yellow."

He chuckled. "Thank you for describing my house like a urine sample."

I laughed. "Sorry. That's not what I meant."

He stepped in and kissed me. "What are you like at gift wrapping?"

"Terrible."

"Then you can keep me company while I do it."

Of course he wrapped presents with surgical precision. Even tied a bow like I'd seen in movies or magazines. "You're so good at this," I murmured.

"You totally saved the entire gift with your Union Jack painting skills."

I chuckled, dropping my forehead to his shoulder, my fingers playing with his. God, I wanted to tell him so bad. I wanted him to know—

"Did you get Chuck's driveway cleared?"

I looked up at him then. "Yeah. His place is out near Vern's Bar. He has a few acres, and he has a mini snowplow he can hook up on his riding lawn mower. But it's still a lot of work. He appreciates the help though."

"I'll have to meet him properly," Rob murmured. "I met him briefly when I delivered the pizza to you at work."

My heart rate kicked up a gear. "Really? I mean, yeah, sure. I'd love that. We could do a dinner or something. His girlfriend, Delaney, is great. Has the patience of a saint, that woman, to put up with him. And I say that with nothing but affection for Chuck. Don't get me wrong. I love the guy . . ."

And there it was. The word love. Even saying it in his presence made my belly knot up. Nerves strung tight, making it hard to breathe . . .

"Maybe after Christmas," Rob said. "We can organize something."

And then he talked about the Kris Kringle dinner tomorrow night. He was excited to see Jayden and Cass's bed and breakfast, excited for a dinner party with new friends.

And my chance to tell him was over.

I mean, I could have blurted it out at any time but I wanted it to be perfect. And he was excited for these social gatherings with friends, something he hadn't experienced in far too long. It felt wrong to diminish his excitement.

I could have told him when we showered together, when we fell into bed together. I could have told him at breakfast the next day or when he was making the potato dish to take for the potluck. I could have told him when he was getting ready, gorgeous and nervous, excited.

But it didn't feel like the perfect time.

Maybe there wasn't a perfect time. Maybe when he was brushing his teeth and I'd made him laugh was the perfect time. Or when he carried the food and wrapped gift out to his car and almost slipped on the path. I'd caught his arm and saved him from falling; our noses were barely an inch apart. Maybe that was the perfect time.

Maybe I'd missed it.

"You okay?" he asked as he drove out along Ponderosa Road. "You're a bit quiet."

"Nah, I'm great," I replied. "Just thinking . . ."

"About?"

While he was driving was hardly the perfect time.

"Just how happy I am," I said. It wasn't what I wanted to say, but it certainly wasn't a lie. "This is gonna be a great Christmas."

He grinned at me, his cheeks darkening by the dashboard light. "I think so too. It's already been the best Christmas I've had in a long time, and we're still a week out. God, can you believe I've only been here for three weeks? Feels like I've been here for years."

Three weeks . . .

Yeah. Now was not the right time. It made me feel a little sweaty, actually. "Crazy, huh?"

"Oh my god," he breathed. "Look at their house."

As we drove up to the house, the grand old manor looked stunning perched up on the hill. Fairy lights lit up the sweeping veranda and stairs, illuminating the size of the place in a muted yellow glow. It was spectacular.

"Wow."

Rob drove around back, parking by the other familiar vehicles. Ren's truck, Gunter's car, Colson's sheriff vehicle. "Are we late?" Rob asked.

"No, right on time."

Before we even had the goods out of his car, the back door opened and Hamish appeared. "Need a hand?"

"No, we're good," I replied.

He was wearing a sweater with a reindeer on it. "Come through here," he said, holding the door for us. "We just got here."

"This place," Rob whispered.

"Gorgeous," Hamish whispered right back.

We walked through to the kitchen where everyone was standing around. The wood fires were burning, something smelled amazing, Christmas lights adorned the most gorgeous tree. It was utterly perfect.

We said hellos and made small talk. Colson gave me a smile and a pointed nod toward Rob. "Things are going well, I see."

"Ah, yeah," I said, trying to play it cool. "He's . . . great."

He laughed. "And the Kris Kringle thing was your idea, I heard."

I groaned. "Okay, so the gift idea, yes. The homemade idea was all Hamish."

He spoke out of the corner of his mouth. "I let Braithe take care of that. He's better at that stuff than me."

I laughed just as two kids ran in from the door we'd come through. "Daddy," the girl cried, running up to Cass. He scooped her up and flattened down her dress.

Daddy?

Cass had kids?

I was racking my brain to remember if I knew that, when Jayden picked the boy up and whispered something in his ear, making the kid giggle and nod.

Then another couple came in. Trey, from a horse ranch

out on Red Cedar Road, and a woman. "Sorry we're a little late," she said, giving Jayden a kiss on the cheek, then Cass.

I wasn't aware there'd be kids coming for dinner, not that it bothered me in the slightest—this was clearly Cass's ex-wife and her new man—they were obviously a close family and could invite whoever they wanted for Christmas dinner.

I was just glad we hadn't made the Kris Kringle gift R-rated . . .

Then Cass's parents came in, waving shy hellos, and when another older couple came in from somewhere down the hall, I could see the surprise on Hamish's face.

But then another woman followed them in. She was mid-fifties, at a glance. Wearing a nice navy outfit, her hair done perfectly, and I assumed it must have been another family member.

But Hamish gasped and he spun to face Jayden. "Nooo . . . You didn't. You did not. Jayden Turner, you . . ."

Jayden nodded, and Hamish burst into tears, pointed to his ugly Christmas sweater, and cried. "Look at what I'm wearing!"

I had no clue what was going on, and from the few other blank looks, I wasn't the only one.

Cass cleared his throat and put his arm around Jayden, then gestured to the swinging door. "Uh, if you'd care to join us, this way," he said.

The little boy asked, very loudly, "Uncle Hamish, why are you crying?"

But as we walked into the next room, it was pretty clear why.

This wasn't a Kris Kringle potluck dinner. This was a wedding.

White chairs with ribbons made a short aisle, and the lady in the navy suit stood at the front. "Please take a seat," she said.

Holy shit.

This was crazy. And awesome.

Rob pulled me into a seat next to his. "Oh my god," he whispered. "Did you know?"

I shook my head. "Hamish didn't even know."

Cass and Jayden stood at the front, their kids standing beside them. And there, in a room lit by a wood fire, Christmas tree lights, and candles, they were married.

Short, sweet, and absolutely perfect.

Hamish wiped away tears the whole time and he strangle-hugged him when the formalities were over. Everyone congratulated them, hugged them, the kids danced with the grandparents, and it was all such a privilege to witness.

I didn't know either Cass or Jayden overly well, but it was impossible not to feel the love in that room. To see everyone talking and laughing, to catch Rob smiling at me from across the room, I felt the need to tell him how I felt more than ever.

My heart decided that tonight would be the night. When we went home, when we were alone, I'd take my heart off my sleeve and give it to Rob.

He made his way over to me, leaning into my side, his eyes shining. "What a beautiful night, huh?"

Okay, so maybe I could tell him now . . .

But then Colson's phone rang. He went to the end of

the room to take the call, but his gaze shot to mine at the same time my pager buzzed.

I checked the screen and my stomach dropped.

House fire.

I could feel Rob's eyes on me, but I couldn't take my eyes off Colson. He was staring at me, walking over as he ended his call.

"We need to leave," he said. "House fire. Off Old Gully Road."

My blood ran cold, my feet stuck to the floor. Colson nodded. "It's Chucky's house. Let's go. I'll drive."

Chucky's house.

Rob grabbed Colson's arm. "Is anyone injured? Should I come?"

I met his eyes, struggling to move, to think . . . Rob gave me a nod. "Go," he urged me. "I'll follow. You need to go. Now."

Colson all but dragged me to the door and I saw Rob standing next to Braithe, both of them and everyone watching us leave.

Then reality kicked in, and I was running.

Chapter Thirteen

ROB

Chuck's house. Soren's partner, his best friend.

God, please let everyone be okay.

My instinct was to go, to follow. To see if anyone was injured or needed assistance. But I was standing in Jayden and Cass's house, at their wedding, and I was so new here. I didn't want them to think I was being rude . . .

Then Jayden was in front of me, smiling, his hand on my arm. "You want to go?"

I nodded. "Someone could be hurt. I'm a doctor. I should go . . . I'm sorry. This was all so beautiful and such a joy to witness. Thank you for inviting me."

He grinned. "You're welcome."

"I feel bad for leaving."

"Don't worry about it," he replied. "Go make sure everyone's okay."

"Come on," Braithe said to me. "I'll walk you out."

I gave a nod and went with Braithe. He basically put me in my car. "I'd like to say it gets easier," he said. "Every time

269

Colson gets a call out, but it doesn't. Soren will be okay. He's very good at his job."

It hadn't even really occurred to me that Soren could get injured. I'd seen many emergency service workers injured on the job over the years, but it never really . . .

Oh hell.

I'd never considered *my* Soren could be injured.

"Tell everyone I said thank you, and I hope you like your gift," I told Braithe. "Sorry I can't stay."

"I'm sure it'll be lovely," he said. "Drive carefully now."

"I will."

And I did make sure to stay under the speed limit, even though my mind kept racing, reenacting every accident that came through my ER, putting Soren in their place.

Or Chuck and his girlfriend.

I could only hope that they got out. Not only for their own sake but also for Soren's. He'd be devastated if the worst should happen.

As I drove into town, the fire engine screamed out of the fire station, siren and lights flashing.

Soren's on that truck.

I followed, turning onto my street. I raced into my house, grabbed my medic bag, and raced back out. I'd heard Colson say the name of the road and I had a vague idea of where it was, but I didn't need directions. People stood in the street, all facing the same way, the red lights fading out of view.

I followed, and soon it was all I could see.

Flashing red and blue lights everywhere and a giant orange blaze against the black night sky.

I pulled off the road, grabbed my bag, and then spotted

the paramedics. I felt a little foolish to think I'd be the only one there but also very relieved.

The back door was open, lights on inside, but the bed was empty. *Thank god.* The paramedic had a blanket around a woman who was watching the fire, her face strewn with ash and tears.

"Hello," I said, addressing the paramedic. "I'm Doctor O'Reilly. I was with Soren and Colson when they got the call. I wasn't sure if I was needed . . ."

The paramedic woman smiled at me. "Name's Chrissie. I think we're good for now."

"Occupants?" I asked. "No injuries? Smoke inhalation?"

"Two occupants, both got out. Delaney here," she said, rubbing the lady's back. "And Chucky. He's over there."

I looked over to the fire engine and sure enough there was one guy not in protective gear. It was hard to tell with the flashing lights and raging fire, but I assumed that was Chucky.

"There was smoke coming from the ceiling," Delaney said, not to anyone in particular. Then she sobbed. "Then there were flames and Chucky knew what it meant. He screamed at me to get out but it went up so fast. He pulled me out."

Chrissie went back to rubbing Delaney's back. "Oh, he's a good one, that man of yours."

Delaney nodded, crying, watching as her house went up in flames.

The three of us stood there, unable to do anything but watch. My attention turned to the firefighters. To Soren.

I could pick him out. The way he gave orders, instructions. The way he moved. How he pulled the hose, how he helped hold it as water burst out of it.

How he yelled at Chucky to get back. He wasn't wearing the right gear.

Chucky stood there, helpless, his hands on his head, watching as the flames engulfed his home. Then he shot a look back in our direction and came running, collected Delaney in a hug.

Then we all watched in silence as Soren and the team did their best. But there was no saving the house. I remembered Soren saying their house was old and they'd been doing renovations . . .

Old houses went up like tinder.

So I'm sure Soren's efforts became about containment, ensuring outhouses and garages were saved.

And if I'd been worried about Soren's safety before, I was wrong. If anything, I got to see firsthand just how capable he was. How safe he was, and how damn good he was at his job.

I stayed until the blaze was almost out, but knowing they'd be here for many hours yet, and knowing there was no injuries—and knowing no one was setting foot in that smoldering and gutted house for a few days yet—there wasn't any point in my staying.

But just then, Soren ran over. He was in full firefighter gear, sweating under his helmet, and heaven help me, I'd never seen a more attractive man.

He went to Chuck and Delaney, putting one gloved hand on her shoulder, his other to Chucky's face. "You okay, brother?" He asked.

I couldn't hear what Chucky said, but Delaney began crying again and Soren put his hand to her hair.

And I was wrong again.

The compassion, the empathy, the pure heart that man had, *that* was the most attractive he'd ever been.

Then he looked at me, his gaze softening. "Hey," he said.

"Hey. I just wanted to make sure everyone was okay. Chrissie's got it all under control. I was just gonna head off."

He nodded. "Okay. I'll be . . ." He turned back to the dwindling fire and billowing smoke. "I'll be a long while."

"It's okay," I told him gently. "You're where you need to be. I'm not going anywhere."

His nostrils flared and he nodded quickly before looking back at the firetruck. "I have to go."

"I'll leave my door unlocked for you," I whispered. "Doesn't matter when."

He gripped my arm tight, scanning my eyes as if he was searching for something, trying to say something, but in the end, he gave a nod and walked away.

I went home, showered, and making sure my front door was unlocked, I went to bed. It'd been a whirlwind of emotions. First, like I wasn't excited enough for the Christmas dinner, then it became a surprise wedding. Such a beautiful, joyous moment.

Only to be cut short by a raging house fire.

Soren's work partner, his best friend. His brother, as he'd called him tonight.

I was so grateful that everyone was okay, but still . . . what an awful thing to have happen.

Homes, possessions, and material things could be replaced. Sorely missed, maybe. But people were irreplaceable, the most important things. That those we love are safe.

Like Soren.

I loved him. I was *in* love with him. The only thing I needed was for him to be safe. Nothing else mattered.

I was disappointed when I woke up alone. I couldn't deny that. But I understood that he'd probably gone home to crash after being at the house fire site until all hours of the morning. Hell, he could probably still be there.

And I'd meant it when I'd said I'd leave my door unlocked for him, and it didn't matter how long it took. Like I meant it when I'd said I wasn't going anywhere.

He had a job to do, and that was something I understood all too well. Not to mention that his best friend needed him right now. So I went about my morning, made breakfast, had a shower, and did everything I could to not think about what Soren may or may not have been doing. If he needed anything, if there was anything I could do, or if, perhaps, I should go over to his place and ask.

But then a truck pulled up out front and two guys went into Soren's place. Then two minutes later, another truck with one guy. Then five minutes after that, the Hartbridge Fire Department 4WD and Doug went in.

Well, I certainly couldn't go over there now.

Oh god, a sinking realization hit me. What if something happened after I'd left. What if someone was injured? What if it was Soren?

Oh dear lord, what if something was wrong?

Then I noticed the sheriff's cruiser pull up and a cold dread seeped into my belly . . . until Colson and Braithe climbed out. Colson went next door to Soren's, and Braithe headed to my house.

I opened the door before he could knock. "Oh, hi," he said.

"I saw you coming," I admitted. "Please come in. I've been watching all the vehicles pulling up next door."

"Yes, Colson was coming down and I knew you lived next door, so I thought I'd drop in and see how you were. And also thank you for the amazing Secret Santa gift. I almost cried when I opened it. It couldn't be more perfect."

"Oh, I'm glad. Soren did the Union Jack. He has more patience than me, apparently. And skill for such things."

He gave me a curious look. "Have you not spoken to Soren? If you're watching next door . . ."

"Not since last night. I left after midnight. They had the fire almost out and I didn't want to get in anyone's way. Did something happen?"

I don't know why I asked him, but maybe Colson had heard.

"No, not that I know of. Chuck and Delaney stayed at Soren's last night. Nowhere else to go," he said with a frown. "Everywhere's booked with the holidays."

God, I felt so foolish. "Oh, of course." Of course they'd be staying with him. "I worried something had happened, and I didn't want to go over there and for his colleagues to think I was being nosey." I shrugged. "Still not sure on acceptable dating etiquette, or small-town etiquette. Or any of it, to be honest."

Braithe gave me a fond smile. "You're doing fine. All I know is Colson and Ronnie, the police chief, and Doug and Soren have to go back to the burned-out house this morning. It's investigative procedure or something. But all the guys are coming to see Chuck and Delaney, that's what they do." He gave me a reassuring smile. "When Colson went in the frozen river last year, all the police on duty came around to check on him."

"He went in the frozen river?"

Braithe nodded. "He did. Saved a boy's life."

"Oh my god."

"At the Christmas street party. You're coming to that, right?"

"Uh, I think the kids at the center were talking about that, yeah."

His eyebrows did a little flick. "Soren will be there in the fire engine, in full uniform."

I had flashbacks of him last night, in full uniform, sweaty, barking orders . . . "Well, then I should probably go."

He laughed. "It's a great night. Lots of families, street food, Santa photos."

"Really?"

"Yes. And it's Clay's dad. And let me tell you," Braithe said with a pointed look. "Picture a silver fox lumberjack, and then put him in a sexy Santa suit."

"Oh."

Braithe laughed. "Yeah."

"Gunter never told me that."

He waved a hand at me. "He probably shouldn't think of his father-in-law in that way."

"True."

Just then there was a knock at my door. I rushed to open it, hoping it was Soren. But no, it was Hamish.

"I come bearing gifts," he said, holding a gift bag.

"Come in."

He stepped inside. "Oh my god," he said. "Your house is so lovely. It's just the cutest thing."

"Oh, thank you," I said, a little embarrassed.

"I have your Kris Kringle gift, and I also brought some cookies," Hamish said. "But I mean, I also want all the goss on the house fire. Please tell me no one was hurt."

"No, thankfully," I replied. "But the house was totally destroyed."

Hamish put his hand to his heart. "Oh, those poor people. Especially just before Christmas. I'm sure Ren will help organize something for them. Everyone in this town will look after them."

I waited for a punchline, given that Hamish was notoriously funny, but there wasn't one. He was serious. This town would look after them, and I loved that.

"Anyone for coffee?"

"Yes, please," Hamish said. "You need to open your gift because you had Jayden as your Secret Santa and he makes the best stuff."

"Oh, Hamish," Braithe said, following us into the kitchen. "Did you not know about their surprise wedding?"

He gasped. "No! I can't believe he kept that from me. I'm going out to his place after I leave here to catch up with his parents. Oh my god, as soon as I saw them, and then the minister, I just knew!" He shook his head. "I'm still not sure if I should be offended he didn't tell me or impressed that he managed to keep it a secret from me."

I chuckled at that. "Are they having a honeymoon? Or are they perpetually busy?"

Hamish put the gift bag on the kitchen counter. "They'll be working through the holiday period, then having a short honeymoon in Australia with Jayden's family."

"How lovely," Braithe said.

Hamish sniffed. "Well, I'm still mad that I didn't know. I told him he's making me lunch as penance. Though his real penance is me wearing that godawful sweater that I thought was funny, and it will now grace every wedding photo of his for all eternity." He sniffed. "And now I will be wearing casual suit attire to every dinner we have in case anyone else wants to spring a surprise wedding on us."

Braithe sighed. "It was so beautiful though."

"It really was," I agreed. "I was sorry to have to leave."

Hamish dismissed it with a wave of his hand. "Everyone understands. After all, it's to be expected when we have one deputy, one firefighter, and a doctor in our midst."

I smiled as he handed them both a coffee and made one for myself. Hamish took a container from the gift bag and opened it. Inside were Christmas sugar cookies in all shapes: stockings, trees, snowflakes.

"You made these?" I asked.

He nodded. "Every Christmas."

The icing and decorations were so pretty. I plucked a red stocking cookie off the top. "Thank you."

"And this," Hamish said, taking a heavier box from the bag, "is for you and Soren. Your couple was Jayden and Cass, so you know whatever is in this is amazing. I totally didn't peek."

I laughed because it was obvious he totally did.

Inside the box were four small mason jars with ribbon

tied around the lid and a small tag. "Gingerbread syrup." I read one tag as I took the jar out. It was heavy, the contents dark. Then another jar was full of what looked like marmalade. I read the tag out loud. "Spiced oranges." Then I remembered the rule of the gift exchange. "He made these?"

Hamish nodded. "He's very clever. Well, Jayden makes the stuff, Cass jars it and does the labels." Then he took out the two remaining mason jars, which were the same. "Two of each. For you and Soren, because you don't live together, obviously, so you each get your own pair."

Braithe sipped his coffee. "You know a lot about them for someone who didn't peek."

I chuckled and Hamish told him to shush.

"These are . . ." I wasn't sure what to say. "Perfect." I cracked the lid on the gingerbread syrup and inhaled the aroma. "Oh my god." I offered them each a sniff. It was out of this world, and I couldn't believe these were for me. "I feel bad that all I did was salad servers."

"No, they're perfect, you don't understand," Braithe said, then made a point of showing me his socks. One USA flag sock, one UK flag sock.

"He cried," Hamish said.

"I got a little teary," Braithe said indignantly.

Then there were loud footsteps across my front porch and the door opened. "Rob?" Soren called out. He was wearing his work pants and a gray T-shirt under his fire department jacket.

I put down my coffee and poked my head out from the kitchen just as Soren came stalking in. He didn't stop, didn't even hesitate. He threw his arms around me, picked me up, buried his face in my neck, and held me so tight. "Oh," I said, breathless.

Oh wow.

"I was going to come over," I whispered. "But I didn't know if I should. I didn't want to distract you in front of your crew."

Soren set me back down, his hands quickly cradling my face. "I'm sorry. I was going to come see you last night but Chucky and Delaney are staying at my place and by the time I got them home, it was far too late. I have to go now, back down to the fire site. I'll be gone all day. I just . . . I just needed to see you. After what you said last night . . ." He shook his head, his eyes imploring.

What I'd said last night.

I'm not going anywhere . . . I'll leave my door unlocked for you . . . Doesn't matter when.

Soren swallowed hard. "It meant so much. I needed to tell you that. It was exactly what I needed to hear." He pressed his lips to mine, my heart squeezing . . .

Until someone cleared their throat.

"Don't mind us," Hamish said.

Soren's head snapped up. He'd clearly not even realized they were there, standing in the kitchen doorway, watching, smiling.

"Oh, I didn't know . . ." he said, now smiling at me.

Hamish bit into a cookie. "No, please continue."

Soren laughed, his eyes soft when they met mine. "I won't be done till late. There's a whole procedure."

"It's okay. I'll make you dinner." Then I remembered . . . "I'll make enough for Chuck and Delaney too. I'll bring it over."

He exhaled loudly, his smile a little sad. "You're amazing. But I have to go."

"Okay. Go be the best captain you can be."

He kissed me again, and when he got to the door, he stopped. He paused for a second, then turned around and came right back, took my face in his hands, and kissed me, hard. "I love you, Robinson O'Reilly. There is no perfect time to say that but I cannot leave without telling you. I *love* you."

My heart stuttered to a stop, as did my breath. "Oh." Then of course, my emotions manifested into tears, and I nodded. "I love you too. I do."

He grinned, and outside a car horn honked. He growled at the sound but kissed me again. "I have to go. See you later. I'll text you when I'm heading home."

"Okay."

He raced out the door, down the steps, and ran to Doug's waiting truck.

And I stood there, my hand to my heart, finally able to breathe, to think.

He loves me. He told me he loved me, and I said it back to him, and I was teary and sweating for some reason.

I think I laughed.

I turned around and Braithe was grinning at me, teary-eyed himself.

Hamish cocked his head, squinting at me. "Your name is Robinson?"

I SPENT the afternoon on cloud nine. As if I were walking on air, breezing around my kitchen, cooking up a storm.

When Soren texted me to say he was finally heading home, it was after four. I gave him time to get through the door at least, and then with a carry bag in each hand, I went over to his place.

He opened the door, sighing and smiling all in one. He pulled me inside, cupped my face, and planted a kiss on my lips. "Hey."

Realizing only then that Chuck and Delaney were in the living room watching, I blushed ten shades of red. "Oh, hi."

They both kind of waved. They both appeared exhausted, drawn out, and I had to wonder if Delaney had stopped crying yet.

"I made food," I said, holding up the bags. "Enough for a few meals, so you don't have to worry about cooking. I'm very sorry about your home," I said to Chuck and Delaney. Sorry felt such an inadequate thing to say.

Soren took one of the bags, looking inside. "You made all this?"

"I did. There's chicken and potatoes, some meatballs and pasta, soup. I figured anything reheatable would be best, given the next few days will be long and busy."

"Thank you," Chuck said. "It's very generous and kind."

"You're more than welcome."

"Come through to the kitchen," Soren said.

I followed him and set the bags on the counter, and he wasted no time in pulling me into his arms. He just held me, his arms around me like a vise, his lips at my neck. "I'm so fucking grateful for you," he murmured.

I smiled and when I pulled back, he reluctantly let me go. He kept his hand on my waist though. "Been a long day, huh?"

He nodded, and I noticed then just how tired he looked. "Their whole house is gone," he whispered. "We saved the sheds, so they have their truck and some farm gear, but nothing else. Not even any clothes. I put them in my room, told them my wardrobe was theirs." He shook his head. "I hate that we couldn't save anything."

"It's not your fault," I whispered.

He shook his head. "I know. It looks like an electrical fire," he murmured. "Started in the roof. There was no way . . . thank fuck Chuck knew what to do." He shook his head. "The only thing he could do was get them both out. It went up like a box of matches."

I pulled him back in for a hug and rubbed his back. "I'm glad he has you."

Soren sighed deeply, letting me hold him. "I meant what I said before," he said softly. Then he pulled back and his eyes met mine. "And I'm sorry for just blurting it out. I was trying to find the right time, but then last night happened and you were there, saying exactly what I needed to hear. You're exactly what I need in my life. I do love you. Pretty sure I did the second I saw you in those flamingo pajamas. I was a goner at first sight."

I chuckled. "I love you too." I let out a shaky breath. "I've never said that to anyone before, so it's kinda scary and overwhelming for me. But you have to know, me moving here, to this town, and finding you was the best decision I ever made." My eyes burned but I refused to cry. "It's as if this town, as if you, are fixing something in me that you didn't break. I feel . . . alive. Happy."

He smiled, his gaze soft and warm. "I fucking love you."

I kissed him softly, but then something he said clicked. "When you said you gave them your room . . . Where are you sleeping?"

"On the couch," he said quietly. "It's fine. More than fine. Just until we can get them a new bed. I can't have them sleeping on the couch while I have a queen-sized bed to myself."

"Sleep at my place," I offered. "Just until you get them organized."

He smirked, his tired eyes slow blinked. "Your bed, huh?"

Then his stomach rumbled, making me laugh. "Have you eaten anything today?"

He made a face which told me no, he hadn't.

"Then let's get you fed."

We settled on the pasta for dinner and the four of us sat at Soren's dining table and ate. They were all so exhausted, but I was pleased by the end of the meal that Delaney had given Chuck a few sad smiles.

With the belly full of carbs, they were a hot shower away from sleeping for twelve hours. Soren wasn't much better.

Once we'd cleared the plates away, Soren came out with an overnight bag.

"Whatcha doing?" Chuck asked.

"Gonna sleep at Rob's," he said. "I'll just be next door if you need anything."

Delaney frowned, teary-eyed again. "No, we can't kick you out of your own house."

Chuck quickly pulled her in for a hug. "It's okay, baby. Pretty sure it's not an inconvenience for him."

Soren chuckled. "No, it is not. I spent more nights at his place these last two weeks than here anyway. Believe me, it's no hardship."

She relented a small smile. "I really do appreciate every-thing, Soren," she said, gesturing to the clothes she was wearing. Which were clearly men's sweats. "Everything."

"Anytime." Soren held the door for me. "See you both in the morning. Use anything you need. I would say that includes my condom and lube supply—" Then he held up his overnight bag. "—but I'm taking it all with me."

"Oh my god," I mumbled, face flaming.

Chuck laughed, holding Delaney in a warm embrace. "And I would say have fun, but I think we all now know that's a given."

Soren laughed as we left, closing the door behind us. And when we got home, I'd have liked to think we were going to put a dent in that condom and lube supply, but he was so tired he could barely keep his eyes open.

"You need a hot shower," I prompted. "And sleep."

He pouted. "I need to hold you all night." Then he shrugged. "And just for the record, if I happen to wake up and you're naked and pressed against me, I will not object. I also will take that as an invitation, so if you don't want that, maybe wear some pajamas."

I snorted. "Naked it is, then."

Chapter Fourteen

SOREN

ROB HAD to work the next three days, and with everything going on at work and with Chuck and Delaney, sleeping at Rob's place was the only time I saw him.

My god, he was an angel.

He looked after me, cooked for me, offered me nothing but long hugs and soft kisses.

I loved him more each minute of every day.

I also loved sharing a bed with him every night. Getting to fall asleep with him in my arms, waking up much the same, was utter perfection. As the snow fell outside and Christmas crept ever closer, I wanted nothing more in life.

And I mean, sharing a bed had more perks than the best sleep I'd ever had, but getting to roll him over any time I wanted and sink my cock inside him was heaven on earth.

Christmas Eve meant the annual Hartbridge Christmas festival, and while Rob helped Hamish and Ren, and Gunter and Clay make preparations, it also meant we had to get the truck prepared too.

Taking the truck down to the park for the kids to see

and play on was a highlight for me. These last few years, getting to see the whole town come out to celebrate their community was incredible.

How the community had turned up for Chuck and Delaney was incredible too. The last three days, people had dropped off food, gift cards to buy new clothing, brand-new kitchen utensils and containers, a new microwave, a coffee maker, gift cards, cash.

It was more than incredible.

Not that they had anywhere to move to, and they could use everything in my house as if it were their own. I was more than happy to stay with Rob.

More than happy.

Like I could get used to it permanently.

And if Chuck and Delaney needed to stay for a few weeks or months, then maybe we'd need to get them that new bed in my spare room, but until then . . .

Until Rob got sick of me, I was happy to keep staying over at his place. I already had my work gear in his wardrobe, some bathroom stuff in his cabinet, because it just made sense.

Made something in my belly warm too.

"Stop your mooning," Doug snapped at me.

I startled, having spaced out for a minute. I was supposed to be polishing the truck. "What even is mooning?"

"Where you get a glazed-over, stupid look on your face." Doug harrumphed. "Always thought you needed to meet someone, and now look where that got us. Mooning instead of polishing. I'm already one man down with Chucky off this week and you're as useless as a bucket under a bull. What did that doctor do to you anyway?" Then he stopped and put his hand up. "Don't answer that. Just get the damn thing polished."

Raf laughed from inside the truck. "No, Captain, please tell him what your boyfriend does to you. I wanna see his face."

Doug pointed at him. "You'll see the toilets cleaning roster for a month if you don't shut up."

Doug stormed off to his office and me and Raf laughed and laughed.

He really did love us.

And by the time we were in our gear and driving down to the park by the huge Christmas tree, I was in the best mood ever.

The street was closed off, the food stalls were getting ready, and the kids' Christmas Winterland train was already in full swing.

It was nothing short of magical.

Colson came by, dressed in his full uniform, huge grin on his face, and he held his hand out for me to shake. "Merry Christmas," he said.

"Same to you."

He nodded to where his boss was talking to mine. Police Chief Ronnie and Fire Captain Doug and the mayor having a good old chinwag. "Who do you think wins when they play poker?" Colson asked.

"Dunno. Who do you think wins the moustache contest?"

Colson laughed. "So, Braithe tells me things with you and Rob have progressed."

My face broke out in a grin. "Kinda crazy, huh."

He shoved his hands in his pockets. "Do you think there's any truth in that Hartbridge Cupid bullshit?"

Then of course, Rob and Braithe walked down toward us, smiling right at us, and my heart felt too big for my chest. "I dunno," I whispered. "But it's definitely something magical."

"Good evening," Rob said, his eyes locking with mine. "Have you ever seen anything so fantastic?"

I couldn't help myself. I pulled him into my side, my arm around his shoulder. I knew he was talking about the Christmas festival, the families, the snow, the way the sunset was painting everything in a soft pink. But he was the most fantastic thing here. "No, I have not."

He gave me a shove and we had a quick conversation, mostly about how Cliff Henderson as Santa was the best part of the whole show. Then Ren, Hamish, Jayden, Cass, and their parents arrived, and I was quick to hoist Cass's boy up onto the firetruck, and then there was a never-ending supply of excited kids.

And so the night went on.

I caught Rob talking with Chuck for a long while, but he spoke with everyone, and man . . . to see him smile.

In his coat and toque, a scarf, and his pink cheeks, the sound of his laughter. It took my breath away. And I even saw him almost slip a time or two, Gunter quick to steady him, or Ren.

That made me smile too.

Because he'd done more than find a community here. He'd gone and found himself a family. A group of friends so beautiful, so welcoming, they couldn't be anything but family.

And I was included in that.

Sure, I'd been included before. Colson and Ren and Clay had always welcomed me, invited me to watch a game, and as a single guy, new to town, I'd always appreciated that. But it felt different now. The whole group just collected Rob and me into their clutch as if we'd always been there.

It was a great feeling.

"You wanna be careful," Chuck said, giving me a nudge.

"Hey," I said. "Didn't see you come up. What might I wanna be careful about?"

"The way you're looking at him," he said quietly. "People might think you're in love."

I snorted. "Pretty sure that ship has sailed."

"I'm damn sure it has." He was smiling, until he looked around at the whole townsfolk and he shook his head. "I cannot believe the people here, ya know? Not just here tonight, but in this town. Everyone's been so great, so kind and generous. Can't believe how lucky we are."

I clapped his shoulder. "You've worked hard for this community. You deserve it."

He smiled and shoved his hands in his pockets. "You sure you're okay staying over at Rob's? You know that's not what we expect—"

"I know," I said. "And believe me, I'm very okay with it."

"Rob invited us over for Christmas dinner tomorrow. To join you guys. Hope that's okay?"

Damn, that made me so freaking happy that he would

do that for them, that he would do that for me. "Of course!"

He was quiet a moment. "I'm really happy for you, man. He's a good guy." It was unlike Chuck to be serious, but given his last week, I'd seen this side of him more these last few days than in the entire last few years. "And you deserve someone who loves you as much as he does."

Oh.

Damn.

"Thanks," I said. "He's kinda great."

Then he rolled his eyes, the serious Chuck gone and the old Chuck back. "Jesus, that's what he said and *exactly* how he said it."

I nudged him with my elbow. "You back at work next week?"

"Yeah."

"Good. I've missed all the stupid shit you say."

He laughed until he sighed. "I better go find Delaney. She didn't want to come tonight but I convinced her. All her friends swarmed her and headed for the churros. First time she's smiled without crying in a week."

"She'll be okay," I offered. "You both will."

He gave me another clap on the shoulder. "Yeah. We will. Merry Christmas, Soren. See ya tomorrow."

"Yes, you will."

The night went on, thankfully without any kids or deputy's going into the river, and before too long, the crowd dwindled and parents took their kid's home with threats of needing to be in bed so Santa could visit.

I was taking the tinsel off the firetruck when a familiar

voice came up behind me. "Excuse me, captain. I was hoping you could help me."

I jumped down and laughed. "Of course, good doctor. What can I do for you?"

He drew his bottom lip between his teeth. "Could you take me home? When you're done here with your very big truck."

I laughed. "Oh, I think I can arrange that. Or," I said, "I can give you a ride in the firetruck up to the fire hall, then I can walk you home."

He grinned. "Serious?"

Hell yes, I was serious. "Climb in."

Then, like he was an excited kid, he climbed up, smile wide. I got in behind the wheel and gave the horn a honk and set the lights to flash, no siren, to warn any stragglers to get out of the way.

It was a short, slow drive up the bank of the park and down Main Street, and when I pulled the truck into the fire hall, Rob was grinning, ear to ear.

I shut it all down and cut the engine. "Fun?"

"Yes."

"Never did that as a kid?"

He shook his head. "Never."

That might have explained the smile. "I need to get out of this uniform," I said.

He sighed. "Shame."

I snorted. "Doctor," I pretended to admonish him. "If there weren't strict rules about civilians being on the premises and security cameras everywhere, I'd totally do you here."

"Oh," he said, blushing. "I didn't mean that . . ."

"I know you didn't," I said. "But I did. We really need to go home. And I could make a crass joke about needing us both to come before Santa does, but I'm a good boy."

He laughed, his eyes dancing. "A good boy? You're on his naughty list for sure."

"I plan to be tonight," I said. "We need to get home."

He climbed down and waited by the truck for me to get out of my gear. He was smiling at the tinsel and baubles hung around the station. "Are you ready, doctor?" I asked.

He nodded quickly. "Very."

He linked his arm through mine as we walked back to his place. The crowd was gone now, all the world quiet. Christmas lights twinkled inside houses, snow flurries skirted the air.

"Would you look at this place?" he said, marveling at the beauty of it.

"Did you have a good night?" I asked.

"I had a wonderful night." Then he slid on the sidewalk and I laughed as I kept him upright.

"I should get you some snowshoes."

He clung to me as we walked the rest of the way, and once we were inside with our boots off and our coats hanging on the rack, Rob took my hand. "Can I make you a hot cocoa or anything? Did you eat tonight?"

His thoughtfulness made me smile. "I'm fine." I pulled him a little closer. "What I need is you."

He hummed. "Just need?"

I pulled him closer, till our hips were flush, my arms around his lower back. "Need, want, love."

He put his forehead to my chin and sighed. "Take me to bed, Soren."

I lifted his face and kissed him. There was no scorching passion, no scramble to rid clothes, no urgency. Every time we'd fucked before, it had been on the more-urgent, rougher side. Where he'd been face down, begging for it, and that was clearly how he liked it. But I didn't want that this time.

I wanted to treasure every inch of skin, caress every part of him, and show him how I felt. I'd told him several times that I loved him, but I wanted him to know it. I wanted him to feel it.

I led him to bed, taking my time to unbutton his shirt, his jeans, kissing the skin I revealed as I went. When we were both naked, he pulled back the covers and knelt on the edge of the mattress, running his hand over his ass cheek.

I stilled his hand and murmured to the back of his head. "Need you on your back tonight," I said.

He did as I asked, lying back and gently stroking his own cock. God, he was so sexy.

My cock jerked, impossibly hard, which he noticed. "Like what you see?"

I shook my head. "Love it."

I threw a condom down beside him and took the lube as I crawled between his legs. I spread his thighs wide and slicked his asshole with the lube, prepping him with my fingers while licking and sucking his cock. He was writhing, getting frustrated, desperate for more.

"Patience," I said. "Believe me, you'll get what you want."

He growled in frustration. He raised his head and snapped. "Soren."

Kneeling between his legs, I rolled on a condom and

smeared more lube over us both. Then I pushed his legs up toward his chest and sank my cock inside him.

Torturously slow, his eyes went wide and his mouth fell open, so I leaned down, pushing in harder and covering his mouth with mine.

I delved my tongue in, tangling and teasing, then sucking on his tongue while I pushed my cock in to the hilt.

The sounds he made sent shivers through me. I had to hold back the urge to give it to him rough.

"Wanna take it slow," I whispered. "Want you to feel everything, feel what I feel."

He arched his back and let his legs slide down my sides, and he hooked his feet over my ass. I had to push up, drive my hips into his, impaling him deeper, and he cried out. I kept my hands on his head, cradling him, and began rocking back and forth.

I kissed his neck, his jaw, and eventually his mouth again, kissing as we found our rhythm. Slow and deep, I poured every emotion I had for him through my body to his. Every touch, every thrust, every kiss.

His fingers dug into my back and his groans got louder as we rocked and flowed with each other's tide.

Then he hooked his arms around my neck and he locked his mouth with mine, head tilted, his tongue sliding with mine as he began to devour me with his mouth at the same time he took my cock into his body.

It was too much. Senses overload, emotions overload.

This was going to be over far too soon.

He was going to end me.

I pulled back and stilled our rhythm.

I waited for his eyes to meet mine, to focus. They were a

flurry of need and arousal. "Please don't stop," he whispered.

"Rob." I breathed his name. "I wanted to take it slow. Wanted to make love to you, but you feel too good."

His tongue peeked out and he licked the corner of his mouth. "Soren," he whispered, voice tight. He held my face in his hands and his body rolled with waves of pleasure. "I can't take this. I need you to move. Make me yours. Please."

Make me yours.

"You already belong to me," I said, trying to move impossibly slow but the pleasure was so intense. "And I am yours," I hissed. "Oh, Rob, your ass is too good. Too tight."

He moaned and rocked us back and forth, and that set off a chain reaction. An explosion I couldn't hold back anymore.

"I love you," I said, my voice tight, my restraint all but gone.

He nodded. "I love you," he hissed, shaking with frustration, with the need to move.

I rocked into him, again and again, driving in deeper with every pass. His eyes went wide again as I came, pulsing inside him and filling the condom.

I bucked into him, crying out with each shock of pleasure, and he held me as I succumbed to the power of my orgasm. Aftershocks, shudders, and spine-tingling pleasure. I collapsed on top of him, too boneless to care.

He rolled us onto our sides, my face resting on a pillow of his hairy chest, and I was out.

I woke up with Rob's head on my chest. "Morning," he said, his voice thick from sleep. "Merry Christmas."

I breathed in deep and squeezed him. "Merry Christmas."

"Do you want breakfast?" he asked. "Or just coffee?"

I tightened my arms around him. "But that involves getting out of bed and not staying like this all day."

He chuckled. "I invited Chuck and Delaney over for lunch. I hope that's okay."

I kissed the top of his head. "I love that you did that."

"It means I'll need to get up and put the turkey in the oven."

"Oh god, doesn't it need forever to cook?"

"It's just a boneless rolled roast from the supermarket. I'm not that good a cook to try a whole bird. But I want to do it slow."

I hummed. "Hmm. Slow is good, like last night?"

He swatted my arm. "No. But also yes, that was amazing."

I chuckled, content and comfortable, never wanting to move. "We can tell them it's a dinner thing and not a lunch thing. We could just stay right here."

He chuckled. "My bladder does not agree." He unfolded himself from me and I whined when he got out of bed.

"So unfair."

But I heard him pee and wash his hands, then a few seconds later I heard the fridge open, the coffee machine beep, and then he appeared in the door with his arms full of the gifts from under the tree.

He was also wearing sweatpants and a T-shirt. He jumped on the bed, making me laugh. "Gift opening time." Then he handed one to me. "You go first."

I sat up, resting against the headboard, the covers pulled up to hide the fact I was still very much naked underneath. His gifts were wrapped so neatly, I almost felt bad for opening them. The first one was a decent-sized box, and it had some weight to it, and I was curious as to what it could be.

Once I had the paper off, I pulled the lid back and grinned when I saw what it was. A fluffy robe, exactly like his. "Oh, I love it."

"It's not that exciting but you liked to wear mine," Rob said. Then he gave me a smaller box. "But this one is the main one . . . oh, well, there's another one still hanging on the tree but you'll have to get that one yourself."

"Hanging on the tree?"

He nodded but waved his hand at the second box I was now holding. "This one next. I want to see your face."

Seeing how excited he was, I tore into the wrapping to reveal another box, which I was quickly learning made for expert wrapping. But then I opened the box and burst out laughing.

Flamingo pajamas.

"I thought you might like your own," Rob said. "Given you stole mine and I never got them back."

I laughed some more, then took one of my gifts from his pile. "Here. Open this."

He looked at it.

"I wrap gifts pretty much the same way I fold a fitted sheet."

He laughed and tore into it. He took one look at it. "You did not."

"I did."

He held up the pajama set. It was the same flamingo design, same brand, but these were mostly navy with the flamingos on the pockets and hems. He hugged them, laughing. "We're going to match."

We totally were.

And I fucking loved it.

The next one was much smaller and just as badly wrapped. "Okay, this one I might need to explain," I said as he opened it.

He took out the gift card box and opened it. Of course he wasn't familiar with the brand or the store. He looked at me. "Uh . . . that's a lot of money."

"It's for a proper riding jacket," I explained. "You need to choose one and make sure it fits properly, but if you want to ride on my bike with me, I thought it was a good idea to get you kitted out."

He held it and nodded. "It's perfect. And a lot more than I spent on you. Now I feel bad."

I took his hand. "It's not about the money. It's about your safety."

He nodded again. "Thank you. I love it. I love it all." He leaned over and kissed me softly. "I can't believe we bought each other the same pajamas. Well, the same but different."

I scrambled out of bed and pulled on my new flamingo pajama bottoms. "Perfect fit."

He was pouting. "I think I preferred the naked option."

I slipped my arms through the robe and tied it off. "Perfect."

He held his hand out to me. "You have one more."

Oh, right. The one on the tree.

I took his hand and he led me to the tree. "Now, before you get this, you should know that I ordered it before the house fire, back when your visits were at irregular times. That being said, it probably makes more sense that you have it now. I just wanted you to know that I wanted you to have this before what happened."

Okaaaay.

I looked at the Christmas tree, not sure what I was supposed to be looking for. An envelope? A small, gift-wrapped box?

And then I saw it.

It was a house key. A front door key. To his house.

It was also red with a green ribbon tied to it, and it hung like all the ornaments. I reached out slowly and gently took it off the tree. My blood pumping in my ears.

For all we'd done in bed, for all we'd declared to each other, this somehow felt bigger.

"You're welcome here, at any time," he murmured. "You don't need to ask, you don't need to knock. And now I don't need to leave my door unlocked."

I clutched it in my hand, and kissed his lips, soft and sweet. "Thank you, Rob."

"You're so very welcome, Soren. Merry Christmas."

"Merry Christmas, Robinson."

He swatted me playfully for using his full name. "Let's have some coffee. I need to get the turkey in the oven, then we can watch Christmas movies on the television and have breakfast, and maybe then some soapy hand jobs in the shower before we make a start on lunch."

I laughed. "Merry Christmas to me."

He shook his head. "No. Merry Christmas to us."

Epilogue

THREE MONTHS LATER

GUNTER and I stood in the empty store next to the youth center, staring at the ceiling, waiting, tapping our fingers, pacing. Outside, through the glass front, the sun was shining, the trees outside that lined the river were in blossom, the flowers were in bloom, the birds were singing, and I was growing impatient.

Gunter hummed. "So, I heard Doctor Humphries is so happy with you he might retire as early as next year."

I nodded. He was only doing two days now and I was doing the three on my own. "It's going well. And he's ready to hang up his coat. He'll be seventy-five next year."

"Can't see yourself working until you're seventy-five?"

I grimaced. "Not if I can help it. When he does retire, I might have to look at getting another part-timer so I can still have my four days off. Going for bike rides with Soren, helping you out whenever I can. Life's too short not to be happy, right?"

"No cap."

I burst out laughing. "Okay, you need to start spending time with grownups."

He laughed. "Oh, Chuck and Delaney's site got cleared and approved for a rebuild, I hear."

The change of topic was welcome. "Yes, thank god. The insurance is all through now. They can finally look at rebuilding; it'll be good for them. Fingers crossed they might have a new home by Christmas."

"That'll be nice." Gunter nodded slowly. "So will Soren move back into his house when they move out."

"Uh, no," I said with a smile. "He wants to rent it out. But he's staying with me." Then I spoke louder to the utility hole in the ceiling we were both impatiently watching. "Well, that's if he hurries up."

Then Soren's smiling face appeared. "I heard that."

"Please say you're done," I whined.

He handed me down his clipboard, then his face disappeared for a second before his boots appeared atop the ladder, followed by long work pants as he stepped down, then a sliver of abdomen showing his very defined Adonis belt, his white Hartbridge Fire Department T-shirt, and bulging biceps as he lifted himself down.

Damn.

Gunter gave me a nudge, but I wasn't even sorry.

Soren was sexy AF.

And I'd learned what AF meant from the kids at the youth center . . .

"And?" Gunter asked.

"Fire regulation check done," Soren answered. "And approved. Congratulations."

Gunter and I hugged each other and then I hugged Soren. "Thank you."

"All part of the service," he said, innuendo fully implied. "For you."

Gunter cleared his throat.

Soren laughed. "No, seriously, it all looks good up there. Circuits are new, wiring's all tagged. Sprinkler system couldn't be more than three years old." Then he nodded to the shell of a storefront. "Once you get any remodeling done and all your displays installed and all that fun stuff, we'll need to discuss operational things, such as fire blankets and extinguishers, of course."

"Of course," I repeated.

He took his cute little clipboard. "It's a great thing you're doing here," he said. "I'm glad you got all the applications and permits approved. Can't wait to see it up and running."

"Same," Gunter said.

The three of us stood there in the little empty store, looking around at what was going to be a café and training center for teens. The plan was to open up and utilize both spaces. In the summer, there'd be tables outside, in the winter maybe a projector screen with movies.

Possibilities were endless.

Gunter nodded slowly. "Sooo, you two had sex in the fire station yet?"

Soren burst out laughing, stunned.

"No. God." I shoved Gunter. Then I mumbled, "Not allowed, and there's security cameras."

He laughed, and my god, it felt so good. Life was good. So freaking good.

"Well, we better get going," Gunter said. "We now have a million things to do."

"Yes, we do."

"Yeah, I should get back and write up this report," Soren said.

We locked the doors, and despite the three of us knowing we had somewhere else to be, we all stood there in the warm sunshine, looking back at the empty store. We had so much work ahead of us that it could have been so easy to be overwhelmed.

But it wasn't.

It was exciting.

I'd gone from feeling helpless, stretched too thin, and being strung so tight I'd almost snapped, to now being the most relaxed I'd ever been. The most content, and definitely the happiest.

"We're gonna do some real good here," I said.

"Yep." Gunter nodded. "Can feel it."

I could feel Soren's eyes on me, and when I turned to look at him, his smile was warm and proud. "I wish I could stay," he said. "But I kinda get the feeling I'll be spending enough time here in the next six months."

I laughed, because we were going to need all the help we could get. "Yes, you will."

"I wouldn't be anywhere else," Soren replied. Then he stepped in close to me, in the way he used his body to press against me instead of leaning in for a kiss. The way he knew I liked. "And you, I will see at home."

It gave me a thrill, as I knew it always would. "Yes, you will."

. . .

~ THE END

About the Author

N.R. Walker is an Australian author, who loves her genre of gay romance. She loves writing and spends far too much time doing it, but wouldn't have it any other way.

She is many things: a mother, a wife, a sister, a writer. She has pretty, pretty boys who live in her head, who don't let her sleep at night unless she gives them life with words.

She likes it when they do dirty, dirty things... but likes it even more when they fall in love. She used to think having people in her head talking to her was weird, until one day she happened across other writers who told her it was normal.

She's been writing ever since...

nrwalker.net

Also by N.R. Walker

Blind Faith

Through These Eyes (Blind Faith #2)

Blindside: Mark's Story (Blind Faith #3)

Ten in the Bin

Gay Sex Club Stories 1

Gay Sex Club Stories 2

Gay Sex Club Stories 3

Point of No Return – Turning Point #1

Breaking Point – Turning Point #2

Starting Point – Turning Point #3

Element of Retrofit – Thomas Elkin Series #1

Clarity of Lines – Thomas Elkin Series #2

Sense of Place – Thomas Elkin Series #3

Taxes and TARDIS

Three's Company

Red Dirt Heart

Red Dirt Heart 2

Red Dirt Heart 3

Red Dirt Heart 4

Red Dirt Christmas

Cronin's Key

Cronin's Key II

Cronin's Key III

Cronin's Key IV - Kennard's Story

Exchange of Hearts

The Spencer Cohen Series, Book One

The Spencer Cohen Series, Book Two

The Spencer Cohen Series, Book Three

The Spencer Cohen Series, Yanni's Story

Blood & Milk

The Weight Of It All

A Very Henry Christmas (The Weight of It All 1.5)

Perfect Catch

Switched

Imago

Imagines

Imagoes

Red Dirt Heart Imago

On Davis Row

Finders Keepers

Evolved

Galaxies and Oceans

Private Charter

Nova Praetorian

A Soldier's Wish

Upside Down

The Hate You Drink

Sir

Tallowwood

Reindeer Games

The Dichotomy of Angels

Throwing Hearts

Pieces of You - Missing Pieces #1

Pieces of Me - Missing Pieces #2

Pieces of Us - Missing Pieces #3

Lacuna

Tic-Tac-Mistletoe

Bossy

Code Red

Dearest Milton James

Dearest Malachi Keogh

Christmas Wish List

Code Blue

Davo

The Kite

Learning Curve

Merry Christmas Cupid

To the Moon and Back

Second Chance at First Love

Outrun the Rain

Into the Tempest

Touch the Lightning

EWB - Enemies With Benefits

Holiday Heart Strings

Bloom

The Men from Echo Creek

Method Acting

The Bait

Nothing Left to Lose

TITLES IN AUDIO:

Cronin's Key

Cronin's Key II

Cronin's Key III

Red Dirt Heart

Red Dirt Heart 2

Red Dirt Heart 3

Red Dirt Heart 4

The Weight Of It All

Switched

Point of No Return

Breaking Point

Starting Point

Spencer Cohen Book One

Spencer Cohen Book Two

Spencer Cohen Book Three

Yanni's Story

On Davis Row

Evolved

Elements of Retrofit

Clarity of Lines

Sense of Place

Blind Faith

Through These Eyes

Blindside

Finders Keepers

Galaxies and Oceans

Nova Praetorian

Upside Down

Sir

Tallowwood

Imago

Throwing Hearts

Sixty Five Hours

Taxes and TARDIS

The Dichotomy of Angels

The Hate You Drink

Pieces of You

Pieces of Me

Pieces of Us

Tic-Tac-Mistletoe

Lacuna

Bossy

Code Red

Learning to Feel

Dearest Milton James

Dearest Malachi Keogh

Three's Company

Christmas Wish List

Code Blue

Davo

The Kite

Learning Curve

Merry Christmas Cupid

To the Moon and Back

Second Chance at First Love

Outrun the Rain

Into the Tempest

Touch the Lightning

EWB

Holiday Heart Strings

Bloom

The Men from Echo Creek

Method Acting

The Bait

SERIES COLLECTIONS:

Red Dirt Heart Series

Turning Point Series

Thomas Elkin Series

Spencer Cohen Series

Imago Series

Blind Faith Series

Missing Pieces Series

The Storm Boys Series

Gay Sex Club Stories

FREE READS:

Sixty Five Hours

Learning to Feel

His Grandfather's Watch (And The Story of Billy and Hale)

The Twelfth of Never (Blind Faith 3.5)

Twelve Days of Christmas (Sixty Five Hours Christmas)

Best of Both Worlds

TRANSLATED TITLES:

ITALIAN

Fiducia Cieca (Blind Faith)

Attraverso Questi Occhi (Through These Eyes)

Preso alla Sprovvista (Blindside)

Il giorno del Mai (Blind Faith 3.5)

Cuore di Terra Rossa Serie (Red Dirt Heart Series)

Natale di terra rossa (Red dirt Christmas)

Intervento di Retrofit (Elements of Retrofit)

A Chiare Linee (Clarity of Lines)

Senso D'appartenenza (Sense of Place)

Spencer Cohen Serie (including Yanni's Story)

Punto di non Ritorno (Point of No Return)

Punto di Rottura (Breaking Point)

Punto di Partenza (Starting Point)

Imago (Imago)

Imagines

Il desiderio di un soldato (A Soldier's Wish)

Scambiato (Switched)

Tallowwood

The Hate You Drink

Ho trovato te (Finders Keepers)

Cuori d'argilla (Throwing Hearts)

Galassie e Oceani (Galaxies and Oceans)

Il peso di tut (The Weight of it All)

Pieces of You - Missing Pieces 1

Pieces of Me - Missing Pieces 2

Pieces of Us - Missing Pieces 3

Code Red

FRENCH

Confiance Aveugle (Blind Faith)

A travers ces yeux: Confiance Aveugle 2 (Through These Eyes)

Aveugle: Confiance Aveugle 3 (Blindside)

À Jamais (Blind Faith 3.5)

Cronin's Key Series

Au Coeur de Sutton Station (Red Dirt Heart)

Partir ou rester (Red Dirt Heart 2)

Faire Face (Red Dirt Heart 3)

Trouver sa Place (Red Dirt Heart 4)

Le Poids de Sentiments (The Weight of It All)

Un Noël à la sauce Henry (A Very Henry Christmas)

Une vie à Refaire (Switched)

Evolution (Evolved)

Galaxies & Océans

Qui Trouve, Garde (Finders Keepers)

Sens Dessus Dessous (Upside Down)

La Haine au Fond du Verre (The hate You Drink)

Tallowwood

Spencer Cohen Series

Thomas Elkin One

Lacuna

GERMAN

Flammende Erde (Red Dirt Heart)

Lodernde Erde (Red Dirt Heart 2)

Sengende Erde (Red Dirt Heart 3)

Ungezähmte Erde (Red Dirt Heart 4)

Vier Pfoten und ein bisschen Zufall (Finders Keepers)

Ein Kleines bisschen Versuchung (The Weight of It All)

Ein Kleines Bisschen Fur Immer (A Very Henry Christmas)

Weil Leibe uns immer Bliebt (Switched)

Drei Herzen eine Leibe (Three's Company)

Über uns die Sterne, zwischen uns die Liebe (Galaxies and Oceans)

Unnahbares Herz (Blind Faith 1)

Sehendes Herz (Blind Faith 2)

Hoffnungsvolles Herz (Blind Faith 3)

Verträumtes Herz (Blind Faith 3.5)

Thomas Elkin: Verlangen in neuem Design

Thomas Elkin: Leidenschaft in klaren

Thomas Elkin: Vertrauen in bester Lage

Traummann töpfern leicht gemacht (Throwing Hearts)

Sir

So Unendlich Viel Liebe (To the Moon and Back)

THAI

Sixty Five Hours (Thai translation)

Finders Keepers (Thai translation)

SPANISH

Sesenta y Cinco Horas (Sixty Five Hours)

Los Doce Días de Navidad

Código Rojo (Code Red)

Código Azul (Code Blue)

Queridísimo Milton James

Queridísimo Malachi Keogh

El Peso de Todo (The Weight of it All)

Tres Muérdagos en Raya: Serie Navidad en Hartbridge

Lista De Deseos Navideños: Serie Navidad en Hartbridge

Feliz Navidad Cupido: Serie Navidad en Hartbridge

Spencer Cohen Libro Uno

Spencer Cohen Libro Dos

Spencer Cohen Libro Tres

Davo

Hasta la Luna y de Vuelta

Venciendo A La Lluvia

En la Tempestad

El Toque del Rayo

Corazón De Tierra Roja

Corazón De Tierra Roja 2

Corazón De Tierra Roja 3

Corazón De Tierra Roja 4

ECB (Enemigos con Beneficios)

Floral

CHINESE

Blind Faith

Bossy

JAPANESE

Bossy

To the Moon and Back

PORTUGUESE

Sessenta e Cinco Horas